The Watchful Dead

A Tale of Old Hastur

by Joe Pawlowski

Glint Media, New Hope, Minnesota

JOE PAWLOWSKI

ISBN: 978-1-7336108-1-0
ISBN-13:

DEDICATION

For the Buddha, the Beatles and Debbie.

"A man is a very small thing, and the night is large and full of wonders."
—Lord Dunsany, "The Laughter of the Gods"

CONTENTS

ACKNOWLEDGMENTS

The author thanks the following people for their invaluable help in the production of this book: my mentor and personal hero, Helen Lloyd Montgomery, without whose guidance and editorial hand-holding this manuscript would never have been completed; my good friend Gregg Gridley for proofing the final draft; Debra Doyle, for her early insights and suggestions; and Danita Mayer, editor extraordinaire, for helping me kill my darlings.

JOE PAWLOWSKI

Prologue

If you search carefully, you can still find remnants of Old Coast Road. Now it's little more than a few paving stones here and there. Not a road anymore. You can't even really call it a cohesive trail. Just spread-out patches of overgrown debris too stubborn to be worn away by the passage of time. Call it a ghost of a trail. But if you search carefully, you can still find it and if you follow it, it will lead you a long way uphill through lush vegetation into the thick forest overlooking the bay.

Be sure to bring a lantern.

Much of the forest is so dense you can barely pass between the trees. Doing so, no matter how careful you are, will eventually leave you bruised and scraped. And passing through the trees while following the remnants of the trail is harder yet. So hard that no one has tried it for more than a hundred years.

But it is still possible. If you work at it with dedication and persistence, squeezing between the trees and squatting to the forest floor to feel with your hands for the road stones and squeezing through more trees and so on, you will come at last to the fallen gate and crumbled ramparts of the ancient city of Hastur.

If you didn't sense it upon entering the forest, you will definitely sense it now: the feeling of being watched. There's no denying it. It hangs over the ruins as palpable as a mist. When it touches you, it crawls across your skin and buzzes in your temples and tugs at you like the oldest and deepest fear you harbor within.

It takes a brave person to press on, feeling watched this way, but if you do, you'll want to pass the fallen gate and follow along inside what remains of the rampart wall to your right. The way is long and the going is slow. The trees, of course, will continue to claw at you and hamper your progress all the way. You will be a tempted to surrender to claustrophobia, given the tight confines in which you move and the knowledge that every toilsome step will have to be retraced when you make your exit. Hopefully, you've begun early enough that you won't be trapped returning through the forest at night.

Along the way, you'll pass broken parts of buildings, mossy and moldy and worm-riddled, cracked and shattered by the forest that has come to claim them. You'll see implements taken by rust and sections of

1

mechanisms and apparatuses so timeworn as to make their original usages pure speculation. And here and there, skeletal remains of gone Hasturians will heave up from the eroded undergrowth.

Don't be distracted by the sounds you hear that seem to have no source: the rattly hiss that wafts up airily here and there, and the groaning noise that reminds you of a full-grown tree bending under great duress. There will be skitters and screeches and a sort of tearing sound and, worst of all, every now and then, when you least expect it, a tremendous crack so loud it billows in the air long after it's passed.

Finally, you will come to a tower: the tallest structure left standing in the city. The tower's roof is gone and fissures breach its shell, but otherwise it remains a sturdy keep. Inside, stone steps wind upward and downward. Looking down, you see a long descent into blackest black.

This is where you need your lantern.

You begin climbing down, maneuvering deliberately, feeling some of the stone steps shift beneath your feet. You step into the smell of wet rock and become vaguely aware of small motions on the dank walls around you. Insects perhaps. Soon you feel the weight of being deep underground, and when you take that last step onto the stone floor so far below, you feel engulfed.

You step into a cavern. Immediately ahead, carved into the cavern wall, is an iron-barred cell filled with boxes. As you approach, rats scurry from your footfalls. Across the cavern on every side, you notice snakes of assorted lengths, mottled and ruby-eyed. They pause from their writhing and coiling to read your presence with their tongues.

The cell door is closed but unlocked. You open it and enter.

There are dozens of boxes made of thick copper, oxidized turquoise, with brass clasps. Each is an arm span wide and knee high. Each is connected at one side to a heavy chain staked to the stone floor. You approach the nearest one, crouch, unfasten the clasp and lift the lid. Inside are stone tablets carved finely with wedged hieroglyphs of birds and sea creatures and bugs and human hands contorted into various shapes. If you can read these symbols, you can learn their story.

They tell the tale of where *he* came from, he who saw things others did not. He who understood things beyond the ken of mortals. He who was the wise man, the keeper of secrets, the bearer of mystery, the traveler who feared no road, the witness of wonders and catastrophes. He who went so very far as to come full circle, who was beaten but never broken, who was weary to the point of exhaustion but did not stop to rest. The man for whom there has never been an equal.

The story is called *The Watchful Dead* and it begins: "I face them, every one."

"It seems to me I am trying to tell you a dream — making a vain attempt, because no relation of a dream can convey the dream-sensation, that commingling of absurdity, surprise, and bewilderment in a tremor of struggling revolt, that notion of being captured by the incredible which is of the very essence of dreams."
—Joseph Conrad, *Heart of Darkness*

PART ONE: SIXTEEN SKULLS

JOE PAWLOWSKI

CHAPTER 1
The Ghost Horse

*I face them, every one. What Darius called "the man-footed beasts."
Molts, Skalks, roundheads, Pyms, islanders. The kidnapped, the castoffs.
Warriors fresh from defeat. Free-walking foreigners with lives so hopeless they
begged me to take them away. The strong and the frail. Beauties and shriveled
husks. Little children. Even the ones already spoken for and passing quickly
through.*

*Some let me read their eyes and some close them or look away, but I
witness every one. I watch the metal collar clamp around each neck and something
blooms in me.*

*There is a thing that feeds every man's soul and, Dagon help me, this is
what feeds mine.*

"Touch it."

Ring Gargery bit his lip.

In the cold dark of the cavernous stable, he stood before the horse pen, chest tight, belly fluttering. Framed in ancient wood and stone, the spindly-legged foal stretched his neck up at him from a distance, pink nostrils sniffing. In the dimness of the stall, the colt's white coat almost glowed.

"Go on," Da's high voice rasped. "Touch it."

The boy huffed into his icy hands and rubbed them together. He tried to recall something useful he had learned in all his 12 years about horses, something overheard or gleaned from watching them cross Maule Square, but nothing rose cleanly to mind.

Uncle Cletus grunted, a low rumble like the bellwether of a storm. "Touch it, ye quail." In the dark, his uncle's voice came at him from all directions: gritty like Da's, but so deep it could have rolled up from a well.

Ring gripped the top board of the gate with both hands and tested it. It wobbled. Lifting onto his sandaled toes, he leaned over the grizzled wood and slowly pushed up. He tipped into the old slat's creak and give, and for a moment, hovering in the dark, he uncoupled from all reality.

In the pen, the creature's bony face fixed on him.

All at once, the board shifted and popped beneath him. He surged forward, nearly toppling headfirst. The blow to his stomach landed like a punch. Blood rushed to his face and sparks danced at the edges of his sight. As he wrenched backward, he saw something stir in the black pit of the stall. *Or could it be the blackness itself doing the stirring?*

Chill air coursed through his teeth. He shook his head to clear it. The worst of the pain slipped free and everything went still again. Everything except the hammering in his chest and the swish of the horse's tail.

The fractured board had come to brace on the one beneath it. His perch now proved firmer, if askew. He drew a hard breath, shifted and adjusted his grasp, breathed out. Several times he breathed the cold deeply, in and out, and, as his mind began to compose, he again felt the men's eyes on him and the urgency to move.

Easing forward, with his pelvis to the cracked wood, he was not so much approaching the foal as immersing himself in the animal's presence. He smelled the sweet musk and saw the light shine behind the creature's eyes. One thing he did know was that the horse could hurt him; even a small one like this could do damage. His mind's eye pictured blunt teeth snapping on the meat of his fingers.

Bearing the full weight of the animal's gaze, he glided one arm out and around and reached for the colt's side.

At his touch, the white hide jerked. The ears went up and the tail went still, but he sensed no malice. Flattening his hand, he stroked the coat's furry smoothness and felt the trembling warmth beneath.

Something within him fell away, some tightness he had carried forever. A wave of calm flooded and lifted him at the center of his being, comforting him in a puzzling way, if only briefly. Then the old trepidations roiled. They lunged up and seized him. They shook him like a sky full of lightning. All sense of control vanished and panic tore through him as if he had gone hollow and open-ended.

When it passed, when clarity resumed and his common way of being returned, he realized he was still touching the foal. Pulling back, he watched his hand shake. His whole body was shaking.

Settling back onto his heels, he looked up over his shoulder at the two shadowy bearded men in loose tunics and sheepskin capes who stood behind him. They stared back sullenly, their breaths fogging in the cold.

"Which one looks paler now?" Da said. "The horse or the boy?"

The stable thundered with their sharp barks of laughter.

Then, looking past him into the stall as if he were no longer there, Da said, "How old, would ye guess?"

Uncle Cletus, monstrously big, studied the tiny horse through bloodshot eyes. "Past weaning age," the giant's great voice raked. "Eight months maybe." Cowled in shadow, with that wild torrent of whiskers and eyebrows and hair, Uncle Cletus hulked like some ominous totem come to life.

Stooped and wiry, Da barely rose to Uncle Cletus' chest. Da's caved and thinned-out face looked like something hacked from wood. Even his prim beard lent little softness. "Just showed up at the flatboat in Morella?"

"Aye, with the molts."

Da's lanky hand bunched the top edges of his pelt cape and pulled it up over his throat. "Any reason given?"

"Andaman said Samira sent it. 'A gift from the queen,' her people told him. Said it was some peculiar kind of horse. Called it, ah,"—the giant squinched one eye—"an Eidon, or suchwise."

"Eidolon. Means phantom."

"Phantom?" Uncle Cletus scowled at the foal. "Ye mean ghost?"

"Aye."

"How do ye know that?"

"Our Luster. He's a trove of knowledge on these beasts. A regular sparkly trove."

Sidling eyes toward Da, Uncle Cletus spat. "Luster?"

"He came by last night."

The red eyes narrowed. "Came to yer doorstep?"

"Aye."

"Last night? To talk about this horse?"

"And about subjects even nearer my heart."

The giant's wooly face went slack. He swiped at his swollen, red-marbled nose.

"What I've been working at, Cletus. For these long months." Da leered, his thin parched lips spreading just enough to bare the sharp edges of his teeth. "Dagon help me," he said.

A year ago, maybe longer, the name Luster Spaulding first entered Ring's world. In the confines of Gargery House, time had a meandering quality. It expanded and contracted and folded in on itself in ways that made gauging its passage tricky. Sometimes he had the feeling he was going through a day twice. Sometimes he would blink and the light would shift, suggesting the passage of hours. Though he was certain the subject of Luster Spaulding first arose after Tutor Will Boyle stopped coming.

It was sometime last winter. Olalla had been treating M's itchy throat with a newly purchased catholicon. Da and Uncle Cletus, just in from the night cold, had been at the small hearth in the entry room, rubbing their arms and stamping snow from their feet. And quarreling about the boatworks. Spaulding Boatworks.

Ring had known the name Spaulding in that sense, as a business entity, as did everyone in Hastur. Spaulding Boatworks at Port Whilom built and repaired most of the city's ships. A vast enterprise, employing hundreds of workers and slaves. It was, Tutor Will had taught him, the heart of Hastur's maritime commerce. The boatworks also constructed and repaired the battleships for the city's 100-ship navy. By consensus, a share of the revenue from the granite quarry just north of Hastur went toward the building and maintenance of these ships, which helped make the boatworks the busiest place in the city.

There were other businesses named Spaulding, he knew, including the notoriously decadent wine hall in the city's upscale Horrocks neighborhood where Uncle Cletus lived. And, of course, there was Spaulding Stables, that relic from the age of the Old Ones where Ring presently found himself. But he had never realized these businesses were all owned by a single clan headed up by a patriarch named Luster Spaulding.

This knowledge he first began piecing together that night last winter.

The squabbling brothers, thawing amber-lit at the fireplace, pivoted before the heat and held up palms to it. A bat had once gotten into Gargery House and Ring recalled thinking how Da's spread fingers reminded him of the bones in that creature's wings.

"Connections, Cletus," Da said sharply. "Are ye brainless?"

They turned to roast their backsides.

"Connections then?" Uncle Cletus replied. "What's wrong with the ones we have? Samira and Wanlo and Enoch Glister? The mines? Killman? And suchwise? They serve us well. We need Luster Spaulding and his boatworks? I don't see the why of it."

Da looked up at Uncle Cletus as if the giant had just sprouted a second head. "The boatworks give us the greatest connections of all. It opens to us new markets in Landor and Pfaal and who knows where else. As both buyers and sellers. We could become the richest slavers from shore to shore."

The giant folded his arms. "More work, more bother."

"And a lot more jingling paldins in our purses."

Uncle Cletus frowned, unconvinced. "How much do we need, Anse? What's the point of earning more if we have no time left to spend it?"

Da lifted a fire-fork and gestured sharply with it. "Don't be a fool. Why not have more? I say let every crawler in Hastur cower in the shadow of my wealth. I promise ye, Cletus, there will be plenty of time left over for intemperance and lechery if that's what worries ye."

Uncle Cletus grunted that low growl of his.

"There are other benefits to having powerful friends," Da continued, "like protection. As it now stands, we alone guard our wealth. We have enough to make of ourselves tempting targets, but not enough to buy the influence that would make us untouchable. What if someone takes from us what we have?"

Uncle Cletus uncrossed his arms and curled his fingers into massive fists. "Let he who tries live just long enough to regret it."

Da busied himself stabbing at the fire. He rolled his neck. "Why think small?" he said at last, the tone of his high, gruff voice now measured. "Small thinking is for fishermen and cobblers. Let's align with those who can help make us true men of substance in this city."

"My friends are fishers and cobblers," Uncle Cletus said. But uncertainty crossed his face. "Even if we could benefit, why should Luster Spaulding help us?"

Da turned from the hearth. "I will make him do it." His narrow face took on a look of steely determination. "I will bring him here and engage him in business and then I will find a way to get from him what I

9

want."

Then one morning two months later—or was it three?— the house's iron street door swung open and in stepped Luster Spaulding, cloaked in a wine-colored tunic and a gold-clasped mantle of rich black wool. He proceeded with the aid of two short walking sticks and was steadied at the elbows by a pair of burly bodyguards. Luster Spaulding, come to talk with Da and Uncle Cletus about business.

This blood leader of the Spaulding clan was unlike anyone Ring had ever seen: a roly-poly man, fleshy and egg-shaped, sickly, with puckered, black-encircled eyes and blotched bronze coloring. A lifeless, limp-bristled beard hung from his face like loose threads. Then there was that awful breathing. Not like M's phlegmy breathing but a tortured crackle and rattle that sometimes filled the room and threatened, at any moment, to explode in ferocious, braying coughs. The first such spasm erupted immediately upon Sirrah Luster's entry. It racked the poor man's body and turned his face scarlet. It so alarmed the boy that fear of witnessing another had clenched at his young heart.

And, yet, this great glob of a man who required steadying and breathed with such difficulty and generally looked about to collapse beneath the burden of his afflictions, had displayed a twinkle of merriment, even teasing Ring about girls. "Are ye putting it to the pudding yet, little Ringy?" Sirrah Luster had wheezed, tapping the boy's shoulder with a walking stick. "Do I need to be caging my young daughter Addie?"

Ring opened his mouth but was lost for words. His face went full and hot. He bit his lip.

Luster Spaulding, moneyed kingpin of Hastur industry and potential champion of the Gargery family fortune, burst out laughing. A bellow that intermingled with coughing and gasping and more laughing: loud, terrifying and gleeful.

The bodyguards also laughed. Da and Uncle Cletus joined in as well with their own sharp laughter. The combined hilarity rose all around and circled in on him. It went on and on, an ordeal to be endured. He tried to merge with the merriment but when he smiled part of his lip briefly stuck to his teeth, presenting to all what he could only assume was a ghastly visage

When the jollity ceased, Sirrah Luster, flushed and somber faced, paused briefly to scrutinize Ring. He gave him a look as if expecting a serious response to his question, before breaking out in a new round of laughter that went on and on some more before dying at last in a dry croak of a chuckle.

Before Ring could make sense of this or say anything, Da shot him a look that sent him up the wooden steps to his room. He climbed in a daze, astonished not only by what he had witnessed but by the revelation that this important man knew his name.

From that day on, under the Gargery roof, Luster Spaulding became a sort of houseguest, appearing sometimes brazenly in scraps of conversation but mostly peripherally in vague phrases, innuendos, significant silences, sideways glances and knowing nods that Ring recognized perfectly and sometimes even understood the significance of. In this way, gradually, Sirrah Luster became ubiquitous, leeching into the very fabric of their existence and over time came to tint nearly every aspect of their daily perceptions. As the boy watched this transformation take shape, he felt the touch of it, and dread began seeping in.

How was all of this going to affect his life?

Shivering in the cold, dark shadows of Luster Spaulding's stable, Ring feared the answer to that question was about to spring out at him any moment with terrifying consequences.

***

The fadumo woke bobbing, her face covered, spikes of pain jabbing at the back of her head.

She had been dreaming and her slow emergence from the dream world added to the surrealism of awakening in an alien space. In the dream, still sharp in her mind, she had been in the caves near enough the overhead opening for daylight to cast a gray glow on her and her immediate surroundings.

The smell of death had clawed up at her.

She bent at the waist to examine something on the cave floor. There confronted her the wizened face of a corpse bitten deep with rot, its features a sunken landscape of bruise-colored flesh rent like tree bark, its hair wisps of cobweb. *Her* hair for now she saw plainly it was the body of a woman.

Sacrificial blood pooled beside the remains and grazed the warding stone.

Beyond the reach of the diffused light something else lurked, something she herself had summoned for this very moment. Both vast and powerfully contained, it thrummed and charged the darkness it had quickly come to own. She felt its many eyes still and blank upon her.

As she studied the dwindled face below, the dead woman's left arm twitched. The corpse's bosom shuddered beneath the stained cerements and began to swell then lessen in a slow rhythm. Breath seeped from misshapen nostrils in a rancid fetor. Eyelids fluttered and cracked lips parted wide enough to reveal a tongue of dried up leather.

As the blighted lips and tongue sought to form words, the corpse's lids snapped open. Shriveled eyes glinted up at the fadumo from deep

11

hollows.

"Who are you?" the fadumo asked, staring into the depths of the cadaver's eyes.

No response. She waited.

"Who are you?" she repeated, leaning closer.

The head lolled as if in protest then paused to focus on her. "Who do you think I am?" the corpse gurgled thickly.

Out of nowhere, a force crashed into the fadumo and her vision spun as her whole body spun. Some nightmare whirlpool had caught hold of her. Then the spinning broke and she was on her back looking up into a blood-specked face no longer hers.

"How does it feel?" her former form asked with a malicious grin. The eyes widened and gleamed.

Looking down at her new self, the fadumo realized the sullied cerement cloth now encased her. She lifted her arms—desiccated boughs, bloodless and deformed in the gray light. Within them, rigid sinews strained grudgingly, threatening to rupture from the provocation of this simple movement. When she looked up again, the figure bent over her had vanished.

The cave opening far overhead seemed to regard her.

The being who owned the dark paused in its thrumming. It snickered.

Then she awoke.

A wave of dizziness rolled through her. *Find it. Concentrate. Locate the pure energy.* Her stomach grumbled and threatened to heave. With a flex of her will, she calmed it and eased more fully into the moment. A familiar tingling roved her skin.

Without stirring, she peered through the sacking that cleaved to her face but the cloth was thick and the outside light weak and all she could make out was formless smudges.

Bulrush cords clung tight to her ankles and wrists. From all around came the sound of waves lapping and the air, cool and cutting, smelled of brine and fish. She listened to the voice of the wind. It told her there were two with her. She listened to the voice of the waves. It told her one was an islander like her.

Her bottom was cold and sopping. She partly sat and partly lay in water on the aft floor of a rowboat—judging by what she took to be the splash and scrape of oars. Her bound hands rested heavily in her lap. The boat cricked and swashed as it jumped and thudded on the water.

Her captors made small noises when they moved. She listened for hints of who they were and what they were up to. She didn't need to know their language to understand the meaning of their words but their voices carried away from her and they said little. She caught the name "Wanlo" which she recognized and some mention of Dagon Bay but that was about it. Nor did the voices of the wind or the water offer anything more.

She felt the jute sack roll against her and knew it must contain her things. She wondered if they had sent the box.

The sea teemed with the spirits of the drowned, the fatally marooned, the shark-eaten. She sensed their presence everywhere. Unfortunately, these gone ones lay well beneath the surface, beyond her funereal reach, water being to her powers the barrier it was.

Still, she was not alone. The pure energy was building around and within her and had already begun to dull the ache in her head.

At her back from the distance came the shrill squawks of flesh-footed storm gulls, the tropical birds unique to the islands of the Amethyst Archipelago. Long-winged and fork-tailed, the birds followed island fishing boats, picking off those quarry that eluded the nets. They also kept the islands all but free of rodents.

As a child on her home island of Presage Cay, when she wasn't in the caves, she and Tarbula sometimes raided storm-gull nests for eggs. Her mother would boil them and serve them up with seaweed salad and coarse root vegetables dug up from the sand. As it happens, that was the very meal the fadumo had last shared with her family. She tongued a scrap of seaweed from between her teeth.

Her mother had taught her how to read signs of the future in the flight patterns of the gulls.

Now the cries of these familiar creatures were fading from her life, perhaps for all time.

She allowed herself to seethe as she pictured the faces of those she had held most dear. Her mother, the Grand Fadumo Olisha; her younger sister, Tarbula, and the stern but warm-eyed elders of her village, including her own father, Mage Medji Zant wa Zant, who presided over all.

As she pictured these faces, she pictured them every one dripping blood, mouth agape, teeth bared, distorted in agony at the thousand tortures she planned to visit upon each of them. In her mind the gruesome images flickered as if in torchlight, pantomimes of terror.

How could they have betrayed her this way? Given her up to a fate she could only imagine? All she had done was take what they had taught her a step further.

A step too far, she had read at once in their distressed expressions. Yet....

The rowboat approached a large ship. The ship blocked the rush of the wind and made noises on the water: the flap of sails, creaking timbers, murmurs of its crew's conversations growing louder, a burst of laughter. Then the rowing stopped and the small boat coasted to a halt. Knocking sounds came from the bow.

The strong hands of her captors seized her at the armpits.

"Almost there, dearie." The islander.

Her bound and numb feet dragged below her as they hauled her to the front of the small vessel. They looped a heavy rope around her and fastened it under her arms where it tightened and pinched as she was lifted.

"Drogo!" someone called down. "Are ye sure she's the right one?"

"She's what they give us," Drogo answered.

"She's the one we want," the islander said. She noticed an odd quality to this one's voice.

Up she went, twisting and swaying, one yank at a time, the fibrous rope burning, until fresh hands wrestled her aboard.

"Take her below but keep her trussed until Wanlo gets a look at her. Who knows what this one might get up to?"

"Aye. Gives me the chill shudders. No luck in it, bringing her here."

They lugged her across the deck and down. Her heels banged against steps as the hollow of the ship encircled her. She banged her head on a doorframe. When they laid her on the damp floorboards, she felt it: the sort of presence she uniquely understood and this one not shielded by water. A woeful presence. Something with which she could work even without her spirit box.

Embracing the divine, she began opening a small space within herself, a welcoming place, dark but warm. She widened it, brushed it clean. Even as she sensed her toters lingering over her and others gathering near to get a look at her, she was lost in her craft. Lost in the flow of it.

When the door shut and she was satisfied all had quit her, she labored to her knees and bowed, still hooded and restrained at the wrists and ankles.

She breathed slowly eight times in and out. She pictured in her mind a circle of light. She touched her forehead to the floorboards eight times, circled full round to her left, and then full round to her right, her movements measured and crablike. She threw back her head at a jarring angle. The power began to build.

Staring fixedly into the chasm of darkness opening within, she began to whisper the warding song. "*Indrin Anarach, indrin retpus,*" she sang in the ancient tongue, caressing the words like threads in a weaving. Even whispered, the sovereignty of her voice was transcendent and her song wandered and flitted in time and space in all directions, seeking out the ghostly ear of her incorporeal shipmate. "*Djamballa andakode oculi imber. Bhaad oina jikan. Zagen indrin. Shug obassi. Obassi rhedrum.*" The strength coursed through her in giddy undulations.

I open for you. Come to me. Come to me. Find your new home.

Eight times she again touched her forehead to the floorboards with vigor, circled round to her left, then to her right, threw back her head and began anew, "*Indrin Anarach, indrin retpus.*" And so on. Now she was the fisher working the hole. She was the storm gull eying her prey. She was the spider watchful on the gossamer web.

Again and again till her mouth went stale and her knees throbbed and the bend of her back seared and a great shadow weighed upon her. Until finally, an apparition began to take shape in the black span she had cleared within herself.

He was coming home.

***

Upriver from whence the flatboat docked lay a forest of blood-thorn greenwoods known as Alburga Crossing. Hidden in that forest's night shade, amid an undergrowth of thistle stalks and frost-blackened witchweed, Andaman Gargery crouched and toyed with his dirk, thrusting it into the snow, wiping it clean, twirling it, watching the stars and the moon dance on its edges, waiting.

The small clearing beyond stretched snowy and moonlit, an oval of calm under a starry sky. Partway across the clearing, two people encamped near the gentle glow of a crackling need-fire. A father and daughter by the looks of them, sitting together on the far side of the blaze on blankets, facing partly away from him. The young girl, quite the charmer, sang in Landorian. Something about a king of suns. Her small voice carried light and sweet in the winter night, setting his yearning to music.

From this distance, these Landorians were nearly indistinguishable from Ligeians. But Andaman had a slaver's eye for race, and he at once had spotted the narrower ears, the wider nostrils, the higher foreheads and slightly oversized eyes that delineated them as natives of Landor. He knew in the clear light of day their bronze skin would appear yellowish and faintly freckled.

Watching the dirk, watching the Landorians, watching the churning whirligig cast off bars of light in his mind, he waited. He was good at waiting.

When he had first arrived, they were collecting dead branches and sticks from amongst a copse on the far side of the clearing. They carried them out and stacked them into a neat pile. The girl was surprisingly determined to be helpful, her small arms wrapped around and dragging some branches that were larger than she was.

When the gathering was done, the father sparked flint into straw, and the wood pile began giving up smoky flames. The pair studied the blaze as it grew with the same awe fire has inspired in this world since the days of the First People and the Old Ones, since back in the time when the

15

shepherd god Hastur first began forming the terrain of the city that now bears his name. If these two had been Ligeian, they would have offered some thankful homage to Osric, the bull god of fire and death—Andaman's personal deity—but the Landorians had their own gods, false as they were, and their own backward ways.

After setting out the blankets, the father made two plates of cold beans and bread and broke out a jug of something they shared.

They ate with their fingers, ripping the bread into smaller bits and scooping the beans. They chewed silently, looking into the fire and nodding. When they were finished, the father showed the daughter how to clean their hands and their plates in the snow.

The father pointed to the sky as he explained something, and the girl looked up and listened wide-eyed for some time.

Then they sat and at her father's coaxing, the girl began to sing about the king of suns who made everyone laugh. About summertime and golden dreams. About wanting to get back home. Andaman's Landorian was serviceable enough to get the gist.

When the last note of the song vanished in the night, the father helped the daughter to settle in, tucking her blanket around her. He kissed her on her high forehead and, bundled snug, she quickly fell asleep.

The father watched her sleep. Andaman also watched her sleep, one hand thumbing the ribbed handle of his dirk.

The man was middle-aged and for some reason put him in mind of a goat herder. He pictured the man with a goat herder's staff, wrangling his small charges about the vales and hillocks of Landor with the young girl tagging along at his side. Perhaps they had brought goats to sell at the market in Hastur and were now headed homeward. He smiled. If they had sold something at the market, they would have paldins, which would be a nice bonus.

Andaman made his way stealthily through the shadows of the forest. He stayed well back from the edge of the clearing as he followed it to where the campers had collected their wood.

The rhythm of the whirligig drove him. In these moments, the rest of the world dropped away and left him alone with his chosen ones. Every detail pulsed with clarity. Every motion thrilled his senses. When he made his destination, he eased into a crouch in a dark clutch of branches and resumed his watch.

At length, the father stood and began walking toward him. The man's outline wavered in the sparkle of the fire and his feet crunched in the snow. Stepping within the treeline, the man lifted his tunic, exposed himself to the night air and released a long, steady flow that steamed in the moonlight. From some hidden perch, a jumbi owl cried *whoot whoot*.

This moment brought all Andaman's life energy to the forefront.

16

He was exhilarated. A light show flitted behind eyes wide with anticipation.

The Landorian finished, then turned to walk back.

In a flash, Andaman was at him, wrenching back the man's head and raking the keen blade of the dirk through the muscles of his throat. A spray of blood fountained skyward as the torso staggered and danced in the assassin's arms. Life left the form in bursts and tremors that radiated in Andaman's bones, filling his brain with blinding light and arching him in an ecstasy that unleashed from his lungs a frenzied whimper.

As the body went lifeless, Andaman fell with it to his knees, gripping it dotingly, as if it were a fallen loved one. He remained in that pose for a long while until his strength of purpose at last returned. Then he dropped the body to the snow and rose, the bloody dirk still clenched in his fist.

He shambled toward the fire's warmth, as if some yoke were being lifted from him. Following back in the dead man's footprints, he came to the brink of the curling flames and stood there for a moment in their glow. It was now his fire, his camp— all the possessions of the dead man, his alone. He bent and lifted a half-burnt branch and slid it into the heart of the fire. With the dirk, he pricked from one finger a drop of blood, which he squeezed into the flames as he bowed his head and said a brief prayer to his god of fire and death.

Then he turned toward the young charmer, asleep in the blanket. Her face small and pretty. A lock of honey-white hair curled over one eyebrow. A silver starfish glinted up at him from a chain around her neck. He studied her lips and her nose and her lashes, absorbing the details of her sweetness. He watched her breathe. A vision of innocence and tranquility in the moonlit snow.

Not a care in the world.

CHAPTER 2
The Prophet of Aungier Street

He came from a hard place. It showed in how he carried himself and in his stony look. Always sizing up. Searching for loose fittings in the scheme of things. A brooder, ye could say. Dour as any who had ever walked this world. Not giant like Cletus but a big man, hard-built, with hefty shoulders and arms bigger than most men's thighs. Thick but taut in the trunk and almost no neck at all. His hands were all calluses and knuckles.

Darius Gargery, my father. Named a whelp of my own after him once. Should have known that would be a curse.

Darius never spoke much and when he did it was mostly lies. He could lie and ye knew he was lying and he knew ye knew he was lying. None of that mattered. Ye listened, not for what he said but for the why of it. What he wanted ye to think or feel or do.

All that was ever given that crawler, he told me once, was Momma, which he viewed as an ugly bargain, her people being poorly off and too spirited for his liking. She came with a fistful of paldins, a pair of oxen and a rickety wagon. The day they wed, he hitched the oxen, rode three days northwest to the market in White Worm and used the paldins to buy at auction his first two man-footed beasts—roundhead sisters named Afra and Trea—then sold them in Hastur three days later at a pretty killing. Or so he told me.

The balance of his gift ended up squandered on his flinty heart.

But she did bear him two sons. Whatever that was worth to him.

*He had this walking staff. Called it Old **Dolge.** Took it with him everywhere. Nearly tall as he was and almost too thick to fully wrap even one of his hands around. A gnarled thing, all scarred and dented. Can't tally the times I endured the crack of Old Dolge, as did Cletus. Momma, too. Though after that time he used it to lay me so low, it became mostly just a threat. And I knew it. Still, years later, whenever* *he shook Old Dolge at me, the breath would catch in my throat.*

Every day, I prayed Dagon would reach up from her watery deeps and rip him from my life. But I learned not to count on the holy ones that way.

One other thing about Darius: never once did I see him laugh or even smile.

An albino spider scampered along the top of the pen gate, crossed the crack in the board and then vanished behind. Ring, still lost in thought, peeked over to look for it when a sound caught his ear. People approaching. Da and Uncle Cletus ignored the commotion but he turned toward it.

The vaulted shaft, walled in huge, colorless blocks of stone, was as murky and cheerless as imaginable. Long groupings of crooked stalls lined either side of a wide, straw-littered aisle. The passage was windowless but along the outer wall large doors hung between some of the stall groupings. Although the doors were shut against the winter cold, their edges glowed with daylight, as did the gaps between their planks. This meager source provided most of the illumination and, since the doors were concentrated toward the shaft's middle, so was most of the light. The additional rays that entered through various roof and wall cracks offered thin and spotty supplement.

In the stalls, horses permeated the brisk air with their earthy essence. They stamped, shook their ears, tossed their long muzzles and snorted. With his eyes adjusted, most of the animals were at least partly visible, but many were just silhouettes and a few of the ones farthest away were completely lost in gloom. The noise of the approaching people came from around a bend somewhere beyond that gloom.

He stared down the stable shaft. The trapped space and darkness felt otherworldly and heavy on him from every side. In the blackest niches, shadows drifted out at him like emanations cast off by the stable walls.

Flee. The impulse yowled up within him. *Flee this awful place.* Fighting that urge with all his resolve sent a heady thrust of nausea cutting through him.

Outside, a sudden gust of wind shook the stable doors. It was as if he had willed the shaking with his desire to rage against this containment. If he could not be home in his familiar places, he yearned to at least be back outdoors in the light and the open.

On the snowy trudge over with the late-afternoon sun on his face, he had concentrated on churning his legs to keep up. "Mind yer da and don't annoy him, boy," M had warned as she clutched at him from her sickbed, her hands clammy and her eyes fevered. "And pay no attention if people look at ye oddly." She was always concerned how outsiders might react to his appearance.

Da, of course, had told him nothing about where they were going or why, nor had he expected an explanation. As he followed Da's heels through the slushy gray of Aungier Street toward Hastur's West Wall—the wall adorned with the shields and scarlet breast plates of the fallen—he tried to remember if he had ever been outdoors in winter before.

The people of Hastur were everywhere, even in the cold and snow. They milled about in the craggy cityscape of upper Allhollon district, crowding the cramped and twisty streets: men and women, young and old, bronze-skinned Ligeians and wayfarers and slaves of various hues. There were merchants, sailors and beggars. Their sandals scuffed and pattered on the snowy, uneven paving stones. Their conversations blended into a vaporous, grumbly drone. Many were days unwashed, their combined feculence assailing him from amongst drifts of wood smoke, challenging his gag reflex.

Already the gnawing cold, driven by bursts of wind, had begun to penetrate him, though he tried to ignore it.

A high-shouldered, droop-eyed peddler in a robe overtaken by patches pulled a handcart filled with damaged pots and rags. He muttered crossly, engaged in some inner debate. His hair was long and matted and wildly hanging. When he curled his upper lip at Ring, he displayed a bloody gum-line.

Two moon-faced girls with the distended features of the simple wove by, holding hands and laughing. One widened her eyes, then wrinkled her long, bony nose at him.

Ahead, a high-wheeled ox-drawn wagon rose from the crowd, hauling crates of roosters and making a ruckus of ringing, flapping and rattling. The wagoner swore and shook a fist at someone whilst the crates spit a trail of feathers through descending snowflakes.

Even as he moved amidst this throng, it all seemed oddly remote. He took it in as an observer, unattached and outside it, unsure how to react to any of it. When he did react, he worried he was being inappropriate, the finer points of interplay lost on him.

Sometimes back at home when he watched the crowds pass through Maule Square a random someone would look up and spot him standing in the narrow window and study him for a moment before passing on. Not often but sometimes and usually for just long enough to recognize and acknowledge his existence, fixing him as a brief encounter in the narrative of someone's day. This experience always unsettled him. He would replay it over and over in his mind.

Once near dusk a child holding her momma's hand had looked up at him. She smiled and waved. He did not smile or wave back, though later he wished he had.

He followed Da through a troupe of scruffy harlequins in pointy hats carrying the long poles they used in acrobatic performances. Or so he guessed of the poles' purpose, based on stories Tutor Will had taught him. He looked back over his shoulder at them. They appeared to be waiting for something. Tiny bells jingled on their hats.

When he turned ahead again, a skeletal, black-toothed crone, her scabby elbows poking through the sleeves of her frock, stumbled by, clutching to her chest a wine jug with one hand and a crying baby with the other. The sight jolted Ring with a pang of disgust.

Across the way, a door flung open and, in the threshold, a thick-bodied roundhead boy with short legs and a long, collared neck materialized. He held out a full chamber pot with his tiny hands. "Out the way!" he shouted. "Out the way!" Then, with no more notice than that, he launched the contents out into the street in a great splosh that provoked passersby into a flurry of leaping and sidestepping.

This activity caught the notice of a pair of sleek, dark-skinned Pyms, festooned with the long, blue ribbons of watchmen. They paused. Their eyes tightened and swept toward the roundhead with the chamber pot.

Officially the properties of the city of Hastur, watchmen were slaves of a higher calling, tasked with keeping the peace. Because searching out and quelling trouble was an undertaking few freemen would choose to pursue, these slaves were trained for the job and enjoyed extraordinary discretion in the handling of such matters. Armed with their peculiar short, braided whips, they always patrolled in pair.

Aware of the watchmen's attention, the roundhead hastened back inside and closed the door.

Satisfied, they resumed their march, synchronized step-for-step, the ends of their ribbons flitted and snapped in their wake.

On a street corner rose a small shrine to Nebo, the bearded and many-breasted goddess of wisdom, its arched scrollwork cracked. The stony beveled sunrays haloing Nebo's chiseled icon were transformed into icy daggers and her eyes had frosted over.

Nebo who lives in the clouds and sees all. She who lit the sun from her torch. Someone had left a bloody sacrifice at her feet.

The fallow cadavers of a dozen plucked and gutted fowls dangled from a line in front of a tall building adjacent to the shrine. The rust-stained abandoned house had a broken door and a swaybacked roof and it leaned to one side, toward a man with no arms and one leg who sat in the mouth of an ice-slicked alley. The man was soiled and emaciated, his ragged, insufficient garb wind-whipped. He seemed to be daring the structure to collapse upon him. Or perhaps wishing it. The boy wondered if this was not the most desolate being in all the world.

At that moment a squinty-eyed mouth breather, naked despite the cold, rushed dull-tinged and goose-pimpled from the alleyway, all in a lather with his feet slipping around in mismatched sandals. "I'm going to die!" he shouted, shaking his hands in the air. "I'm going to die!"

The crowd parted as he charged through. Tears streamed down his face. As he approached, his lower jaw outthrust and quivering, the distraught proclaimer jabbed his finger at people nearby. "Yer going to die! And yer going to die! And—"

He shuffled toward Ring and held out open hands as if to show there was no helping it. "We're all going to die," he said.

He took up this new cry. "We're all going to die! We're all going to die!" He lurched past and evanesced from sight and sound, leaving Ring stupefied.

Da paused and looked back. His face blanched. Every witness to the naked prophet had ceased movement as if time itself had stopped.

Then by unanimous decision, everyone moved again, including Da who pressed on down the street.

Trailing in his stooped father's silent and frigid wake, Ring spotted the gated entry with the name Spaulding Stables etched in high-reaching, greenish hieroglyphs. As his father worked the spiked iron open on whining hinges, Ring observed down a narrow side street a small girl with tangled hair and a dirty face tossing bits of meat to a cluster of black-throated butcherbirds, her bare feet red and raw in the snow. Far beyond her, in a grimy gutter, a pair of fat wharf rats scampered for their lives as the city rat-catcher, Ratter Lumen, and his ferrets closed in.

Somewhere nearby an agitated dog barked and growled. A waif with a fighting stick backed into sight from around the corner of a building and swatted, presumably, at the cur who growled all the more fiercely.

Inside the gate, across the white foot- and hoof-printed field of the stable's central courtyard, Uncle Cletus towered casually in one of those rare doorways sufficient to accommodate him fully upright.

"Brought the whelp along, then?" the giant called out. "What's the occasion?"

"Winter in Hastur," Da replied, stomping on a road apple. "Thought the pretty snowflakes might cheer the little villain."

Their voices, low and high, burred especially reedy in the outdoor cold.

As Ring crossed the field of snow, the wind took to moaning like an injured animal. His eyes began to water. His feet had gone numb and leaden, and chills had commenced chasing one another up and down the length of his frame. Leaning forward, scrambling to match the progress of Da's long strides, he had yearned with all his heart for the shelter of the building they were approaching.

But now, in the bleak shaft of the stable, he found himself feeling worse than he had outside. Not as cold, but cold just the same, and heartsick, so heartsick he half feared the weight of it would crush him somehow. As he cupped hands to his lower face and breathed warmth into them and tried not to fidget, the heavy darkness of the stable seemed to be forcing itself into his very pores.

"What did Luster say to ye, then?" Uncle Cletus asked. "Did he beg ye for help?"

Da, still clutching the cape to his throat, frowned and pursed his thin lips. Then enunciating carefully, he said, "*First*, he told me about this beast." Da nodded toward the foal, his demeanor indicating he would relate the night's events in the order of his choosing. "Ye did right bringing it here. Our Luster was quite impressed by it. According to him, our Samira has presented us with a rare and valuable gift."

Uncle Cletus looked dubious as he considered the colt.

"Luster says these ghost horses are sacred," Da said. "Priests raise them."

The giant frowned. His expression was almost menacing when his red eyes slid toward Da.

"Says ye normally never see one outside Morella. This might be the first one ever in Hastur. Maybe the first in all Ligeia. According to Luster, we could name our price for it." After a pause, Da added, "Half expected him to make me an offer."

From the thick gloom at the far end of the passage, figures emerged. Laborers and metal-collared slaves in work gowns and aprons began drifting from stall to stall with buckets and grooming tools. Some workers spoke to one another whilst others spoke playfully to the animals. "Hey there, yellow legs," chimed the accented voice of a Morellan slave girl. "Oats for dinner. Just what ye like."

"Four times a year, our Samira holds a festival," Da said, his high, coarse tone adopting a storyteller's flavor. "In the city of Karain. Gathering her freakish denizens from all corners."

The Morellan slave girl caught sight of Da and Uncle Cletus and stopped.

"Molts" these Morellans were called, because someone had once decided the color and texture of their silver-white skin resembled the sloughed-off casing of a molting snake. Tutor Will thought the term a slur though just about everyone in Hastur used it commonly. Like this girl, most Morellans had distinctive amber eyes with silvery sclerae. Aside from these colorings, though, Morellans looked like Ligeians, and in most ways, within the limits of their station, acted like Ligeians. "People everywhere," Tutor Will was fond of saying, "are much more alike than we are different." It was that kind of talk that had gotten the teacher in trouble.

The stable slave studied the men. Recognition dawned on her face and her features went still and bereft of emotion. She edged past them with downcast eyes and an economy of movement.

Ring turned away toward the foal, resting his elbows on the pen gate's cracked board.

"The galas last three days. Performances, contests, banquets. Like ours in Hastur, I suppose. But there, on the first morning, priests draw a full-grown ghost horse from their cloister. Dress it up in gold-threaded finery and a plumed headpiece. They display it before their thatched temple for all comers to behold, and the slack-jawed molts flock there in droves. Ye know how they are."

Ring looked back over his shoulder at Da's face.

"When night falls on the third day of the festival, Luster says the priests, attired in shiny white, fetch the beast. Chanting their chants, they parade torch-lit through the streets with it, accompanied by jugglers and clowns and reed-pipers and soldiers. Others collected along the way join in and follow to the queen's palace, where bonfires roar and Samira herself sits waiting. There before the feasting eyes of the queen and her servile assemblage, the priests bind the sacred horse. Then, with their long knives, they offer it up to their holy ones."

A smile split each man's lips.

"And the ghost horse becomes a ghost," Uncle Cletus said.

"Aye, for the gone to ride in the next world ... or so the molts believe."

The men's faces clouded over and they regarded the foal.

No sooner had the Ring settled into this quiet, when his uncle's bloodshot eyes turned on him. "What do ye say about the little beast, Ring boy? Ye like it well enough, then?"

Both men watched him with rapt curiosity.

"Speak up, whelp," Da said. "Ye like it well enough?"

They looked at him as if he were some new kind of life form they expected to transform at any moment in some amazing way.

Ring stepped from the pen and turned toward them, his shoulders bunched tight. He searched for a response, something of substance to get them nodding and back to conversing between themselves, but nothing came to him. All his thoughts fluttered out of reach like veils taken by a breeze. The only thing he could think to say was, "Aye." After he said it, the single word, foolish and empty, echoed in his head like the clang of a bell.

Finally, when their responding silence had lasted long enough to change the color and feel of the air, his father spoke. "That's it, is it?" After another pause, Da added, "Brilliant. A regular beacon of brilliance ye are. Do ye agree, Cletus?"

"If he was any more brilliant, my eyes would go blind."

However, this time they did not laugh at him. Da's face became a mask of mockery, with his eyes incredulous and his mouth gaping horribly. Looming Uncle Cletus similarly gawked.

Ring's footing wavered. He felt himself go loose-kneed as the strength left his body. Despite the cold air, his skin went hot and sweaty. He licked his lips.

"I like him very well, Da," he said at last. To his own ears, his voice sounded muffled and distant. "He is a beautiful horse."

Da glared back speechless, teeth gritted, his bearded wedge of jaw set at a slight angle. His bent, lanky form was so still as to appear petrified and so foreboding that it seemed to pull the darkness in around him.

***

Night fell before the pirates got around to removing the cloth sack from the fadumo's head. By then, sweat saturated her frizzy hair and dripped from her chin. The bulrush cords used to bind her chafed at her wrists and ankles, and the long stretch of cramped mobility had bedeviled her with cricks and soreness, and one leg had gone to sleep.

But she brimmed with accomplishment.

The warding song had succeeded in drawing out her incorporeal shipmate and attracting him to her and to the welcoming place she had opened within herself.

At first he approached cautiously, drawn more by curiosity than by the power of her spell. As he did, she breathed to him a litany of encouragement and mystical enticement. Luring him in was a long process, her without her warding stone and this gone one being a mere child unaccustomed to trusting adults even in his mortal life. But in the end, he entered and swelled up within her, not only filling her space but curling into it. That's when their dialogue had begun in earnest.

As the cloth of the sack swept from her face, exposing her skin to cool air, the fadumo rode the pure energy back into the outer world.

She lay in a small forward hold compartment. Two figures on the far side of a lit candle huddled over her. She squinted as her vision adjusted to the brightness of the flame and began taking measure of her visitors and her surroundings. Her empty stomach growled.

"Sounds as if our guest could do with a morsel," said the smaller of the two—the one holding the candle and the sack removed from her head—"but otherwise not much worse for wear. As a practice, what does yer island brood eat, Wolfdog? Monkey brains and such?"

"Fish," Wolfdog said gruffly, setting down an empty slop bucket. "Gull eggs, berries, tubers and no end of fish."

Their speech was some mongrelization of Pym, Landorian and

island talk but filtered through the pure energy she understood it perfectly and could even speak it with them, if she chose to.

"Then—what a coincidence—her personal gods have smiled upon her because if there's one delicacy I'll wager we have onboard it is fish."

Wolfdog shrugged. "There are no coincidences at sea."

"Spoken like a true outlaw."

The smaller one's details took form in the candlelight: face gaunt and leathery: a son of Pym, his coloring the purple-black of an overripe grape. One eye was dead, its blue iris swathed in a murky film to shocking effect. A rich black mustache of uncommon thickness fell past this pirate's chin. Gem-encrusted gold gleamed at his neck and one ear, and ruffled garb of assorted bold fabrics emblazoned his slender frame.

"Why have you taken me?" she asked sharply in her husky voice.

They started at hearing her address them in their unique vernacular. They looked at each other, and then looked back at her, as if doubting their own ears. After a long delay, they elected to ignore her question.

"Ye certain she's the genuine article, Wolfdoggie?" the one-eyed one asked at last. In the bleak pool of his good eye shined cunning alertness tinged with depravity. "We don't want to disappoint our good customer."

Wolfdog's garments were more muted and practical than the candleholder's, though they were stiff, stained and rank from being long worn unwashed and sea air had begun rotting their threads. Like her, this one had an islander's coloring: light ochre tinged with burnt orange. And there were the other distinct physical traits like the deep clefts at the chin and tip of the nose. A small, wine-colored birthmark stained one of the pirate's cheeks. One hand rested on the curved handle of a sword.

The fadumo didn't recognize this fellow islander but that was no surprise given more than four hundred bodies of land composed her native archipelago. However, there was something off the mark with this brigand that she noticed at once. Something that rippled false in the pure energy.

"Aye, sure and certain she is one of them," Wolfdog said, "and then some. It's plain as day. I'll show ye."

They hauled the fadumo to a sitting posture and Wolfdog took her hands, large and mannish. He held them up to display their backs. Decorous scars covered each: elaborate, raised, intertwining scars that began at her fingernails and traveled up the backs of her hands and wrists. Wolfdog bared her arms and the scars crept all the way up to her shoulders.

The scars formed symbols. There was a fat spider with a dragon's head wearing a crown; a three-bladed axe in a circle of fire; a demon with a flared, furrowing tongue; disembodied wings impaled with tridents and arrows; and leaping stick figures composed of jagged lines and elongated circles and squares.

"What do they mean?" the one-eyed pirate asked.

"They identify her to the spirit world as one unique," Wolfdog said. "They mean she can talk to ghosts."

"Ye believe she can?"

Wolfdog shrugged. "I wouldn't misbelieve it."

The scarred images just went on and on. There were hexagrams, interlocking rings, animal skulls, daggers, ghosts with stars for eyes. A lizard-headed bat strummed a lyre. Thorny vines entwined a horned crow. There was the vivid profile of a snarling dog with serpent fangs and a pig's snout. There were twisted hands formed from tree roots, hungry-eyed wolves, a thick falchion in a skeletal fist, flying fish, bleeding flowers.

The one-eyed pirate studied them all carefully. "These are amazing."

She grimaced at them. "What do you want with me?"

This time, the one-eyed pirate met her gaze brashly. He gathered his words, tapping his fingers one at a time against his thumbs. Then he said coldly, "Let me apprise ye of yer situation, dearie, so we are clear on all counts. I am who ye fear me to be, Wanlo, Wanlo the Freebooter, scourge of the foaming seas and bringer of bloody death. This is my ship, the *Pillager*, and this fine fellow is Wolfdog. He and the others who have chosen to sail with me are all the brothers I have ever had. That's all ye need know about us."

Wanlo scowled at her before proceeding.

"Ye are our prisoner who we are transporting to someone who has engaged our services for that very purpose," he said. "Our preference is to make our delivery and receive our handsome payment. But, just so there is no misunderstanding, let me assure ye that if ye bring us any depth of misery we will gladly put an end to it by showing ye the color of yer insides. Does that answer yer question?"

She dipped her head and peered up at him, her face blank but her half-lidded eyes made fierce. So, this was the notorious Wanlo the Freebooter. At once, she felt his resolve soften under the power of her gaze, felt him pulling into himself. But he masked it well and gave no quarter.

The fadumo could have left it at that, but she was not accustomed to men trying to frighten her and her anger took hold.

She flashed them both an illusion, a brief amalgamation of the same myriad symbols burned into her arms, only lifelike and menacing. Demons flapped and scratched and crawled through the air toward them, talons gleaming, tongues lashing, clamorous, oscillating the air with their hot, stinking breaths,

The pirates shrank back. Even Wanlo's dead eye seemed to beam with terror.

As she watched this reaction, she barely managed to withhold the

28

pleasure from showing on her face.

Much of what Wanlo revealed she had already wormed from the ship's gone one, though Piran—that was the spirit's name—much preferred talking about his own tragic story to answering her questions.

Born to a Pym slave and an unknown father, Piran had found himself orphaned at age five on the perilous streets of Bethmoora in western Usher. Bethmoora was a lawless land overrun with disease and poverty and Piran quickly learned to survive by rooting through market waste for spoiled food and sleeping in alleys. When that wasn't enough, he learned to get what he needed through stealthy theft. During the ensuing years, he endured beatings, illness, lice and vermin bites, rashes and sores, exposure and sexual indignities too appalling to relate.

At age 10, having had his fill of life in Bethmoora, he hid in a wagon that was part of a caravan headed north for Usher's coast. He arrived in a blighted warren called Red Mouse. It was there whilst watching a fellow thief being stoned to death that he encountered amongst the witnesses the seaman he thought to be his savior.

Not that Drogo Scuttin was any vision of salvation, with his bloated Pym face. The bridge of his nose was flattened and one earlobe was missing, but still he cut a fair figure in his long, banded seacoat, and he spoke with a flow of words that captivated the boy. Over stone plates of warm barley and groats, Drogo spun tales of life on the sea, of adventure and riches and riotous good fellowship.

"My crewmates are my brothers, fine fellows every one," Drogo said. "But there's always room for one more, say, a fine fellow like yerself, willing to start at the bottom as cabin boy. Willing to work hard and prove he has the sand to be a seaman and take his place amongst the bravest of the brave. There'd always be room for a fellow like that."

Drogo winked at him.

The next day, the *Pillager* set sail with the size of its crew expanded by one small cabin boy.

But it wasn't long before Piran found his new life to be every bit as treacherous as his old.

The crew amounted to 48 and all were hard-hearted brigands quick to scoff and cuff at the cabin boy. They insulted him mercilessly, played tricks on him, rudely ordered him about and thought up the nastiest tasks for him to perform. Not even Drogo, his recruiter, came to his aid.

A common sport was to trip him from his feet. Then, just as he was about to crash to the deck, the tripper would shout, "Watch yer step, sealegs!" and laughter would roll up all around him.

The first time, he was so taken by surprise that the impact slammed the wind from his lungs and left his head spinning. When he realized what had happened, he lay sprawled in stunned disbelief. The second time, which took place later that same day, he at least had the presence of mind to hold his breath and brace for the collision. The third time, also that day, he was carrying off a full pail of slops from below when the ambush arrived. The resulting clamor sullied both the deck and him and added measurably to the subsequent laughter. The putrid cleanup, of course, was left to him.

Day after day, they tripped him. His knees and elbows were all scrapes and bruises and he was soon walking with a limp. They took to calling him sealegs, then seahag and then sea- other things lewd and licentious beyond belief.

The meanest amongst them was an oafish Landorian boatswain named Red Judoc. Red Judoc was especially fierce with the boy when under the sway of grog.

Indeed, that was how, after several long months of abuse, the end came for the 10-year-old boy. Feeling the danger amassing that night as the grog flowed and the pirates' songs grew louder and more raucous, Piran hid beneath a tarp in a rowboat at the ship's aft.

He laid still and quiet as Red Judoc shambled near, cursing and calling him.

Some of the pirates were laughing. "Come on, Red, let the sprog alone. Enjoy the song and drink."

"Show yerself, ye little coward!" Red Judoc called. "Show yerself or ye'll pay dearly for defying me."

Then, "Look in the rowboat," yelled Obie Morag, the ship's carpenter. "Under the tarp." The words turned Piran to ice and squeezed all hope from his young heart.

The tarp lifted and the stubbled face of the bleary-eyed miscreant loomed over him, wreathed by night stars. The seaman drew back a hand and came down with it clutching a fat wooden cosh. Piran's palms went up to block the blow but to no avail. The cosh came down on his head and the last sound Piran heard in his sad life was the buckling of his own skull.

The fadumo wondered what Wanlo thought about the cabin boy's fate, whether he had any pang of guilt or admonition for his pirate brother who had performed the senseless slaughter. Wanlo the Freebooter, bringer of bloody death. Even to young children.

After nervously removing the cord from her wrists, the two pirates backed toward the threshold of the small chamber, watching her keenly, their faces still horrorstruck. As he backed out of the room, Wanlo the Freebooter, without realizing it, left behind a small remembrance. A curled hair the length of a cat's whisker came free from his lengthy mustache and eased downward to the floor. When the door shut, the fadumo retrieved the strand and tucked it into the hem of one sleeve.

Shortly another pirate arrived with a bowl of tasseled blobfish. The fadumo looked into the bowl and her stomach went sour. It smelled terrible. She poked at the fish with a spoon. It languished in pale and slimy chunks in a thin broth. She sampled the broth. Not exactly prepared in the savory manner of her mother. Her meal came with a flask of weak wine though, so that was something.

She looked up at the pirate who delivered these delicacies and could see at once he meant her no good.

This Landorian needed a shave. His narrow ears were swollen and deformed, and his freckled nose was fleshy, with gaping, hairy nostrils.

"Maybe I'll come back later and give ye some company," he said, leering at her. "A strapping, sweet thing like yerself shouldn't be left to go cold in the night."

Within her, Piran writhed angrily, frantic as a trapped squirrel.

That night she did not sleep. Outside the door of her cramped compartment, their lusty shouting and horseplay kept her alert. She heard some of them talk of her. They called her the conjure woman. They said she could create visions. They said she could speak with the dead. Some sounded wary, whilst others joked about her. About visions they had of her shorn of her clothing and on her back and so on. She expected at any moment for someone to stumble down the steps and burst through the door. She imagined filthy hands clawing at her.

And her last defense? A muddled and angry young wraith not yet up to the task of protecting her. But, given the time, she would get him there. Anarach willing.

Late in the night, the pirates' reverie faded. She heard them collapse, one by one, into drunken slumber in their berths or massed together on the steerage floor or elsewhere above or below deck. Their snoring overwhelmed the sounds of the ship and the sea. Using the pure energy, she drifted along the boundaries of their dreams, sifting for bits of useful information amongst the refuse and wreckage of their troubled nightscapes.

In the morning, the one with the hairy nostrils staggered in, passed her a bowl of dried apricots and faro bread and a jug of water. This time he didn't speak or wait for her to finish but lumbered off with her slops, putting extra effort into every weaving step.

By then, Piran had told her what she had already suspected. The brigand serving her meals was none other than Red Judoc.

***

Ring only came when she summoned him. Usually through his nursemaid, Olalla, or, before her, Everild, or before her, the one who wasn't around long and whose name he couldn't recall. Sometimes a house servant other than the nursemaid would come for him, though only a few times because M believed strongly in each having assigned responsibilities.

It had always been like that: him only seeing her when she called him to her sickroom. Except maybe it hadn't. He retained a sliver of memory of her holding him in her arms outside at some public gathering: a festival or an execution. The memory nestled distant and dreamlike, and it seemed unthinkable they would both be outdoors together that way, yet he chose to hold onto its possibility.

When he entered her room, he stepped into different time and another way of being. Here she existed as some figment from the past and he was a younger version of himself. Things felt all-encased, as if in cotton: the compacted darkness, the oppressive air laced with her sickness.

Her breath was phlegmy, her features drawn, and sweat seeped from her hairline. Beneath her blankets she lay, neither dead nor fully alive but haunting some restless middle ground.

Surrounding her, the dressers and tables were covered with engraved figures, talismans and fetishes. She had dioramas of each of the four holy ones: Nebo on a blanket of billowy clouds; Dagon amid a tangle of seaweeds, her tentacles fanned out around her in a demonic nimbus; Osric, encircled in flames, with his great horns and mammoth ballsack; Hastur asleep beneath the soil, cradling his shepherd's crook. There were silver carvings fashioned by her father and brother: blood hawks, temples, a crescent moon, her name in hieroglyphs. There was a soldier with a spear, good luck phalluses, and one of those starfish necklaces so popular with the young. There were also painted tiles she had collected as a girl, bracelets he had never seen her wear and small containers of powders and fluids: nostrums purchased from the endless parade of beggar priests who went door to door peddling them as curatives. And always a bowl of smoking myrrh, lending a languid tang.

When he came to her bedside, all he saw was her face as she spoke. After the first few sentences, her voice turned unaffected and took on a lethargic quality, as if she were reciting lines from memory. He didn't always understand what she was talking about but he paid close attention. He didn't want to miss anything, so rare were these opportunities.

Sometimes she would tell him what it was like when she was a girl. Her recollections drifted. They were broken and were not always believable, but he listened through all that to get to the bits of truth. She told him how she and her brother, Zath, and sometimes her mother, used to sing and dance in their kitchen or play some game called "knucklebones." How her father would come through the door in the evening with open arms to hug them, his hair sparkling with silver dust.

Sometimes she asked him if he remembered his brother, Darius. He told her he did because that made her happy but the truth was all his thoughts about Darius were cobbled together from what others had said.

He did have one memory but it was elusive. It was there but he just couldn't get at it. It was about the night Darius died but something about it was so painful he could never fully realize it. Whenever he tried, it would slip away. Of course, he had been very young back then. She said when Darius died, her world had turned black and upside down and had never again righted itself. But she was so given to exaggeration he wondered if that was true.

M was eager to give him advice, to pass on something of value to him whilst she was "still around." After all, she was not long for this world, she liked to remind him, and when she was gone who would be left to understand him? Him with his horrid features and dim wit and childish impulses? Not his father, by any stretch.

"Ye will be alone, boy," she would say. "As alone as anyone could be. But it's better to be alone than to bring false people into yer life. Trust no one. Always remember that."

She also told him time was his enemy and the only thing worse than the drudgery of life was death. And she told him other things of which he could make no sense.

What about the terrors from the dark, Momma? The night gaunts and the Gloamer who assails and overwhelms? What about the cold creeps, the empty cravings, the doubts and uncertainties that worm in the bones, the life expenses incurred for which all currency is lacking? The thorough vexation of the spirit? What about the dead weight of exile on a young heart?

But he would never raise such worries with her. He knew if he did she would talk right through them. Early on he learned that his concerns had no perch in this room.

Her eyes always drew him eventually. Eyes that ultimately focused elsewhere, as if peering through a spyhole at a distant object in some foreign territory. Sometimes her eyes took the form of bleak spheres, protruding and glassy; sometimes they turned wooden and flat, like Da's eyes could be, almost as if painted on; sometimes her irises sparkled and seemed to circle downward in an endless spiral, from whence his reflection looked back up at him.

No matter where in the sickroom he stood in relation to her, even when he was close enough to sense her wildly fluttering heart, even when she did reach out and touch him, even when he leaned over her and put his ear close to her words, somehow she always remained a furtive figure, distant. Hopelessly beyond his reach.

***

When Wanlo the Freebooter returned to the forward hold compartment after breakfast that morning, the fadumo studied him for

33

changes in his appearance. What she saw were small differences: some flaking at the eyebrows, a little less sheen to his mustache and hair. Some minor flagging in his posture, perhaps.

He eyed her warily.

"Cause me no grief today, conjure woman," he said in a tone more pleading than commanding. "Last night's drinking, I fear, has done me in."

He blames his state on too much grog. Let him think what he wants.

"The winds are not availing us today," he explained, his voice a little foggy. "The sea is black and smooth as midnight. We'll make slow progress. May add a day to our voyage. Feel free to roam the ship, if ye like. At yer own risk, of course."

The fadumo said nothing.

He shuffled out and closed the door, leaving her to her thoughts, which turned at once to the stubble-faced pirate who brought the fadumo her meals and carried out her slops. The boatswain Red Judoc, the treacherous scoundrel who, in a drunken rage, had slain Piran and had personally threatened her with defilement.

The shade painted Red Judoc as a villainous rogue, as villainous as any who had ever put to sea, but the fadumo perceived as much herself. To some, pirating was just a way to get by; to others, it was a true calling. When Red Judoc wasn't measuring his greatest joy in the slicing of captive flesh, he did so in the wanton conquest of female honor, these latter assaults so loathsome that not all survived, and some who did may have been better off had they not.

At midday, having fully recovered, Red Judoc delivered the fadumo's meal—the woeful tasseled blobfish again—with a generous side dish of lechery. He remarked in detail on the lure of her thighs and the swell of her breasts.

"'Twould be a shame to leave a strapping, sweet thing like yerself longing amidst the rough and tumble of a seafaring night," the boatswain said. "Better to have a fine fellow like myself putting ye to use, as nature intended." He winked an oversized Landorian eye at her. "I'll bet ye buck and squeal with the best of them, dearie."

She gave no reply but peered at him in the same way she had Wanlo the Freebooter and Wolfdog, her hooded eyes slits of contempt. He met her gaze unwavering.

Infuriated, she sent out a burst of horrifying visions to his mind's eye of the pirate. Writhing depictions from the scars on her arms: dragon-headed spiders, wide-eyed demons, horned crows and dogs with serpent fangs.

But where Wanlo and Wolfdog had blenched at her venomous images, Red Judoc bared his teeth and laughed. He peered into the onslaught of illusion as if wildly entertained. When it ended, he seemed invigorated.

"Are ye done now, conjure woman?" he asked. "It will take more than tricks like that to dissuade this fine fellow from his purpose."

With the pure energy, she sent a wave of chill his way. He shivered briefly and lost his smile but not his resolve.

She felt an uncoiling from the spirit cove within her. In her peripheral vision, she watched Piran's form taking shape darkly.

Red Judoc regarded her with his cruel Landorian glare, unaware of Piran's emergence. "Maybe ye need a bit of hard play to get ye in the mood." The pirate flexed his fingers at her and took a step forward.

Before he could make good on his threat, the door swung open and a short-limbed, flat-headed Pym with a scent reminiscent of moldy cheese thrust his top half through the threshold. "There's a hitch in the rigging, Red. We need ye to have a look."

Red Judoc halted, anger quaking his features, his clenched hands trembling with rage. "Aye," he said, choking out the word hoarsely. Then he spun and bolted from the compartment, slamming the door in his wake.

The fadumo turned to Piran. "We need to do something about that one soon," she said.

The ghost swirled, dark as a thundercloud.

* * *

As his father's eyes bore into him, Ring recoiled. He folded his hands behind his back and braced himself, unable to move or breathe.

Just like those nights he felt the mantle of fear descend; his stomach churned, his skin prickled, and half-formed thoughts flooded wildly through his mind. Also like those nights: the anticipation was nearly as chilling as the ultimate outcome itself.

Embodiments of rage. During his brief life, he had faced his share.

But this time, almost at once, the danger passed.

Da's neck rolled, and his face drained and went expressionless. His wiry body shrugged off the fervor that had seized it emphatically enough to elicit a faint chink from the paldins in the purse beneath his sheepskin cape

After several moments of silence, Da turned slightly and pointed in the distance over Ring's head. He said quietly, "See that one? The spotted roan?"

Uncle Cletus squinted.

Then Da showed his back to the boy and pointed in the opposite direction. "And that one over there? Just like it. Near the far door?"

Ring's uncle followed the gesture.

"Tull Fennel's," Da said. "Both of them. Our Tull surfaced in the chinwag last night, as ye might suspect."

Uncle Cletus crossed his arms and nodded, as if appraising the horse.

Satisfied they were through with him, Ring loosened and straightened and began breathing again. He felt a curious debt of gratitude toward Tull Fennel, whom he knew only by reputation as being some cavalry officer in the city's army, the Vermilion Shrikes. Owning a horse was a luxury only the truly rich could afford and cavalrymen were amongst Hastur's richest and most prestigious citizens. Cavalrymen owned most of these horses, he guessed.

"Tull Fennel," Uncle Cletus said, dragging the name scornfully across the low rasp of his voice.

"The crawlers will be carving marble into his likeness any day."

"Shrikes." Uncle Cletus grunted. "Pompous braggarts with their ribbons and flags."

"Don't forget the bird hats," Da said.

The men barked out a laugh.

"Let him have his trophy," Da said. "After tonight, it will be the summit of his achievements."

Uncle Cletus gave a start. "Tonight, then?"

"Gibbous moon."

"Gibbous what?"

"She says it's what we want."

"The conjure quim?"

"Dagon help me, with luck, this time tomorrow, we'll have Luster's problem all sorted out."

The men exchanged looks and said nothing for a long while.

Luster's problem. There was the crux of it. Of all the references to Luster Spaulding that had circulated in Ring's presence, those alluding to this mysterious problem had emerged as the most urgent to Da and Uncle Cletus. Ring had come to understand that the success of whatever plot the brothers had hatched to gain favor with Sirrah Luster hinged on resolving this particular difficulty, though he had only the dimmest idea of what that difficulty might be or what solving it might entail, aside from the distinct impression that the solution somehow involved him.

The first time he recalled hearing a reference to "Luster's problem" was some weeks after Luster Spaulding's visit to the house. It was late winter or early spring—the snow was gone, he remembered—and M was feeling particularly nauseous that day.

The spy, a stubby, feral-faced creature named Killman, had arrived at the door with news of a battle in a valley two and a half days northwest of Hastur.

Killman was a longtime associate of the Gargery brothers. He had bulging eyes and prominent temple veins and a wily way of gesturing and moving that Ring found unnerving. But Da, not a man long on trust, relied on this spy's reports and Killman's information, gathered from some vast nebulous network, invariably proved accurate.

According to the spy, a large band of Skalken nomads had attacked the shantytown of Scylding Tangle, just south of White Worm.

On hearing this, Da went a shade paler. "Scylding Tangle, ye say?"

He and Uncle Cletus locked eyes. The giant's lips curled within the shaggy beard.

"Good fortune to us," Uncle Cletus said dully.

Killman said the Skalkens, having terrorized the citizenry in all the horrendous ways typical of barbarians, had set up camp in the ravaged village. Unfortunately for the raiders, word of their initial trespass of the Ligeian border had made its way back to Hastur days before and the Shrikes' Fourth Legion had immediately set out in search of them.

"The army arrived at dawn," Killman said, sweeping the Gargerys with a sly gaze, "and they caught the savages unawares."

Those Skalks left breathing were up for sale, the spy said. If the Gargerys set out at once, they could scoop up dozens of the prisoners at a bargain price.

Because of the Skalkens' uncivilized and devious ways, few city merchants or householders had use for them. But at the copper, gold and iron mines north of Melmoth near the Ligeian River, it was a different story. They were always in need of fresh, strong backs, given the harrowing conditions and brief life spans of miners. The mines paid slavers well for anyone strong enough to chisel or swing a pick. Of those not suitable for the mines, the better-looking women could be sold to outlying brothels and the older children could go to rural farmers for field work.

All told, if they acted now, the Gargerys stood to make a pretty killing.

The veins in Killman's temples pulsed as Da crossed the spy's palm with gold paldins.

"And don't forget yer seafaring friend tonight," Killman said. "He will be at the regular meeting place at the regular time with the special cargo ye requested."

Da smiled and added another coin to the spy's stack.

Then, without a word, Killman opened the iron door and whisked off into the street. Da stood at the opening with his long fingers hooked on the door handle. Uncle Cletus loomed nearby. For a while, the men gathered their thoughts.

Outside the door, Cousin Andaman, not privy to the Killman meeting, stood waiting, focused darkly on something across the square. A good-looking young man but uncombed and disarrayed, with ill-fitting clothing. He toyed absentmindedly with his dirk, holding the point to a finger whilst twisting the handle with his free hand. Sunlight caught and flashed on the flat of the blade. A silver starfish swayed from a chain at one wrist.

"We should send Andaman with a wagon, then?" Uncle Cletus said at last.

At the mention of his name, Cousin Andaman turned.

Da nodded. "We should send two wagons."

"Aye," Uncle Cletus said, his lips curling again. "If I go, what will ye do about tonight?"

"I can handle our pirate alone."

The giant nodded.

"Looks like Wanlo has come through for us again," Da said.

Uncle Cletus shrugged.

"Hopefully, he'll have just what we need to finally settle Luster's problem," Da said.

Uncle Cletus looked doubtful but kept his tongue in his teeth.

Then the men nodded to one another and the giant ducked through the threshold into Maule Square and he lumbered off, Cousin Andaman tailing behind him.

Ring had worked the details of this encounter around in his head, sifting what meaning he could. The next day, he would learn what Wanlo's cargo was, and eventually he would piece together what Luster Spaulding's problem was. But he would never fully understand the significance Scylding Tangle held for Da and Uncle Cletus.

Ring's memory of the spy's visit had faded when an event some days later refreshed it in his mind.

He was downstairs playing in the main room at the time. It was a favorite game of his, developed bit by bit over years of long hours in the house. In the game, he was an explorer, worldly and brave, renowned for his many great discoveries. Walking barefoot, slowly, heel to toe, along the very edge of the room's conch-patterned carpet, he imagined traversing a treacherous ledge on a mountain. Beyond the ledge lay an abyss of unfathomable depth. The game was not just to maintain his balance but to do so whilst envisioning every aspect of this fantasy as vividly as possible.

When he played it right, the game absorbed him, drawing him away into a sort of mournful trance. There, as he treaded the brink of annihilation, every contour of the stone ledge, every pebble, every sandy grain took form beneath his feet. A breeze whispered down from storm clouds just above him where the upper reaches of the mountain vanished. Sometimes he glimpsed a presence in the clouds, amongst the roiling black and glints of lightning. A presence that seemed to follow his progress. *Is that ye watching, goddess of wisdom?* The air, raking at him softly, was cool and thin and smelled of coming rain. As he stepped, he felt the pull of the great void beside him and knew in his heart it was the pull of the Netherworld, coaxing him to obliteration. Sometimes, from deep in the void, he even heard the faint roar of the death god Osric, calling to him. When this happened, the boy would pause and his foot would hover uncertainly in the dead space beyond the rim of the ledge.

That day, he had just begun playing the game when, stepping into a warm patch of sunlight near the shelves that held the skulls of his ancestors, he was roused to reality by the sound of Da's voice coming from M's sickroom. So rare was it to hear his parents speaking to one another that curiosity drew him within earshot.

"Why do ye hate me?" she asked in her rheumy voice. "It's the illness, isn't it?"

"I don't hate ye."

"Ye hate me, and ye wish I was dead."

"Don't say that!"

"Him, too. Ye always have."

Da said nothing.

"Yer own blood."

Da said nothing.

"Ever since...."

"I told ye not to bring that up again."

"Ever since then, ye have no time for us."

"I'm a busy man. The rest of it is all in yer head."

"Ye seem to have enough time for yer island woman."

"Enough! Dagon help me, why do I bother with ye?"

"She frightens me, husband."

They were silent for a while, then Da said, "What I do with my property is my business. But I'll tell ye this much: That woman is the key to solving Luster's problem. I'm convinced of it. If I told ye what she is capable of, ye wouldn't believe me." After a pause, he added, "I hardly believe it myself."

"What about *him*?"

"When the time comes, I need him to do his part."

"To do what?"

"I don't know yet. But something. To abet us with Luster somehow."

She made that helpless sound in her throat, the one she made when compelled to speak but was unable to find words. Finally, she said, "How is he ready for any of this? What will they think of him, the way he is?"

"They'll think he's a boy like any other. They'll think what I want them to think. Don't fret the hows and whats. I'll take care of it. This is about *outside* business. Yer dominion is the running of this house."

She sobbed. "I have a terrible headache. Please leave me now to my suffering."

"If what I ask is beyond him, Gracie, then he is useless to me."

Just then, two girls with damp sleeves swept into the main room from the scullery next to the kitchen. Ring's nursemaid, Olalla, and the maidservant Bartine whispered sharply in their flute-like Morellan tongue, all-consumed in their exchange.

Not much older than Ring, Olalla and Bartine were willowy and tight-breasted, their silver-white skin contoured with the palest of pink and lavender, their amber eyes clear and deep, their necks, circumscribed by metal collars, rising statuesque, their forms caressed by the sheerest muslin as they flowed barefooted across the room toward him. Yet the inevitable sadness tugged at the corners of their features and a hint of resigned dullness veiled their countenances, even in this moment of agitation.

Da said he kept for himself only the best. But his keeping reduced them, every one.

They spoke of discovered broken cups; a cupboard full of broken cups. How would they explain this to their masters? Would the blame turn on them?

Slaves weren't supposed to talk in their native language in front of Ligeians, but the rule was lightly enforced and Ring had heard enough Morellan over the years to pick up a rough understanding of it.

Not wanting to be caught eavesdropping on his parents, not even by these two, he returned to playing on the carpet. As the girls passed, their young womanhood imbuing the air, he heard Bartine's whispered suggestion that, perhaps, it was the new one, Aneleh, who had somehow broken the cups with her island magic—perhaps she had stirred some spirit to the task.

As they made their way to M's bedside to share the news of the cups, he envisioned his headless ancestors sleeping beneath the floor of this very room. Sometimes when he was playing here, he sensed their company through the soles of his feet, though he didn't sense it now. Could someone really call up the gone from their repose? A question he should have thought to ask Tutor Will.

Finally, late last night he was in bed, ears keen for the sound of any approach. Gargery House was dark and quiet and, despite his best efforts to stay awake, his consciousness was giving ground. He was about to drift off when a knocking from downstairs roused him with a start.

Overhead, Da's footsteps moved quickly and precisely on the stairs. The flame of an oil lamp cast a glow into his room, forming shadows that slid across the wall before sliding away again. M, who had complained that day of chest pains, called out from her sickroom downstairs but received no reply. The air in his room stirred as the front door opened and Da greeted Luster Spaulding by name.

Careful to avoid the board that groaned, Ring crept four steps down the stairs. Luster Spaulding's tormented breathing was now clearly audible over the night sounds let in by the open door. One more step down the stairs and he could just glimpse the figures at the entry. He sat very still, studying them in the weak light below. The outdoor cold streamed up to him.

The roly-poly, egg-shaped man coughed several times, obscuring the thud of the shutting door and the squeal of the sliding bolt. This time, no bodyguards accompanied him.

Gathering himself, Luster Spaulding said in a choked voice, "Forgive the hour, Anse. This night holds no peace for me." He wore the same black wool mantle he had worn on his first visit and an azure tunic with a purple sash, snowy and wet at his chest and his knees, as if he had fallen. He wobbled on his two short walking sticks.

"Of course," Da said, holding the oil lamp. He stood stooped in the familiar fringed sleep gown that so loosely overhung his frame, his hair comically mussed. He started to near his visitor but hesitated.

Sirrah Luster chuckled. "Quite a pair we make in the dead of night," he said. Then he gasped, from either shortness of breath or the press of despair or maybe both and, after taking a moment to compose himself, said, "Apologies for visiting my problems on ye at this hour. We have no long history and ye owe me no special consideration. However, ye have given me some small indications that ye are aware of my difficulty and are, perhaps, sympathetic to it. And ye strike me as a singularly resourceful fellow." The patrician smiled. "I'm not too big a man to ask for help."

Easing forward, Da used his free hand to brush snow from his visitor's rounded shoulders and the plush mantle. "Come in," Da said, taking an elbow. "I'll start a fire. Warm yer bones. Of course, I'll help ye. I know what yer problem is and I think I know how to make it go away."

"Go away?" Sirrah Luster took one shaky step and halted. "Ye don't know how happy that would make me. But how? I've already tried the usual persuasions. What have I overlooked?"

"I promise ye there are avenues ye have not considered," Da said levelly. "There is definitely a way."

From his vantage, Ring couldn't see very well but he sensed a change in Sirrah Luster's demeanor.

"It may be a bold way, though," Da said warily, "and maybe even a wicked one. Not a way around our obstacle so much as through it. Would this kind of solution interest ye?"

Sirrah Luster cleared his throat and, leaning heavily on the walking sticks, rocked his bulk back and forth. "I would never become a party to murder," he said, though some aspect of his manner suggested this was not strictly true. "My preference is to face my enemy after his downfall. To joke

41

and smile and laugh with him."

"No, not murder," Da reassured, "but murder is not the only evil possibility. Perhaps not even the most evil one."

The patrician went noticeably still and alert, the crackle and rattle of his breathing filling the silence. "At this point, short of murder, I would be open to almost anything."

They retreated from the entry and their voices faded. Hours later, long after the visitor had departed and Ring had gone back to bed, he was still pondering the meaning of what he had witnessed. What was this oft-spoken-of problem that brought Sirrah Luster to their door in the night and what deviltry was Da hatching to solve it? Ring especially feared any role in it planned for him.

Now, back in the dark stables, these thoughts and worries continued to gnaw at him. He rubbed the cold from his upper arms.

Da and Uncle Cletus still stood with their backs to him, talking.

"In the meanwhile," his uncle asked, "what do we do with our ghost horse? No selling it, then?"

"Samira would be furious. Besides, I have a better use for it."

"What are ye thinking?"

"The beast opens another door, once we've settled Luster's problem."

The men shifted to face Ring and the white foal.

"We keep the ghost horse here," Ring's father said, his drawn face displaying renewed sternness around his eyes and bearded mouth.

Uncle Cletus nodded, though he appeared uncertain. After a brief silence, he said, "How much will that cost us?"

"Nothing."

Uncle Cletus frowned in that disturbing way of his.

"Luster and I reached an agreement on that," Da said.

Ring watched his father slide eyes toward him for Uncle Cletus' benefit. The giant spat and considered the boy blankly, looked at Da, then looked back at Ring. Even through the shadows, Ring could see realization light his uncle's face.

The men exchanged looks. Then they both turned to Ring with a shared grim expression that brought a fresh dread crawling up from within him.

He returned to the foal. Slight and alien and penned in. Surrounded and threatened. Ring wondered if this Morellan colt, uprooted and so far from home, didn't feel the same way he did.

CHAPTER 3
Things Invisible

Looking back, we must have been nearing them for some time. But that's not how I remember it. As I recall, I just gazed up and there they were: this great gathering of birds in the sky. Pulsing clots of them, clustering, falling away, coming together again. All black and wavy. Swarms of them pouring forth from the clouds and the sun. Black-throated butcherbirds, bloodhawks, crows. Cawing and chittering. Every bird in Ligeia, it seemed. Their cries and the flutter of their wings soon prevailed over all sounds.

A wonder for a young boy to witness, really. Me, maybe seven, with Da and Cletus in that rattly wagon on a crisp afternoon. Part of a caravan headed for White Worm with less than a half day's journey to go. Coming to buy roundheads at auction. Bumpy riding all day through rutted, late-autumn meadows of failing grasses, sheaves brittle and brown, and wild groves of trees. All around us, the smell of plants returning to the soil.

Da was in one of his moods, with Old Dolge at the ready, so there was no talking. Me, I was famished and my tailbone hurt. Blister flies snapped at us. Dagon help me, I never wanted to get anywhere as much as I wanted to get to White Worm that day. Then we came upon the spectacle of these birds and I forgot all that.

The lower ones by turns swept in and lighted. But ahead the ground fell away and I couldn't see where they were coming down. I should have been able to see something but I don't remember it that way.

As we cleared a rise, I turned to Cletus, two years my junior but already a head above me. His eyes on the birds were wide with amazement. I was enjoying watching him when at once all the color fled his face. His expression dropped and those eyes began brimming with tears.

Turning front, where the wide basin had opened before us, I saw what he saw.

And cold terror gripped me.

Dead men lay everywhere. On bellies, backs and sides. Hundreds of them. Maybe more. Caped in fur, half naked, pale-skinned and hairy, their long faces painted blue. Blood-slaked and fanned across a rock-strewn, weed-choked landscape dotted here and there with twists of trees. Disjointed these dead men looked, pierced and torn, some impossibly angled, some missing parts. Some little more than parts. Many with aspects showing awful recognitions of their fates.

Even our oxen cringed at the sight.

Dozens of Vermilion soldiers paired off amongst the fallen. One soldier would hold a sack, the other would bend and carve at a corpse with a dagger. Collecting ears for an accurate tally of the enemy dead, I later learned. All the while, the soldiers talked lightheartedly. One waved to us with a bloodied hand.

And throughout all this hopped the birds, footsure, with flitting movements and onyx eyes. Beaks slashing and snapping horribly amidst their carrion.

"There'll be prisoners," Da said, shouting to be heard over the racket. "Man-footed beasts for sale. Good fortune to us."

The caravan, keeping as much as possible to an outer edge of the grim assemblage, wound toward a great blaze in the distance where most of the Vermilion soldiers had collected.

As we passed by the carnage, I observed a stirring and a pitiful moaning coming from the dead men nearest us. I studied a figure wincing amongst his vanquished fellows and the birds. A sorry survivor, not quite gone. But near enough for the black-winged feeders.

Ring reached beneath his cloak and rubbed himself through the sleeves of his robe. His sliding hands warmed his surface but were unavailing against the deeper chill in his bones. He tensed to contain a shiver.

In the dark of the stable, his father leaned a bit to one side and towering Uncle Cletus bent low to align their heads. For a good while, Da hissed smoky whispers into the giant's ear. When the whispers ended, they stood upright—or, in Da's case, as upright as normal—and they studied the boy, their eyes gleaming ghostlike.

"So, Luster will set the bait, then?" Uncle Cletus asked.

"Any time now," Da said.

"And all is arranged at the fane?"

Da snaked a hand beneath his sheepskin cape and patted the paldins in his coin purse.

Uncle Cletus spat and nodded. The great wooly face slackened and the glow in his eyes faded. Ring sensed that his uncle was no longer looking at him but toward him in a general way, as people sometimes do when lost in thought. Then, mercifully, the giant turned his back on him and regarded a stable hand currying the mane of a brindle in the shadowy distance.

"Is it true, do ye think?" the giant said at last. "What they say about this place? Going back to the time of the Old Ones and the First People and suchwise?"

Da peered about the dim shaft, high and low, grimacing, then also pivoted from the boy. "I know it's older than Grand Da," his high, gravelly voice said. "Older than Great Grand Da, as well. At least that's what Da used to say, if ye could believe a word from his mouth."

Ring mistily recalled his father's father, a surly old man who mostly avoided him. In a way, he knew his other dead ancestors more intimately. Although he had never met them in the flesh, he saw them every day. Or what remained of them. Theirs were the 16 skulls on the ornate wooden shelves in the main room of his home. The harvesting and presentation of such remnants were common until recent times—until the emergence of Mount Dnarden as the preferred repository for Hastur's gone. The cranium of his father's great grand da, Odgar Gargery, was amongst the oldest in the collection. Brown-tinged and deeply pitted, his was one of two in want of a jawbone. Died of the fever. Da's grandfather, after whom Uncle Cletus was named, had a skull distinguished by deep temples and a pronounced brow crack. It lacked several teeth and rested back in a way that made it look as if it were shrieking. Fell dead out of nowhere whilst working at the mill.

Ring had grown up his whole life under the eyeless gaze of these gone Gargerys, whilst their headless torsos rested in the floor beneath the room's conch-patterned carpet.

With their backs to him, the men were now exchanging observations on the stable. With their scrutiny withdrawn, relief swept through him. Still, he sensed that, behind their words, he remained in their thoughts—in some dreadful role he couldn't imagine. What was it Da had said to M? *I need him to be involved.*

Ring now listened to his da launch into a discourse on proposed improvements at the stable, about new stalls and grooming areas and replacements of decrepit boards and stones, and the boy wondered why his father found the prospect of such alterations intriguing.

Looking around, he tried to picture the changes as Da described them, as things of promise. He could see the merit of replacing rotting wood and masonry, but what rose foremost in his thoughts was a vision of the existing strangeness of the place—which already competed from all angles to affront his comprehension—growing more aberrant and complex.

His perceptions tripped over the distinguishable length and breadth of the cavernous maw: the visible nooks and rims, the washes of shadow and light, the myriad textures, movements, vibrations, odors, sounds, and, permeating every aspect of it, an embedded, tactile weightiness that seemed to gather from the stable's endless pools of darkness. Small tremblings flittered at every edge. Like Da and Uncle Cletus, he watched the workers snake through it all, dispatching their tasks with purpose and ease and, certainly unlike Da and Uncle Cletus, he wondered what it was these workers had in them that allowed them to function here under these circumstances with such purpose and ease.

And he wondered more than ever why Da had brought him to this place.

Something fist-sized flapped moth-like past his ear but, when he turned to look after it, whatever it was had already been claimed by blackness. In disbelief, he studied the gloom for movement but saw nothing. Nothing certain anyway.

Had he imagined it?

Swiping at his ear, the boy swung his attention to the frail creature that seemed to be at the heart of this undertaking, this gift to his family from the queen of Morella. The white foal stood vigilant.

He watched the horse. He watched the horse watch him.

As Da droned on, Ring's head so flooded with thoughts and speculations unrelated to the thread of his father's oration that he briefly lost all awareness of his periphery and the passage of time.

A hand brushed his neck and lighted on his shoulder and he realized his father was addressing him. With a start, he looked up. Da's ashen-gray eyes peered flatly down at him.

"I said, I give it to ye. And ye say?"

Fingers tightened on his collarbone. He stiffened.

"Answer me!"

The shout set his heart storming. Blinking up at Da, he said, "Y-ye give it to me?"

A thumb found the tender spot midway between his shoulder blade and spine and dug in. The pain arched his back and lifted him to his tiptoes. His throat went dry and he couldn't swallow.

"I give it to ye," Da said, his voice scraping like a blade on a whetstone. "And welcome to ye, my thankless whelp."

The thumb thrust deeper, unleashing a lightning bolt of pain. His head snapped toward it, his neck pressing against his father's cold fingers. His thoughts went white as agony consumed him and his whole body clenched and shuddered. All the air left his lungs and he was unable to draw new air because the pain was so powerful it clouded his ability to breathe. He regarded Da and Uncle Cletus through welling tears that brought their images sliding in and out of focus. Both men scowled at him. He bucked in a frantic attempt to restart his breathing and keep his knees from folding and from some primal compulsion to fight to save himself any way he could.

Somewhere a door clamored open loud enough to penetrate the rioting of his senses. Light flooded in and a new clatter approached. Da let go and Ring stumbled forward. Instinctively, he ducked, but a sharp blow caught the back of his head, knocking him roughly against the pen gate and spilling him to the ground. The impact jolted his face and chest. He lay for a moment, in the sour reek of urine, with his head and stomach spinning, the taste of blood in his mouth and the sensation of blood in his nose and the muscles of his back still seized in fiery pain.

He worked his hands under him and gradually pushed up and tottered to his feet. For a moment, just standing took his every effort. He wiped back his tears with the clutched sleeve of his robe and looked at Da to see if it was over.

Da's attention was elsewhere now, as was Uncle Cletus'.

He touched a slender knuckle to his nostril and it came away with a thin smear of red. He wiped it off with his thumb. He didn't look to see if any of the stable workers were watching him. Most of them must have seen what happened. His face went hot with shame.

The phantom horse, now lit more brightly, had wedged backward into the corner where the stall trough met the stone wall. The creature regarded him with wild eyes.

He wiped pebbles and dirt from his face and hands, rolled a shoulder to loosen some of the pulsing ache in his back, then he, too, turned toward the source of the clatter and brightness.

Wind burst through an open door about 30 strides away. From outside came a huffing, a clumping, a jingling and the sound of a dog barking. The same barking as he had heard in the courtyard.

The thrown-open door deluged the area with golden-white daylight, revealing details of the stable the darkness had hidden. The walls were iced over in patches where moisture leeched in from outside, and hieroglyphs and other scrawlings in assorted sizes and styles popped up on several flat surfaces: a prayer here, a name there, a phallus, a proclamation of love, an obscene limerick and, prominently, a remarkable rendering of the god of death, Osric—the fire-breathing bull, black horns poised, balls the size of overgrown melons. Osric, suzerain of the Netherworld. They say the dying hear the approach of his hooves. How many of these scrawlers had since heard for themselves?

Through the open door, amidst the howling wind, a snow-dusted boy about Ring's age with darkly handsome good looks and wearing a gown and apron like the other workers swaggered forward, pulling a fistful of reins. His footwear betrayed one foot as clubbed but his wide-stepping gait and the ease with which he carried himself showed no hint of the constraint that sometimes marks the afflicted.

Ring recognized this stable boy at once and the realization sent a surge through him that awoke his full attention. This was someone he knew well, though they had never met.

From the tall, narrow window at his home's third-floor landing, he often watched Maule Square below where people milled all day past the blue-veined marble statue of the great cavalry General Drummer Maule. All manner of people swept into and out of the square through six arched side streets that opened between the tall buildings.

Over time, some of these pedestrians became so familiar he regarded them as acquaintances. Their brief passages through the square day after day combined to form a narrative in his mind. He studied their clothing and manners, and watched them interact when they were alone and in groups. He imagined from whence they came and where they were going, what their lives were like and even what their names might be. Based on his observations, he took a personal liking or disliking to each. And, in his mind, he wove himself into the lives of some of them and imagined accompanying them through Maule Square into the outlying streets of Hastur, most of which he had never set foot upon.

In his daydreams, this black-haired boy was named Arvin and was the son of a ship captain. Arvin's da brought spices and fruits to Hastur from exotic island ports far across the Sea of Broken Light and was almost

always off sailing, whilst Arvin, like himself an only child, and Arvin's
mother lived inside the city's East Wall near the banks of the Redgauntlet
River in Wharf Town, where most of the families of Hastur's sailors,
shipbuilders and dock workers lived.

Nearly every morning, he waited for Arvin at the statue of General
Maule. Sometimes Arvin came and sometimes he didn't, but when he did
the two friends proceeded west through Allhollon, walking briskly and
confidently, as good friends do, to the academy at Hastur Fane, where they
learned about arithmetic and science and philosophy from the city's
foremost teachers.

Afterward, on their way back home, they sometimes stopped to
kick a ball in the park with their classmates or to share a copper paldin's
worth of grapes bought from a street vendor or to joke with the slave girls
fetching water from the city fountains.

Some days, he even returned with Arvin back through Maule
Square and down Ausiel Thoroughfare all the way to the Redgauntlet River,
where they watched flatboats bringing in gold from the mines near
Melmoth, or, during the summer months, they sometimes spent all day
trekking down past the busy port to the sandy stretch of Dagon Bay where
the sunbathers swam and the stork like stilt fishers angled in the sparkling
emerald waters offshore. Some days they stayed until the sun began to wane
on the far horizon, skipping stones, chasing razorbill gulls and searching for
the perfect seashell.

With these memories awakened, he now watched the stable boy
lead in a pair of magnificent grays, warhorses with tooled armor on their
faces and chests. Vapor jetted in squalls from the animals' nostrils and their
bits dripped with foam. Snowflakes clung to their sable manes and muscular
backs. Behind the steeds, on gilded wheels rattled in a shiny bronze chariot,
its bow huge and curved, its surface emblazoned with battle-scene reliefs. It
was scraped and slightly dented on one side.

As every eye in the stable fixed on the black-haired boy with the
horses and the chariot, the youth shook the reins and called out, "Verger,
Willa," and the response was instant. A teen-aged, metal-collared groom
with the ashen countenance of a Morellan hurried toward the stable boy.
He moved in a side-to-side, loping gait, hitching a shoulder with each step.
"Coming, Master Paulus," the slave said, whilst a thin-boned, oval-faced
Ligeian girl in the distance clanked down a pail and scrambled forward. A
scarf covered her hair but a strand of yellow curled out onto her forehead
and wisps escaped around her ears. The girl's nose was oddly asymmetrical
but she was pretty in her own way.

The two workers took the reins and calmed the horses, whilst
Paulus-not-Arvin approached the chariot's left wheel. The stable boy bent
over and examined it, shook it, scrutinized the hub, worked fingers around

it, twisted to see the inside of the wheel where it joined the axle, then shook the wheel again.

"Luster's youngest," Da said.

Uncle Cletus nodded and both men crossed their arms.

Willa and Verger unfettered the steeds and set the chariot's yoke on the ground. As they led off the warhorses, Paulus abandoned the wheel and followed them as Da and Uncle Cletus and Ring made room for them to pass. First Willa, then Verger, with the great warhorses huffing. Then Paulus, moving assuredly. He caught Ring's eye and mouthed the word "Gargery."

Before Ring could react, Paulus, the chariot, Willa and Verger were past. They pulled up to a now faintly visible far-end wall near where the shaft of stable turned sharply left. There, at a grooming station, the three tethered the animals and began stripping away the metal plates.

The other workers resumed their duties.

Rolling his shoulder some more, Ring looked at Da and Uncle Cletus when, with an iron certainty, it seized him: he knew what Da had meant by, "I give it to ye." He looked into the pen. The foal had eased out of the corner and was once again stretching toward him.

***

Things invisible lie hidden in the open: the inner workings of light, the displaced energy of thoughts and motions, physical embodiments of smell and sound and of heat and cold. Gases, vapors, miniscule specks of life and death. They crowd the air, surging, flowing, confronting, amalgamating, slipping through and around one another, dividing into layers. Within their smallest bits lurk whole worlds with teeming, transparent airs of their own.

High up, a party to all this, another construction altogether but no less magical, reposes, coalesced from centuries of hope and heartfelt sighs. Amid dense and heavy firmament of rippling gray and white, where her winter sun shines unobstructed, the many-breasted goddess of wisdom, naked, pink and fleshy, strokes her beard and, through the falling snowflakes, languidly observes and contemplates her subjects far below.

Dolt urchins in an alleyway slap at each other with sticks, as snot bubbles from their noses. *Don't put out an eye, boys.* In that same alley, where it opens onto the street, a uni-limbed raggedy man, warrior turned pauper, shivers in a sprawl, beggar bowl empty and overturned. She pops an olive into her mouth. *Bask in yer glory, hero.* Now, for some real entertainment, she turns her attention to the city rat-catcher, his terrier yapping, leashed ferrets frantic in their collars as they strain toward their whiskered prey. The ratter lets go the leashes and the ferrets squiggle forward as one in a ripping, clawing churn. The rat squeals wildly. The goddess rolls the olive on her tongue, sucks juice from it, begins to chew.

A gust wipes clean the snow from the marketplace image of her coupling with the shepherd god. The mosaic, once brilliant and vibrant in color and line, is now cracked, chipped and dull, but still carries an erotic charge. She smiles at the spread of warmth it brings her. *Awaken, my lover, and take me again.* But buried in the groans of the winter wind are the snores that rise from the depths of Mount Dnarden.

Meanwhile, her devotees as always cry up to her from their houses, shrines and fane. "Queen of the heavens, save my brother from the fire that burns in his bones." "Mother of great wisdom, favor me with the embrace of the one for whom I yearn." "Holy Nebo, smite my enemy ... watch over my child ... bring me wealth ... raise the fallen ... make me beautiful ... give me strength ... let me win." And on and on, the never-ending clamor for her assistance in their mundane affairs. Happily, an actual response is unnecessary. The only true duty of a supreme being is to observe, she reasons. If fate gives to her disciples what they seek, the goddess of wisdom has answered their prayers. If not, who are they to question her will?

The olive she works in her mouth is from a tree 1,500 years old. She can taste every day of those years. With her teeth and tongue, she separates the fruit from the pit. She daintily ejects the pit into her palm, makes a fist over it, then opens her hand one finger at a time. Her palm is empty. The pit is gone, vanished from this world like the Old Ones and most of the First People. *Into the ground, under the sea? Who knows where?*

She swallows. Fingering another olive from her golden bowl, she props up on her elbows and resumes watching.

Look at them, so impressed with themselves, with their small lives. Enthralled with the trappings of human exceptionalism. See them build. See them create. See them transform the world around them whilst the other animals slink from their path. Those they don't subjugate or devour.

Yet their human distinction is the very thing that ultimately leeches their joy. After all, knowledge is power, except when it's not. She has seen it over and over: their paralyzed vigils, open eyes in the grip of night, cold sweat breaking on their brows, tortured, as only humans can be, by the realization that one day the spark will cease to glow. And therein lies the true source of divinity.

She pokes the olive into her mouth and licks juice from her fingers.

Rather than face the possibility that at the end of road lies only the end of the road, they had fetched their tools and begun building. Too bad their tiny minds couldn't conceive something worthier than that ridiculous bull.

***

The next day, rough seas roiled the *Pillager*. They growled in the ship's timbers and engorged its air. Rain fell in torrents. Pirates scrambled up and down the steps outside the fadumo's door, snarling orders and oaths. Her door was unlocked and nothing prevented her from venturing outside for a survey of the action but inside was her place for now, and not only because it felt safer. Let their activity distract them for a while. She had work of her own to tend to.

The ghost Piran squirmed within her, aroused by the siren call of nature tossing and churning. The dead have their affinity with storms. Knowing this, she whispered to him and he heard her words in the language of his native Usher: "Bridled lightning roars within you. Your breath can be a gale, your will a tempest. These are yours to set free. Pelt your enemies. Quake their sky. Whip the water until they wash away wailing in foam to the ends of the world."

And so on, she worked to embolden him.

She felt his timidity fading and none too soon.

The foulest of moods took hold of Red Judoc that day, turning him all bluster and rage. Wet with rain, he muttered and slammed down her food, sending some of it bouncing across the deck. He didn't speak to her but regarded her savagely, shooting looks of derision her way.

He did not visit her last night as she had feared he would, but she sensed this night would be different.

All day, she worked with the shade, pumped him up, cajoled him, gave him confidence.

They had sailed at length out of the squall and into relative calm, but not until the last of daylight was squeezed from the heavens. What was that Landorian song her mother used to sing to her as a young girl? Something about the sun turning out its light, her mother's voice clear as a bell. *Olisha, why have you forsaken me?*

Needless to say, the crew embraced the calm with good cheer. Their voices built to a swelling drone punctuated with easy laughter. They shared their tales of the storm. She could hear the scrape of their dishes as they ate.

Red Judoc brought her dinner, barely containing himself as he grimaced at her, eyes shiny with lust. "Eat up, dearie," he said simply. "Ye'll need yer strength."

The voices of the pirates grew boisterous and full of cheer. The grog began to flow.

With a final word of encouragement, she dispatched Piran and she was left alone in the forward compartment to see what her fate would be. She prayed to her spider god Anarach. What else was there to do?

Finally, the moment came. She heard his voice, goading her. "I'm coming for ye, conjure woman." He was above deck, wild with drink, his voice cutting through the fog of a dozen conversations. "Get yerself ready for the ride of yer life."

There was motion on the stairs. Her stomach filled with a cold weight as she listened to his approach. Then something unexpected happened. She heard Red Judoc curse, stumble on the steps, wail and fall heavily, three solid crashes: *ka-thunk, ka-thunk, ka-thunk*. He rolled to her door, the dead weight of his body pressing against it. There was silence. And then....

Otherworldly laughter. It echoed in the hollows of the ship. The crew went still at once and the only sound the fadumo could hear was the laughter, mirthless and savage, bellowing in the night. It was the sound of retribution, pealing triumphant, and it went on and on and on.

Then Piran's voice powerful beyond its years gave utterance to a single cry. "Watch yer step, sealegs."

And he laughed. And he laughed.

***

The yearning took form gradually. Bits of color running together, lighter than vanity, gleaming, fashioning itself into a whirligig of sorts, a tangible embodiment with many moving parts. Silvery, like a young girl's necklace. All reflection, dancing and watery. In his mind, it called to him with solemn purpose. He stood in awe of it. *Feed me*, it commanded.

As he created it, Andaman examined it from all angles, like a craftsman, attentive to detail. He watched it quiver and ripple, nurtured it. He saw it grow until he faltered under its heft and his mind strained to contain it.

He went through the motions of his other life, dutiful worker that he was, but his creation once conceived was never far from his thoughts. He owed cousins Anse and Cletus for seeing to his care and making him a part of things. When first his mother, then his father, then his brothers were felled by the fever, Cletus had found him residing amongst them, a toddler alone in the house of the dead, frightened, filthy and nearly starved. Andaman wondered how long he had been in there alone with them.

He claimed not to remember any of it. But in truth, it came to him sometimes in fragments and dreams: the cramped space, the silence, the hollowness of their features, the fulsome stench, the darkness closing in, the hunger.

He lived with relatives, shuffled from house to house. He even lived with Cousin Cletus and Everild for a time. Then he stayed with the workers at the slave pens in the Gondemar district, learning his trade, until he was old enough to earn a living and pay for a room at Nilus Margrave's

Inn. He was adequate at his work, rounding up man-footed beasts and barking orders at minions. Moving things along from one spot to another, whether by boat or wagon. He was dependable and that was good enough.

But it was his other life that made him feel alive.

He had been waiting outside Anse's black brick three-story. Half his job was waiting. Spider oak leaves clogged the gutters and a hint of winter was in the air. The square was all but empty, owing to a performance of "Jocasta in the Sky" at the Magnus Theater. It was still cold but he didn't mind. Cousins Anse and Cletus were inside meeting with the spy Killman, and Andaman sensed travel in the offing.

He was toying with his dirk, spinning it, sunlight flaring on the blade, when he spotted the charmer across the square: a young, freckled thing with a divot in one cheek, her hair done up in auburn ringlets. She wore a blue and silver dress edged in lace with a sprig of rue for luck. Lost in play with a straw doll, her nose running in the cold, she chewed on the neck of her dress.

Andaman was thunderstruck.

Then the door to Gargery House opened and someone spoke his name.

On the trip to Scylding Tangle, the young girl from Maule Square was with him in every way except physically. He imagined her looking up at him, again and again, her face lighting up with terror as she glimpsed the first stirrings of the whirligig inside him. Two and a half days out. Two and a half days in. Collecting the wretched Skalks, their smell hideous, their features streaked with blue, barbaric beyond all measure. They should be glad they weren't captured in Kempelen, where they blinded slaves to keep them from running. But he only half saw them, only half smelled them, so entranced was he by his yearning.

Digna, he learned, was her name. Sweet Digna Greavor. She reminded him of Tilda Tambernich, his first charmer. Her hair, also, had been done up in ringlets. She weighed almost nothing, he remembered. The memory brought him a grin.

Back from the trek, he had left the Skalks safely shackled in their berths in Gondemar. It would be another week before arrangements could be made with the mines. Then they would load up the wagons again. But tonight....

Tonight was all his.

The front door was locked and unassailable, but a gate in the back off the alley opened onto a small courtyard and he made his way slyly across. The back door rested in a scoop of shadow. Over it hung an ancient starfish, crooked and sun-faded, placed by someone long ago to chase off bad fortune. The door was locked but vulnerable to the pry bar he carried beneath his cloak. The wood splintered and moaned as he leaned into the bar. All at once, it gave. He stepped within and listened.

He was in the kitchen. The wood stove had gone cold but the oily scent of roasted goat and chards lingered in the air. Ahead the black night coagulated. Stowing the pry bar, he gave his sight a chance to adjust. Slowly wan outlines grew until he had a sense of the house's layout. He moved across the kitchen into the dining room.

Alban Greavor was a cavalry man with the Vermilion Shrikes and he favored the trappings of a soldier. Correction, "doomsmen" was what they called themselves. The fireplace, still sizzling with a semblance of flame, was draped in the bunting of the Fourth Legion. Its mantle held spoils of war: a dented helmet, Arnheimian by the looks of it; a feathered spear probably taken from a Skalk; some foreign coin with an octopus on one side and a waterclock on the other; a sleek obsidian dagger that drew Andaman's particular attention. The far wall held a shield that was battered and scarred, and a pennant of some sort. Even the dinner table had something of a military bearing. And, of course, the room was exquisitely carpeted, as was most of the house.

The stairway ahead loomed wide and inviting, stripes of shadow cast by the banister. Its forging featured a carved griffin, oversized head resting thoughtfully on clenched claws, tongue extended, nubs of horn rising above pointy ears. A fern-colored runner overlaid the middle of the stair steps.

Andaman tested one of the steps. It gave softly beneath his weight with a faint mewling sound, like a baby's whimper. Best to keep to the outside of the stairs near the banister. Light-footed, he crept up past the watchful griffin. Two steps, three steps. An upstairs landing came into view. As he ascended, he became aware of a hall, open doorways and blissful snoring. The snoring, that of an adult, came from the first room. Probably old Alban himself, sleeping the sleep of the conqueror. The next room, on his left, was some sort of sitting room, which he ignored. There was one more room on this level on the right. He paused at the steps to listen but heard no noise from above. Slave quarters up there probably. He glided to the threshold of the third room and looked in.

A tiny window let in icy moonlight that limned the edges of cabinets, a chamber pot, some small toys, a bed-stand and a bed. Asleep in the bed on her back, clutching her straw dolly, was the girl, her hair fanned out in dark curls. She'd kicked off her blanket, exposing a thigh, much to his delight.

Andaman closed the door behind him.

As he approached her, a chill passed through him. The clean lines of her bedclothes and her lack of adornment carried an artless sophistication beyond her years. He trembled and throbbed in the grip of her presence, the yearning coming to a head. Lights of the whirligig shining within, he edged onto the bed, careful not to wake her prematurely.

He forced one hand down upon her mouth. Her eyes popped open, shimmering with terror. Shushing her, he said softly, "Relax, my love. It will all be over soon enough."

He saw in the shadows of her frightened eyes the silvery light of the softly whirring mechanism within him and something else: the hooved approach of his bull god Osric.

***

At dawn the first of the soldiers, crouched and silent, slipped from the tree line at the valley's crest. Two hundred Vermilion archers in their distinctive helmets and scarlet breast plates spread wide in a single row. Each fell to one knee, set his shield in the grass of early spring and clasped his bow in its familiar place. Two hundred arrows notched.

The general, standing just within the spreading spider oaks, gave a signal and the javelin throwers flowed out into the fresh light. Nearly five hundred strong, wearing shields fastened to their forearms, they grouped behind the archers. Each drew a sturdy shaft from the clutched handful he carried, slipped fingers into the throwing strap and snapped the weapon into his grip.

Skirmishers in place, the general turned to his second in command, Brigadier Tull Fennel, a gangly, square-jawed man with acne-scarred cheeks and said to him, "If we don't meet again in this world, my friend, may we meet in the next."

Tull brushed aside his russet hair, long and thick as any woman's, and they stood together in silence in the way only soldiers on the verge of battle can be.

Then the men clapped shoulders and separated to mount their chariots.

The general took up his shield which bore the likeness of his personal goddess Dagon, as his other hand gripped his snakeskin-wrapped spear. He arose into his car, then set the shield into the slot designed to hold it. His attendant, Spearman Alban Greavor handed him the reins to the grays and then climbed in behind him.

In combat, as the general's extra eyes and backside defender, Alban possessed a riveting focus developed in part from years of scrutinizing the weaves and threadwork of the carpets he traded. A plucky, thick-lipped, bald man with a divot in one jowl, Alban had served the general in the tight quarters of the war chariot for nearly a decade. Spear at the ready, Alban squared off in a bent-knee stance, his free hand fastening on the car's metal curve.

The general had only to rock on his feet and the horses started to move slowly past the archers and the javelin throwers to the lip of the crest.

Below him he watched the enemy encampment, spread throughout the conquered town, easing to life.

Nearest, a cluster of mostly women attended to pots at cook fires whilst children in various stages of dress and wakefulness stayed close at their mothers' hems. They were a hairy people, these Skalken nomads, even their women and children, with their furry arms and legs, and overrun brow ridges; a long-boned people with hard, elongated faces and noses, angular, every edge sharp and their skin pale as rock salt. Across the valley, each, from infant to codger, wore some measure of wolf's hide.

Smoke from the fires wafted up in the still air to the general and to the archers and javelin throwers, who awaited his command to let fly. The general saw the smoke and felt it in his eyes but the sense of smell had never taken root in him.

A generation ago, this area, known as Scylding Tangle, had been a wild valley, the site of another battle with the Skalks. Afterward, squatters had begun moving in: exiles and vagrants and assorted sloggers headed to White Worm or some other place where they were unwanted. They had abandoned those journeys for lives of squalor here, where they lived amongst their kind and worse in a makeshift camp of sprawl and scarcity. Whole families came to live in these crude lean-tos and hovels fashioned from branches, stones and mud. Now they could only look back fondly on even that wretched existence—those lucky enough to have escaped with their lives.

The few hundred warriors visible were surprisingly inattentive for being so deep within Ligeian borders. They gestured and conversed in small circles, their voices too low to carry, their faces still stained with the lurid-blue paint they had worn into battle when taking this town just yesterday. Many of the enemy warriors were still out of sight, just beginning to rouse from their coarse blankets in the odd, slanted huts these Skalkens favored. They were clearly not expecting the 5,000 soldiers of Hastur's Fourth Legion to pass through the forest at night and swoop down on them from above.

The massacred village stretched largely flattened and diminished to rubble across the valley floor as far as the general could see. The bodies of people and animals lay amongst the ruins, some burned, some headless, some showing signs of having been dragged behind the half-wild ponies these Skalkens rode. Corpses hung by their necks from ropes tied to tree branches. He counted 11 of these. Some bodies had been dressed out and butchered like wild game, making him wonder what simmered in the cook pots.

The general took all this in instantly.

Then, after a glance at the soldiers behind him to his left and right, he slapped the edge of his spear on the shiny bronze chariot. The metallic clack rang in the morning air.

Below, faces turned and looked up at him. Their expressions came alive with awareness and seemed to pulse in the new light of day. Behind him, the forest stirred with a great rush of movement.

In that instant his depth of vision intensified. Every detail sharpened to a stunning clarity.

Two hundred arrows leapt to the sky, arced in the dawn light, and rained down the first wave of death. The javelin throwers rushed partway down the hill, set their feet and flung their volley. Behind them, grim rows of spearman emerged from the trees and, forming a protective wall with their shields, descended in lockstep.

The bowmen fetched up their shields, moved forward and replanted. They notched and pulled at their strings, unleashing a fresh barrage.

The valley filled with screams and gasps and frantic scrambling and the sounds of bodies collapsing to the ground. Dozens of the pallid savages lay pinned by arrows or javelins. A warrior's life gushed out of him as he pulled with bloody hands at the shaft that impaled him. A woman roamed in circles, trying to make sense of the spear that thrust out her middle, some remnant of her dangling from the spear's tip. Tears flowed from the faces of children—some hurt, some orphaned—terrified by the carnage all around them. Lucky were the fallen who succumbed impassively to the black swoon of extinction.

The javelin throwers snapped fresh shafts into their hands, scrambled ahead several steps, aimed and fired. The spearman closed on their rear. The cavalrymen, some on horseback, some in chariots, their steeds fortified with armor plates, appeared in a great din on either flank of the advancing spearmen.

Below, the camp became a frenzy of sound and motion. They barked at one another in their vulgar Skalken tongue. Mothers with infants on their hips bolted in desperate retreat. Warriors rushed for arms, cover, mounts. Some with weapons at the ready took up war cries and closed in, their blue faces twisted, teeth clenched, froth forming on their lips. The hoofbeats and nickering of ponies rose from the distance.

Within those sounds, he heard a woman's voice whisper to him; the voice of his sweet familiar, whose cloth bound the bicep of his dominant arm.

"Hold yer lines, doomsmen!" the general shouted. "Ready in the front!"

The spearmen, advancing to the fore with the first light of day flashing on their stylized, bird-shaped helmets, showed their bronze points to the advancing enemy. A dozen Skalkens lunged at the front line, growling and snarling, hammering at the shields with swords and axes and cudgels. The Vermilion spears, driven by powerful curled arms, ripped into the attackers' chests and throats. Flesh shredded, bones cracked, blood sprayed and cascaded. The Skalkens fell in heaps to be trampled beneath row upon row of spearmen sandals.

As the general's troops descended into the valley, a great tide of defenders rushed forth with weapon arms cocked. The howling of their war cries saturated the morning air, their chiseled blue faces raw with malice. The surge on impact flexed the front as their advance was hindered. A filmy ripple like heat shimmer radiated up the rows of soldiers. A tumult of metal on metal resounded.

Skalken archers opened fire in ragged volleys. Most of their arrows careened off helmets and shields, but two bolts bit true. One found unsuspecting Spearman Zath Mallock, husband, father and smith, whose intricate renderings in silver were unsurpassed in Hastur. With an ugly sound, the barbed shaft sank into his eye, dropping him to his knees yowling and jerking, all his talent dwindling with him as he gave up his final breath. The other took down tanner Petrus Geb, piercing the soft spot at the base of his throat, sending him coughing and twisting to the Netherworld and rendering destitute his aged father, Hedwig, who himself had lost two arms and one leg to the waging of war.

The front line, heavily engaged, spurted ahead several steps. As the lines following advanced, a spearman in the sixth row tripped on uneven ground. He tumbled, as if into a sinkhole, and took several of his comrades down with him. As they were helped to their feet the lines wavered and buckled and stalled anew.

A Skalken horseman, burning with rage, charged through the front lines into the gap formed by the fallen soldiers. With his battle axe flailing in a crimson blur, the rider opened a wedge in the Vermilion formation.

Spearman Cyril Carver, a breadmaker and father of three, lost his helmet in the jostling and the final vision this world held for him was the edge of honed metal slicing down between his eyes. The axe blade buried itself deep in the spearman's skull and when the horseman, in a ghastly display of crazed fury and strength, yanked at his weapon with both hands to free it, the body of the spearman lifted from the ground and flew overhead before coming loose and sailing through the air. Hardened Vermilion veterans shrank at the sight.

Shrikes swarmed the savage, jabbing pitilessly at him and his mount with their spears until both came crashing down. The pony screamed, bucked and kicked, sending soldiers flying and bounding in all directions.

"Heads in the game, doomsmen!" the general shouted. "Mind yer formation!"

Soldiers tottered to their feet and coalesced unsteadily around the now-flat horse and rider, both still alive but motionless except for their breathing. Fisted spears thrust down on the two from all sides until the barbarian and his mount slipped beyond the agony of retribution and the points began passing through them effortlessly.

"Dress to the right!" the general commanded.

The soldiers regained their poise and wheeled into place, reforming their lines. The battle march resumed, the columns dividing just long enough to bypass the carcass of the horse. Somewhere in the rear, Tull hollered encouragement.

The general turned to the bowmen and gestured with his spear hand.

Taking up their helmets and shields, the archers advanced several steps into the valley, knelt, aimed and let their bow strings sing. At much the same moment, the javelin throwers added their bolts to the deluge of arrows, and scores of enemy warriors collapsed wounded and lifeless throughout the melee.

"Horsemen to the ready!" the general shouted.

Moving to help advance the lines, Vermillion riders swept in from either flank and cut before the besieged spearmen at the front. The cavalrymen chopped at defenders with their glistening swords. Their armored horses reared and stomped and brayed, their sun-dazzled armor plates clanking.

The general gave a signal and the javelin throwers followed several steps in the cavalry's wake.

"Slay these wretches!" he ordered. "No mercy given or taken!"

A fresh barrage of Vermilion arrows and javelins sliced the air, taking out Skalks in swaths and sending many more recoiling and retreating from the onslaught, even as their barbarian brothers stormed in bareback on naked ponies to engage the Shrike cavalry up front. One of the fleeing savages caught a javelin in the back of his skull.

"Forward, doomsmen!" the general ordered and the spearmen pressed on, stepping over their slain fellows as needed.

The general urged his grays to the left flank and down, then halted to oversee his spearman descending past.

Up front, the horsemen clashed and flailed their weapons, sending riders on both sides smashing to the turf until the barbarians, feeling the worst of it, broke it off and pulled back.

The Shrike cavalry repositioned at the flanks as row upon row of spearman pressed forward, rolling through enemy warriors with machinelike purpose.

"General!" Alban Greavor said from behind, pointing to the right. "Over there!"

Three Skalken horsemen had doubled back and slipped behind the cavalry on the right flank. They trampled through javelin throwers and tore a furrow through the spearmen columns, knocking over soldiers, left and right. They thundered toward the general with axes at the ready, their eyes stark and furious and fixed on him with grim purpose.

The general yanked his reins and the grays reeled to face the enemy. The chariot careened on one wheel before crashing level. The jarring dislodged the spear from the general's grasp and upended Alban, pitching him rolling from the car. The general, still grappling with the reins, found himself braving the enemy charge alone and spearless.

As the lead pony appeared out of nowhere, a Shrike arrow skewered the creature's throat and the pony went down hard, choking and kicking. The second pony tripped on the first, staggered and flipped and also went down, quaking the ground and wiping out spearmen on all sides. In a brilliant execution of horsemanship, the third rider guided his steed in a magnificent leap that cleared the fallen ponies and sent rider and mount hurtling at the general's chariot.

As he closed, the blue-faced savage raised his axe high overhead and swung it at the general's skull.

The general reached for his sword but there wasn't time to draw it.

Just then, in a blur and a great pounding of hooves, a second Vermilion chariot burst in, clipping the side of the general's car whilst ramming the advancing pony hard enough to knock the creature off balance and sideways. At the same time, Tull Fennel used his sword to cleave through the attacking savage's axe arm, separating it from its shoulder and sending the severed limb and its weapon spiraling into the air in a trailing gout of blood.

The general, tottering, wrestled with the reins. He pulled back on them and they bit into his hands. The grays slowed and that's when the wheel started knocking and the chariot began to shake. The vehicle shuddered to a halt.

Around him, the battle sounds faded into a silence broken only by the distant squawk of a razor-billed gull.

The Vermilion soldiers and the barbarians and all their mounts and weapons turned to wisps of smoke and evaporated before him.

The ravaged town of Scylding Tangle, with its devastation and its rocks and trees and grass, wavered, sunk slowly into the ground and covered over in a cloak of snow.

It had all just been one of his visions.

He twisted and, over his shoulder, he saw the snow was rent with looping tracks that wound on and on and crisscrossed in a patternless frenzy.

He recognized the tracks as his alone.

Facing front, the general found himself a solitary figure, breathless, cold and sweaty, his arms wrapped in a lion's-hide mantle. Looking at the sky, he wondered how much time had passed. He examined his throbbing hands, uncurling his fingers, and saw where the reins had left his skin torn and bloody.

Old Coast Road, half buried in snow, wound upward to his walled city. Far off, a straggler made her way into a gate. Still breathing heavily, he gave this fresh perspective a moment to settle in.

"I see," he said aloud, acknowledging the whispered words of the woman who was speaking in his head.

He swung the horses round to face the road and he followed it, the wheel knocking and the chariot shaking the whole way.

***

Two men followed the chariot's wet tracks into the stable, one of them breathing loud and crackly.

"I cannot think what possesses ye," wheezed Luster Spaulding, maneuvering on his short walking sticks like some ungainly, four-legged creature. Snow lightly veiled the patrician's arms and chest and frosted the limp strands of his beard. His bulk rocked and jiggered with each step and his swollen feet overfilled their sandals.

The second man wore the high, black-and-gold, bird-shaped helmet, the scarlet corselet and pleated skirt of the Vermilion Shrikes, and a mantle of what appeared to be lion's hide. Oddly enough, this soldier also looked familiar; though it was improbable Ring could have seen this man before and not immediately recognized him now, considering that bright-orange chin beard and those glassy, jade-green eyes.

Though there were no active campaigns, the soldier clutched a thrusting spear and a shield. Worn snakeskin covered the spear's long handle and the tip of the weapon's blade curved slightly, either by design or from usage. The shield was a scarred oval of bronze-covered wood and featured a stark silhouette of the tentacled sea goddess Dagon. This man, Ring guessed, was the charioteer.

"I am trying to be honorable here, Luster," the soldier said, "but my loyalties are divided."

Before either could add another word, the soldier spun into a crouch, shield raised and spear at the ready as if challenging some threat approaching from his rear. But there was nothing there to confront. The motion drew the attention of everyone nearby but they looked away as he straightened and turned back toward Sirrah Luster.

The two stepped over to the chariot and faced each other. Sirrah Luster erupted in a deep, hacking cough that lasted for several moments, darkening his face and leaving him gasping. He wiped at his mouth with a rag.

The charioteer leaned his shield and spear against the vehicle. The spear slid to the ground. As he bent to pick it up and lean it more carefully, he said, "As ye know, this matter involves a friend of mine, as well. A brother in arms, a son almost, to whom I owe my very life."

Sirrah Luster cleared his throat. "Ye made a promise. Ye gave yer word and not just to me."

"If she were still here, 'twould be different. Then Tull would understand."

"This is still a family matter."

"There is more than one kind of family, Luster."

"Family is in the blood. Lucrezia's blood runs in my veins and in the veins of my children."

Removing his helmet, the charioteer raked a hand though damp orange hair that steamed in the cold, but in the process, brushed against the shield. It hit the ground with a muted thud. Sighing, he righted it against the chariot. He perused the stable, pausing intently on Da and Uncle Cletus.

"Maybe now is not the time for this talk," the soldier said.

"Time is running out. I need to know I can count on ye. Seth needs to know. We're all aware of what she wanted."

"Luster, she is gone."

"Gone and forgotten, it seems. What has it been? Less than a year?"

The soldier, wincing, said nothing.

"Ye think she doesn't know, Drummer? Ye think she doesn't see from the other side? See how ye betray her?"

The soldier, looking horrorstruck, took a step backward. His green eyes flashed briefly on the carving of Osric and widened.

Drummer. Of course.

How could Ring have not seen it? The charioteer was General Drummer Maule himself, the cavalry commander represented by the statue in the square. The statue had stood within a few feet of his front door since before his birth. This realization swept through Ring with surprising force, though he found it difficult to reconcile this shaken wretch with the vision of triumph he had lived with all his life.

"How she must seethe, Drummer."

The general looked at Sirrah Luster quickly. "Ye can't know that!"

"There are those who can." Sirrah Luster leaned toward the general. "Go to the fane, Drummer. See the oracle. Ask Saga Eldritch if ye can break yer word to the dead. Ask the seer if my dear cousin watches."

"The fane?" His voice had a restricted quality, as though he was trying to conserve his breath whilst speaking.

"Go to Dagon Fane and put to Saga Eldritch the question of whom ye should support in this election and whether yer lost beloved can still hold ye accountable. Look into the Netherworld and see the truth for yerself."

The general attempted to say something but failed.

Clumsily, he donned the high helmet. "Just fix the wheel," the general said, clutching the spear and shield. Then he shambled off in a kind of swoon, nearly tripping.

Da plucked the coin purse from beneath the sheepskin cape and tossed it to Uncle Cletus.

"To the fane," Da said. "Be quick." And the giant slipped off without a word.

Then Da swerved toward Ring and said, "Come along," They walked over to Sirrah Luster, who watched Uncle Cletus leave before turning toward them.

"That Drummer is a stubborn one, Anse," the patrician said of the general.

"But no match for ye in a war of words, my friend," Da said.

"Perhaps. But it will take more than words to win his support."

"Leave the rest to me. I promise ye, ye will get what ye want from him."

"It saddens me ye had to witness that, Ringy," Luster said, swaying on his walking sticks. "Sometimes business and politics can be heated and show an ugly side. But a greater good lies behind it. Never forget that." Small black eyes glittered at him from their dark craters.

Ring nodded.

Sirrah Luster coughed again.

"Now, do ye see the boy in the back over there?" the patrician asked, gesturing with a walking stick. "The one who brought in the chariot? That's my son Paulus. Go talk to him, Ringy. He expects ye."

Ring stood a moment, stricken with fear. Then he nodded again and turned away. The path before him darkened and narrowed. Lightheadedness swept over him and he moved without any real perception of owning his movement. All round him, edges twitched. He stepped deliberately as, from the corners of his sight, he seemed to glimpse threatening apparitions. But when he looked directly at them, they were gone. He felt his father's eyes upon his back. He felt the stable hands watching him from all angles. Paulus, Willa and Verger paused in their grooming and looked up at him. As all these eyes crawled over him, he felt like some kind of imposter, unsure of what to do or say. All he could think to do was keep moving.

Sensing his trepidation, Paulus stepped forward. "Paulus Spaulding, at yer service. This is Willa Lumen, daughter of Ratter Lumen, and Verger, who has been with my family for five years." He clapped Ring on the back and stepped behind him. "This is Ring Gargery, everybody, son of the slaver Anse."

There was no mistaking it. Paulus had a presence, a keen visage and an ease of manner that bespoke confidence.

Ring and the others exchanged nods.

With a glance, he took in Willa Lumen: her scruffy sandals, bare ankles and soiled work clothes, the hints of her form against stiff fabric, her hands from the dirty nails to the wrists, the smooth lines of her neck framed by loose hair falling from beneath her headscarf, her ears flat and oval, lips sweet but plain and the odd nose which he now realized had been misshapen by a bad break. She carried herself like a person capable of taking on responsibilities far beyond her years.

Verger, the Morellan slave, eyed him suspiciously, grooming tool in hand. When he met Ring's eyes, he looked at the ground, hitched a shoulder and, after a suitable pause, went back to work on a horse. He wore a string of spider oak acorns: a charm against the fever.

"Do ye like horses, Gargery?" Paulus asked, stepping around to face him. "These are two of the finest grays in all Hastur. Chariot horses, battle scarred. Owned by the great General Drummer Maule himself. Ye can touch them, if ye like."

Up close, the grays were monsters. Shaggy maned, sleek muscled and powerful. Their teeth were gigantic. Their eyes looked almost human.

"No, thank ye," he demurred, his mouth suddenly dry.

"Do ye know much about stables, Gargery? This one has been in our family for as long as anyone can remember. When it's full, we can service up to 200 horses. We feed them, water them, keep them clean, take them for walks. Most of the cavalry horses lodge with us. Taking good care of them is quite a responsibility."

Ring nodded, cleared his throat, acted interested.

When he looked again at Willa Lumen, she met his gaze. When it came to her eyes, the casual nature of his inquiry shattered. He locked on them, locked in a stupor on their boundless depth and on the stark vulnerability they displayed. He was unable to look away even though a frantic impulse commanded him to. Equally frightening, he sensed she saw things in him he did not want to show.

She blushed.

Just then, Da called to him and Ring looked back over his shoulder. Da patted Sirrah Luster high on the arm and stepped aside.

"Nice meeting ye, Gargery," Paulus said with genuine good cheer.

"Look forward to seeing ye again."

He looked from Paulus to Willa to Verger to Paulus again and nodded.

Biting his lip, he turned and followed Da from the dreadful stable.

***

The night was not Ring's friend.

Like black sand it would whisper down on him one grain at a time. He would lie in bed and watch it build, his heart gripped with apprehension. Must stay awake and be vigilant, he told himself. Vigilant for motion or the sound of any unwelcome approach. He rubbed the lucky stone he relied on for protection in his times of peril.

Most nights that was all there was to it: him lying nervously in bed until he couldn't fight it anymore and sleep came crashing down on him.

Most nights.

His earliest memory of the visitor came when he was four, shortly after Darius died.

The loss of his infant brother, unmarked by any ceremony, was not explained to him or discussed by anyone, not even the servants, and this silence, as much as the vacant cradle in his room, contributed to the sensation that everything in his life revolved slightly off center, as if on an axis: a small, uniform movement of reality slid off kilter. Even at that young age, he knew better than to ask anyone about any of it.

He was lying in bed that first time, eyeing the empty cradle, when from somewhere in the twilight of his room there came a sound like someone walking through tall grass on dry leaves. *Swish, rustle, crunch.* He listened attentively as the measured steps grew louder.

He wanted to turn his head toward the sound but couldn't bring himself to do it. He tried to cry out but fear gripped his throat too tightly to allow words to escape. He tried to sit up but his body was weighted down, as if turned to lead. He was unable to command it to rise.

Am I going to die, too? Like Darius? Was this how it felt to die?

He tried clenching his fists, but his hands wouldn't move. He tried closing his eyes but the lids wouldn't shut.

The floorboards creaked.

On the ceiling, a dim glow spread and caught on the edges of his room. Another creak. Shadows stirred in the dark around him and the source of the dim glow neared. Creak. The air went cold and enveloped him, squeezed him, pulled him down. Throughout him, panic screamed in his veins. One last creak and he went delirious with tears flowing down his face, his breath burning and wrenching.

From the shadows a mass materialized, a manlike form impossibly long and thin; so thin its torso was not much wider than one of its arms or legs. Said arms and legs were impossibly long and thin, as well. Its fingers, too; half the width and twice the length of a normal man's. The glow came from eyes possessed with an eerie vacantness. An aurora backlit it's sticklike outline.

With the rest of Gargery House in hibernation, the figure had him to itself. It taunted him with sudden gestures, widening its eyes and pumping its legs up and down. It cried out at him in a sound like timbers snapping. He shrieked for his da, for M and the others, shrieked until the sound he made was just gagagagagaga, and he realized his mouth wasn't moving and the shrieking was taking place entirely in his own head. The figure lengthened and hunched out at him, reaching.

Whatever happened after that was lost in oblivion. The next thing he knew, he awakened to the morning.

But that was far from the end of it.

Shiny Man. That was what he called the being before he knew it had a name. Frightful and unwelcome, Shiny Man came to him, not every evening, just often enough to keep the fear in him. And to compound the fear, its appearances grew gradually longer and more intense.

Always under cover of the dark when he was on the verge of sleep, the determined footfalls would approach.

In subsequent nights, the footfalls came running. Running through the grass and the leaves, running through his room. Pounding out a rhythm that came to echo like thunder in his chest: *here-I-come, here-I-come, here-I-come.* The veil of dread fluttered down on him. The weight of his body once again pinned him coldly to his bed.

Frozen in place, frozen in time, awaiting the first blur of movement. Nearing light limned the ceiling and the edges of the small hearth and table past the foot of his bed.

Something new: a brilliant white flash. *When had that become part of it?* And there it was, aglow and shimmering, eyes now balls of blue fire, limbs stretched ever more exaggerated, fingers turned to claws.

If that wasn't bad enough....

Springing, whizzing, bouncing Shiny Man lurched out at him and over him and around him, throwing shadows everywhere. It came closer with each passing visit. Spectacular, hypnotic and terrifying all at once. First it was here, then it is there, silent now save for that sizzling hiss. The air ignited with sparks of blue and white flame, as the boy lay leaden and spellbound, mouth agog, the blood gone effervescent in his veins.

Over time, as he grew older, Shiny Man would touch him with those icy claws, poke at him, pinch his nose, thump his ears, ruffle his hair, grab a clawful of Ring's nightshirt and shake and swing him in the air, fiery eyes glowing malevolently.

The cry that strained to clear his throat was weighted down, lucky to emerge as a faint gurgle. Shock upon shock flared through him, his eyes stinging of sweat and he unable to shut them against that scorching onslaught of awe.

Then he awakened in his bed, covered in a cold sweat.

As yet another day dawned, he already he feared the coming of the next night.

"... In the presence of death reason and philosophy are silent."
—Ambrose Bierce, "John Mortonson's Funeral"

PART TWO:
THE SUMMONING

JOE PAWLOWSKI

CHAPTER 4

What They Have Chosen

We met at night on a hillside just beyond the Horla district. Outside the city walls, where he could move freely. A familiar place to us both, but the figure that greeted me there was not familiar. In fact, he was so unfamiliar that at first I was confused. Who was this broken down, old man?

Wasted and waxen. That's how I would describe him. His breath labored, his motions sluggish, his eyelids red and crusted. Cracks formed at his mouth and a vicious rash bloomed across his forehead. Skin so thin ye could almost see through it. What remained of his mustache hung in tatters. The only constant was the eye. A milky caul over one eye.

"Wanlo?"

"Aye," he croaked. "Wanlo the Freebooter, scourge of the foaming seas."

I was lost for words.

He brought along a minion. An islander named Wolfdog, whom I had met once before. Wolfdog looked anxious, fidgeting with a sword. They both looked anxious. Wanlo had brought someone else, who I guessed was the source of all that anxiety.

Bound at the wrists, Fadumo Aneleh Zant wa Zant stood near the oxen. She was silvery in the moonlight, buxom, with frizzy hair tumbling about her round and placid face, her eyes heavy-lidded and piercing. An islander's clefts at her nose and chin. Her arms a spectacle of scars.

"They give her up, her own people did, for a song," Wanlo said. "Not sure who got the best of that bargain."

I watched her over Wanlo's shoulder as I and he settled up the agreed-upon amount at a crossroads where suicides lay buried in unmarked mounds. She did not look away. I knew she would not either when the time came for the metal collar to kiss at her throat.

Wanlo shakily handed over a jute sack and a wooden box. The box was heavy and filthy and foul-smelling, and had an odd clasp shaped like a spider. When I took hold of the box, it seemed to stir in my hand. Just touching it made me go all prickly.

"Her things," the freebooter said.

I nodded.

I wanted to inquire on his health but thought better of it. Whatever sickness he had, I didn't want it. As we stood there in the moonlight, I could almost feel the illness reaching out at me.

His working eye was on me unsteady and he looked to be hunting words. "Tell me to dance off into the deepest deep and I blame ye not," Wanlo said at last with no trace of his usual bravado, "but I feel remiss not to offer a cautionary word." His thumbs worked at the tips of his trembling fingers. "Between what we see and what we think we see, there is sometimes a world of difference. And that difference can turn on a man in ways he never imagined."

His good eye was still on me, and I felt he was waiting for me to say something. But what do ye say to that?

When I didn't reply, he reached out and weakly clapped my shoulder. "Be well, Anse Gargery," he said, as if he knew in his heart they were the last words he would ever speak to me.

As General Drummer Maule moved across the stable's back lot, a scarred, yellow dog, walleyed and missing a back leg, approached yelping. The animal, a frightful-looking cur of average size and above-average fierceness, seemed particularly angered by the general's incursion on his turf. His bark, mixed with growls and punctuated by the snapping of foamy teeth, was beyond threatening, as was his gaze, which seemed to shift angrily from eye to eye.

Still stung by Luster Spaulding's harsh words regarding the general's obligation to the now gone Lucrezia and her family, the jolt of this barking dog added a disproportionate layer of anguish to his misery.

He walked slowly, keeping his shield between himself and the mongrel. If the creature attacked, he would stab him with his spear. One blow, maybe two, and it would be over. He backed away cautiously, through the creaking gate into the snowy, stone-paved streets of Hastur.

He breathed deeply, expecting to pass out at any moment, yet forced himself to keep moving. He turned and stepped forward. Gradually, his agitation subsided.

Then suddenly he caught a blur of motion.

From the corner of his eye, he saw something closing in on him and knew it had to be an illusion but his soldier's reflex made him reel anyway, spear and shield at the ready. Of course, there was nothing there but the cockeyed cur, a frosty road and a stable lot awash in the golden light of dying day. Still, in that glow, he felt curiously exposed, as if someone was watching him.

The feeling remained even when the stable disappeared behind him, even when he had followed the downhill slope around a corner to the long blocks of two- and three-story buildings that led to the home he had lived in all his life.

Fat flakes of snow drifted again from the dimming maize-colored sky and resumed their gradual, pale-white cloaking of the people and structures of Hastur. It had snowed like this years ago at his mother's funeral. He remembered watching the flakes strike the red-painted wood as he, Ash, Uncle Lafe and Da carefully let out the ropes, hand over hand, and lowered the coffin into the ground. They could have afforded a tomb, but Da preferred the ground out of fear of the rats getting at her. Da had a deathly fear of the rats.

The general looked up at wooded Mount Dnarden, the gray

branches of its trees etched white with snow, rising in the distance behind these buildings. At its crest stood the twisted monolith known as the Beckoning Stone. It stood so tall it dwarfed the surrounding trees. Many times, he had felt the pull of that stone.

Flocks of skull grebes, butcherbirds and red-throated creepers circled and rippled amongst the treetops. They would drift off soon, whisked to the safety of their nests in roof overlays, low bushes and burrows throughout the city. Leaving the graveyard to night things.

Troubled by his uncertainty, he thought about Lucrezia and his mother and others he knew who slumbered in Mount Dnarden's caress. *Do the dead hold the living to promises made?*

Chimney smoke hung in the air and the street rabble moved with and against him as he followed the familiar path. He knew these pedestrians were eyeing him, remarking on the sight of a uniformed and armored soldier in their midst, some perhaps aware of his celebrity, but they were just smudges in his periphery and he felt wholly unconnected to them, until he heard something in the shuffling of their footsteps that moved him closer to their sphere.

The scuffing cadence that swirled about him took the shape of whispered syllables. Not full-formed words at first, but fragments that repeated again and again in the same order, a brief string of word bits that slowly built against the overall scraping din of foot traffic. Halting, he strained to decipher its message, and when it emerged it erupted in a burst that seized him at his gist: "She watches, Drummer."

For an instant, his heart stopped. His head and shoulders jerked around and he nearly stabbed a pedestrian with his spear.

"She watches, Drummer." The shuffling sounds returned to normal but the words echoed inside his head as he scanned the procession of humanity all around him. Someone must have spoken those words. He had not imagined it. He had not imagined it.

The pedestrians became grotesques: demonic, horned and camel-faced, with huge, glowing eyes and black wings. They glowered at him as he passed through them. A few took flight and their wings flapped like wind-blown fabric as they wheeled high overhead. But he had seen this kind of thing happen before and he knew it was not real.

He walked on, refusing to be panicked.

An eternity later, he stood at the threshold of his house and knocked.

The door opened and one of the winged and horned monsters greeted him, but only briefly. Then its features ran like wax until it transformed into another form altogether: a pole-thin man, pouch eyed and crinkly faced, with thick gray brows and thin gray hair, and the powdery off-white skin of a Morellan, his metal collar tarnished from years of service.

Ash who had been with the Maule family since before Drummer's birth. Something softened inside the general at the sight of this lifelong companion.

"Why knock, dear fellow?" Ash asked in his melodic accent. "Come in. Come in." He took the spear and shield. "Ye'll catch yer death." He eyed Drummer warily.

In the background stood Ash's common-law wife, Huldra, 10 years her husband's junior, yet similar-looking to him in the way longtime mates come to resemble each other. She was, of course, Morellan, and was drawn and gray and carried herself in the same calm manner as her partner. When she looked up at Drummer, she mirrored Ash's expression of concern. Huldra set on the table the tray containing the remainder of the food she had been dishing into red clay bowls: barley groats and cheese, smothered in onions. One of her signature dishes.

Grady Maul who was Drummer's father, and Uncle Lafe, his father's brother, looked up from their steamy bowls. In a rare display of agility, Drummer's da, straggly white-haired and straggly white-bearded, with sagging skin and age spots, in a felted gray robe, bolted to his feet and hurried forward. Uncle Lafe, who was much younger than Da, followed. Though he never spoke of it, Drummer had always seen more of himself in Uncle Lafe than he had in his da, though maybe it was because of Uncle Lafe's closer proximity in age. Still, his uncle's build was quite similar to his, and there was a matching sharpness in their cheekbones and a squareness in their jaw lines, and the shapes and color of their eyes were the same.

"Ye were gone so long," his Da said, "we were getting worried." He embraced Drummer.

"Took out the chariot to practice some maneuvers," the general said. "The left hub wrenched in a furrow and now it needs a wheelwright's attention. Hopefully, I won't require it for a bit, though Luster Spaulding's people are usually prompt with repairs."

"Come along, General," Uncle Lafe said. "Ye're just in time to have a bite. And something warm to drink?"

"A spot of groats might do me good," he said.

The three men pulled up at the table.

Later, the groats still warm in his belly, the general rested alone in his room upstairs. His sheathed sword and the swath of cloth he wore into battle lay on the covers beside him.

He held a hand up to his face and, by the light of an oil lamp, watched it tremble. Turning the palm away, he examined the ends of his fingers. The flesh encircling each nail was notched and scarred, and many of the marks were an angry pink. He brought his ring finger to his mouth and touched his teeth lightly to a tiny ridge of hard skin before biting in.

The bed rested in an alcove. He looked across the foot of his bed through the parted bed curtains to the small window on the other side of the room. Frost swept across the lower pane but through the top one he clearly saw a thinning sky striped with bruiselike shreds of purple clouds. A light snow was still falling. He considered getting up and walking over for a better view, but didn't.

On a cool spring night when he was 14, he and his father had sat in chairs in the living room downstairs toasting bread in the fireplace, when Da turned to him and said, "Drummer, we have selected a bride for ye."

In the hearth, a burning wood knot popped and sprayed a burst of sparks. When the sparks hit the floor, they turned into gold bugs that scurried away in all directions.

"Who is she?" Drummer asked. By then, he was long used to the apparitions and knew better than to mention them.

"Garner Spaulding's daughter Lucrezia, the little thin one with the dark hair."

Drummer nodded.

Garner Spaulding was part of the Spaulding clan, which owned Spaulding Boatworks on Dagon Bay, along with other concerns. The boatworks, at Hastur's bustling Port Whilom, included a shop, a factory and a warehouse. Hundreds of workers and slaves built and repaired military, commercial shipping and fishing boats and they sold supplies, including flax-spun sails and nets made at a factory owned by Grady and Lafe Maule.

At the time, Drummer had tried to picture Lucrezia but could only summon the vaguest recollection. After all, she was only 12 and not one of his regular playmates.

As betrothed, they met for the first time two weeks later at a Spaulding family dinner. Garner and his wife, Aella, had welcomed Drummer and his parents warmly. Young Lucrezia wore a fiery fuchsia dress embroidered with gold trim and, for protection, an amulet shaped like an open hand.

He bowed politely and kissed her fingers. She smiled at him, her eyes a warm and brilliant blue. His heart opened to her.

After a year they married and Lucrezia moved in with Drummer, his parents, Uncle Lafe, Ash and Huldra. In this very room, she had let the wedding gown slip from her shoulders and had taken that first slow, single stride toward him, like some princess in a painting stepping from a palace bath, all fresh and clear and shiny as a pearl, her skin so smooth and soft he could feel it from across the room with his eyes and with his own skin.

They were four months married when he first put his military schooling to use by joining the Vermilion Shrikes as a young doomsman.

He lifted the sword beside him and pulled it from its sheath. The blade was sharp but nicked in more than a dozen spots and the handle was slightly bent. Resheathing it, he laid it back down.

He had continued his study of warfare and horsemanship with the best teachers, not only in Hastur but throughout Ligeia in Melmoth, Carcosa, Moonstone and White Worm, quickly moving up the ranks in the Shrikes until the reins of the Fourth Legion were his and he became a hero. Through it all, she was his strength. Over the years, when he rode into the rain of spears and arrows, and the dust and the blood and the heart-wrenching cries of the wounded and dying, and as he barked orders that sent fear-shaken men moving into harm's way, he drew on the part of her he carried within him always. In the halls of government, when he addressed the archons and the high priests, and had to impress on them not only the details of his warfare but his command of the cavalry and the vigor of his courage and the wisdom of his strategies, the words he spoke came from a heart brimming with her love and confidence. She had made him everything others imagined him to be.

They shared this very bed for nearly 20 years, until she became so terribly ill she had to move downstairs. The fever attacked quickly, reducing her to a stupor. It lasted three weeks.

When he came to her sickroom bed that morning, his presence pierced an awful silence. Her raven hair lay tangled, her bosom still, her eyes and mouth open in an expression of quiet awe. He leaned to her, closed her mouth and one last time kissed her lips, already bluing. Then he looked into the eyes that had once filled him with purpose and pride and saw nothing but his own ghostly reflection. He slid them closed.

Death, that cruel and vicious takeback, had robbed him of the being he loved most. He railed against it as a cheat, a sadistic prank. With its grim finality, death made a mockery of beauty and compassion and hope. It may spare the severely afflicted of suffering but these poor sufferers were already caught in death's spiral. Their torment was just a part of it. *Her torment.*

On the battlefield he had witnessed so many fall, hardy and full of life one instant, diminished and hollow the next. Empty vessels.

Death, so terrible many pretend it will never come for them, even though we all cross the same floor, never knowing when the trap door will spring and spill us into darkness.

He sat with her that day, beside an effigy of Dagon, taking no food, taking no consolation from his family, watching her still and slender form, heartsick.

He now picked up the scrap of her fabric, which he had worn into battle since the day she left him. He examined the cloth thoughtfully, fondling it, and he made up his mind. He would go to Dagon Fane tonight and have his answer. He would see Saga Eldritch and ask her, once and for all, if the dead are truly watchful of the living.

***

Ever sullen, ever still, the hamlet on the hill broods against the city skyline.

At its crest towers the Beckoning Stone, a twisted obelisk of runic images and hieroglyphs. The stone overshadows a nearby forest of blood-thorn greenwoods and spider oaks, leafless and oyster gray in the dusk, shrouded in snow. A solitary jumbi owl hoots from some hidden branch, its cry a chilling lament.

Households of dreamers lie along the mound's walkways in dark, steepled chambers guarded by ghostlike statuary: carven likenesses of deities and dolphins, soldiers and sylphs. Many of the sleepers, though, blanketed in snow, sleep with the worms in the ground. The high and the low, brought together by the taking away of breath.

Here lie the denizens of Mount Dnarden.

They say that beneath the mount lies Hastur himself, not dead but asleep. The shepherd god—some say exhausted from his toils, others say exhausted of his patience with humankind—curls in a coma from which he may never awaken. If you listen closely you may hear his snores in the whistling wind. Some say if he wakes, all the dead of Mount Dnarden will arise with him.

Enshrined here is Cyril Carver, breadmaker and soldier, his head stove in by a Skalken axe, his secrets buried with him. He once speared a Skalken infant from her mother's arms and held the wailing babe aloft in triumph, blood dripping down his arm, whilst the mother collapsed heartbroken to her knees. He then raped and killed the mother and collected her ear for a trophy. The child's, as well. As a breadmaker, he sometime urinated in the dough, serving it up with a smile to the unsuspecting.

And here is Jemmy Lumen, wife of Ratter Lumen, mother of Willa; all her adult life associated with her husband's grim calling. The smell of ferrets in their cages permeated their meager one-room dwelling. Corners clogged with traps and skins. Her husband's hands scarred with bites and scratches and his clothes smelling of the dank alleys and the dark places he frequented. Over time, he even took on something of a likeness to the creatures he hunted. Eventually, she took the rat poison herself, not all at once but a bit at a time. She suffered a terrible death, protracted and wrenching, but it appeared to all as if a sickness had taken her, saving her from an unmarked grave outside the city gates at the place called Suicides Crossing.

Her neighbor is Undine Maule, mother of famed General Drummer Maule, insulated by snow and dirt from the cares of the world.

And from the sum and substance of the wicked life she led. The child she baked in her womb was a lunatic, born of an intrigue with her husband's brother, fashioned into a man by her relentless will and subterfuge. Her tools, bolstered by her place in the community of aristocrat wives, included the spreading of venomous rumors, character assassination and lies, all carefully placed and nourished. She paved the way for her child's success by heartlessly taking down his rivals one by one, many of them upright and faultless.

Down the path from her lies Petrus Geb, the tanner, only son to the war hero Hedwig Geb who gave up all his limbs save one for the glory of Hastur. Petrus, it turns out, spent his last shiny paldin on the building of his stony sepulcher. The rest of his money was long gone to games of chance at which he was luckless, women to whom he was meaningless and lenders who were both ruthless and scurrilous. He left his father destitute and homeless until the day arrives when Hedwig joins his son in this gloomy chamber.

Beyond him lies Zath Mallock, husband to Casilda, father of three, and brother to Grace Gargery, Ring's mother. Another one taken on the battlefield. As skilled a silversmith as ever huddled before a bellows, most agreed. Unfortunately, he was as much a perfectionist in other areas of his life: harping on Casilda's running of the household until the poor woman second-guessed her every decision; his children cowering under their father's critical eye; the workers in the foundry pressed to unrealistic standards and always treated as if they were coming up short. They all shed tears for him but secretly felt a heavy weight lifted.

In a tomb the next row over is young Digna Greavor, daughter of Alban Greavor, the carpet merchant. Digna lies beside her mother, who died giving her birth. One of many children gone in a time when reaching adulthood was, at best, a 50/50 proposition. However, it was not sickness or accident that claimed her, but the lust of a mad intruder, who took her innocence along with her life and left her to be discovered in the shocking light of day by her grief-stricken father.

Down from her rests Darius and Savina Gargery, parents of Anse and Cletus. Savina, broken in body and spirit by the bitter and cheerless man she married, in the end simply lost the will to live. Darius, gored by a wild boar—or so they claimed—left this life as violently as he lived it. On the day they learned of his death, the slaves of Hastur rejoiced. Although they hid it well, secretly so did his own sons.

Next we come to Lucrezia Maule, wife of the general, daughter to Garner and Aella Spaulding, buried, along with her husband's secret, not in the ground as the general's mother was, but in a suitable vault with space for the general to one day lie beside her. The beautiful Lucrezia, gone of the fever, too soon, buried in a red-painted coffin full of flowers in a shroud

79

with a square of fabric cut from the hem.

And so the histories go, on and on, until one day, with the rarest of exceptions, they are consigned, at best, to seldom-read footnotes in faceless eternity. The denizens of Mount Dnarden will get fewer and fewer visitors until the mourners stop coming altogether and, over time, the dead merge into the anonymity of ancestry. Slowly, they are forgotten. Gone to seed. For all the fullness they felt of life, it was almost as if they had never existed.

***

Ring had lived his whole life in the black-bricked house on Maule Square. A sprawling, well-worn edifice, spread over three stories, it felt bigger on the inside than it looked outside, especially to Ring, perhaps in part because, from roof to floor, it was the boy's entire world.

Who knew how old it was? Some said Gargery House had been built long ago upon a hanging grounds, and a tapestry from the appropriate period seemed to support the claim. The tapestry, owned by Aylmer Wilf— the retiring archon, who said it had been in his family for generations— appeared to show a gallows approximately where the house now stood. The threadwork was faded and moth-eaten and it required some scrutiny, and perhaps a bit of imagination, to spot the detail. There was no proof that the hanged appeared every year—on the anniversary of their deaths—in the square outside the house, though the rumor circulated widely.

Upon entry through the iron street door, a visitor would first encounter the ground-floor entryway with its fireplace and clothing hooks. A pinched high-ceilinged space, it exuded not so much warmth as a sort of a hard-fisted tolerance. The entry gave guests a taste of the architecture, which could charitably be called discordant.

Wooden stairs fed up from here, their contours mildly warped and slanted. Many times he had lurked on these steps, watching and listening to whatever transpired below. When Ring was younger, Grand Da Darius would clamber up and down the stairs barefooted, his feet making an awful slapping noise on the wood. Curiously, Ring remembered the sound, though little else of his grandfather.

The entry floor and all the floors on the ground level were black flagstone, which tended to rob the rooms of light.

The entryway led to the main room with its splendid, conch-patterned carpet, purchased from the carpet merchant, Alban Greavor, who lived just across the square. The carpet, though beautifully rendered, was really too big for the table and chairs set in the middle of it and made them look tiny, like a knot of flotsam in a sea of conchs.

Stepping into the spacious main room always brought the boy a sense of relief. Here, daylight was most plentiful and activity of one kind or another was generally at hand. Meals were prepared and delivered, cleaning chores undertaken, attention given to assorted errands. The servants, wisping about in their clinging linens, provided as much entertainment as utility. Here he played his mountain explorer game, walking around and around the carpet edge.

Gargery House was never as silent as it was when its main room sat empty.

Here was a larger fireplace with an ironwood mantle that featured fang-toothed fish and viper sharks swimming along its edges. On the mantle was an immense clay vase, a polished whalebone and a decorative phallus, gleaming gold. Also displayed prominently in the main room was the ornate shelf containing the sixteen skulls of Ring's ancestors. And feeding off this room was a scullery, a kitchen and M's sick room. Beneath the floor were the sixteen headless corpses from which the skulls were harvested, sunk in the masonry when that was still the custom.

Some said the skulls of the ancients were emptied of their brains as part of a ritual cannibalism designed to allow the living to feed on the skills and memories of the dead. But this may have just been made up to frighten children.

The second floor contained his bedroom, the area where he spent much of his time. This was where he had taken his lessons from Tutor Will. Sometimes he could still feel the reassuring presence of his former teacher.

The room consisted of a small, straw-mattressed bed, a bedstand, a meager fireplace, a desk, a chamber pot, a wardrobe closet and a small window. The wardrobe closet contained six changes of clothes, which was more than sufficient, a seldom-worn winter cloak and an extra pair of sandals.

Down the corridor, which some days seemed to extend forever and other days seemed truncated, were the quarters for the household staff, currently just two but sometimes as many as five. The two rooms contained three beds each. There was also a spinning and weaving room and, at the end of the hall, in a shadowy niche, lay the room that had belonged to Grand Da Darius but was now Fadumo Aneleh's. Before Fadumo Aneleh, no one had lived in the chamber since Grand Da's death. Ring had always avoided the room because something about it made him uneasy.

The third floor, which included the landing and window from which he viewed Maule Square, contained Da's bedroom, a sitting room, Uncle Cletus' old room and a large room sometimes used to house slaves when the pens in Gondemar were full. Ring had many times watched said wretches file up the stairs past his room in shackles, Uncle Cletus or Cousin Andaman silently spiriting them along. Without exception, these boarders were gone the next day.

As with most old houses, this one had shifted and settled and didn't always line up exactly square which gave it a feeling of being not quite right. There were cold spots and places where light leaked in as smoky beams. You could feel Da's presence in Gargery House even when he wasn't there, and the servants, as always, came and went. M was a presence but a distant one. There were traces of gone Gargerys and the people who had lived in the house before the Gargerys, their invisible hands and feet having smoothed the floors and the railings: their sins and guilt and depravities had left a faint, moldlike whiff in the darkest recesses —or maybe that was just decay. Like most old houses, this one spoke in creaks and groans.

As he looked out from his narrow, third-story window on the darkening twilight and the trickle of day's-end stragglers crossing Maule Square, Ring felt as if time were standing still. He was now once again one with the house, back in his familiar places, where he understood the daily comings and goings. Where he could figure things out. The day's trip to Spaulding Stables had jarred his sensibilities and left him exhausted and confused.

Rubbing the glassy surface of his lucky stone, he thought about the foal. *His* foal. The boy had no frame of reference for this ownership. But the instant his young hand had reached out and stroked the animal's white coat, he had connected with the tiny horse as he had never connected with anything in his life. He relived the trepidation of his approach, the feeling of furry warmth beneath his fingers, the jolt that transported him whole to another plane of existence.

What was that feeling?

Across the square, Alban Greavor shuffled to the doorstep his young daughter had once played upon. He looked around, scratching his bald head, as if he had misplaced something.

"What is death like?" Ring had once asked Tutor Will, as the boy practiced his hieroglyphs on a soft wax tablet.

To him, it was just another question, but it brought to his teacher a profound stillness. Studying Tutor Will's raven eyes, Ring waited.

"It's ... a shadow," the teacher said at last.

"A shadow?"

"Aye." A sparkle came to the dark eyes. "In his shadow, a man is neither absent nor present and, yet, he is both. That's what death is like."

The boy had thought about this many times. *Was this pronouncement whimsical or pithy?* With Tutor Will, it was sometimes hard to tell.

Digna was the dead girl's name, according to the maidservant Bartine, who knew all about the neighbors from gossip exchanged at a nearby well. Digna Greavor, a spindly imp who usually jumped rope but sometimes played instead with a doll or a top or some other toy. She'd been younger than him but only by days. Whenever he saw her, her hair was done up in a bouquet of ringlets. He had sometimes dreamt about her and he would wake up from the dreams with fond thoughts of her that carried through into his waking life. It was one of his few dreams that didn't terrorize him.

When he watched her, he imagined the sound of her voice, the smoothness of her hand, the smell of her hair, the taste of her lips.

Now that taste would be forever denied him. Digna. Murdered in her sleep, much to the alarm of households throughout the city. Gone to Osric and the Netherworld. When he learned of her death, he secretly wept. He felt as if she had been stolen from him, though the two had never actually met.

Sirrah Alban shuffled inside and closed the door behind him.

From the floor below came the sound of motion. Fadumo Aneleh's room. The boy had quickly gotten used to odd noises coming from there. The soft singing and chanting, the muffled and sometimes violent knocking. Bartine, who brought the fadumo her meals, had remarked on the room's having acquired a gamey smell, though this may just have been Bartine's way of being scornful.

His thoughts returned to the foal and the stable. To General Maule and Sirrah Luster, to Paulus, Willa and Verger. Where did he fit in with these people?

He knew from Da's exchange with Uncle Cletus that tonight would hold some answers for him. Whatever was taking shape, it included the fadumo and something called a "gibbous moon." An answer to Sirrah Luster's problem, once and for all?

He eyed the lucky stone in his hand. An adder stone, Tutor Will had called it when he gave it to him as a parting gift. Shot through with pink and green sediment, the adder stone had a hole clean through its middle. Tutor Will said it was called an adder stone because some believed it was formed from hardened saliva left by mating serpents, though the teacher, skeptic that he was, doubted the story was true.

As the boy rubbed his thumb on the stone, he sensed a great change coming. It mewled to him in the winter breeze that swept the city. It rang in the footsteps of the passersby in the square below and rattled his narrow pane of glass. Whatever form the approaching change might take, the boy feared he would have no choice but to surrender to it completely.

***

A dry boil of blistering air thick with glowing ashes and scalding grit howls down at the mount and his naked rider as they come to the passage entrance. By now, the young rider is a broken thing, clenched and shaking, out of her mind with terror.

Halting, he shrugs in the way he has shrugged off her countless predecessors and he feels her slip reluctantly from him to the ground. He turns to her. Dark ringlets frame her tear-stained face.

The lord of death, black-horned, baleful, his thick-boned frame jutting muscular, his fur matted and singed, his scrotum calloused and leathery from centuries of dragging his enormous balls across the sizzling, gravelly slate of the Netherworld floor, steps backward and watches, a lick of flame escaping one nostril.

A frail twig she was, even in life, but here in the enormity and perpetuity of this lonesomest of end-road places she is barely a speck of dust. Let her quiver and weep. There is no shame in it. He has seen the bravest and strongest men do the same. But neither does he feel sympathy for her. This is, after all, the way it ends for everyone.

Turning from the vacant black of the passage threshold, she asks, "How can it all be over so soon?" Her small voice cracks, frantic but barely loud enough to be heard above the howling wind. "I never married. I never had a child. I never even got to say goodbye." She sobs. "What's the point?"

A ball of flame crashes behind Osric, sending a wildfire snaking in the violent wind, cascading hot ash.

Facing him, she says, "I want my Da. Bring me to my Da."

Long streams of fire spurt from his flared nostrils, a warning that cannot be misunderstood.

He turns and leaves her watching after him, a bronze and naked child at the doorway to doom.

He shakes his massive head and tells himself, *It's what they have chosen.*

***

The fadumo dreamt of the charnel caves again. The corpses, the smell of death, the pooled sacrificial blood. Again she fluoresced in a glow, not the gray of the overhead opening but an emerald glow. Again she huddled over a particular body under the watchful study of her thrumming god in the shadows.

This time, she focused on an old man who had been dead perhaps a week. He sat up slowly. It was painful to watch him rise, this ancient bag of bones, his joints clicking, his tendons stiff and testy. She recognized him as one of the village elders, not her father, Mage Medji Zant wa Zant, but the oldest of the elders, Mage Solon Worthy, his ochre skin wrinkled and loose on his frame as old people's skin sometimes can be. He looked at her, eyes already beginning to recede into their hollows, and pursed his lips almost to the cleft of his nose. There was a defiant air to him.

"You are a wicked, wicked child," he said in his chalky voice. "You bring great shame on your family and your people."

"But I have breathed new life into you, Mage Solon."

"My life was not yours to give. And I don't recall asking for it."

She had thought he would be pleased.

He pushed a hand through thinning white hair, wincing at the effort. Sniffing, he made a face.

"Do you understand what you have done to me, child?" he asked. "My place amongst the elders has been taken. My house and boat have been sold. My family has wept for me and is beginning to move on. All of life has moved on." He looked around him. "Even if I wanted to, I don't have the strength to climb out of this cave."

His deep-set eyes went moist.

"But, Mage Solon, where there is life there is hope."

"Not for me. Not now. Where would I go from here?"

Unable to respond to this, she let her dream world fall apart and melt away.

The fadumo awoke on her new life. A single oil lamp flickered on the bedstand. The dim room, still used for storage, was choked with linens and clothing and odd bits of furniture, but the bed was large and comfortable, and, though the room's fireplace had gone out, she was tolerably warm beneath the threadbare covers. Beside the lamp lay a pitcher of water, a clay cup and the spirit box with the spider clasp.

A month had passed since she landed with Wanlo the Freebooter and Wolfdog in moonlit Dagon Bay. The cold weather of Hastur's autumn had seemed far removed from her sunny island. Even with layered clothing, the damp chill bit into her. She witnessed the exchange of her ransom, witnessed the two men awkwardly swap pleasantries. The slaver seemed genuinely touched by Wanlo's deterioration. Poor pirate. Not long for this world and not much hope for him in the next. Inwardly, she beamed.

Piran had, once awakened to his powers over his former oppressors, gone on something of a rampage. Red Judoc had been the first to fall, his neck twisted round by the plunge down the stairs. Then there was Drogo Scuttin, Piran's recruiter, who, wearing his banded seacoat, mysteriously jumped overboard and was promptly devoured amid a cacophony of horrible screaming by a school of hungry viper sharks. Obie Morag, the hard-featured carpenter who had once gleefully boxed the boy's ears and had given him up to Red Judoc's rage, came crashing from the mainsail to the deck, landing smack on his head. Then there was Rance Philo, the paunchy surgeon with the menacing eye, who had hit Piran and kicked him and threatened to kill him. Rance apparently sliced himself to ribbons with his own surgical tools.

When the fadumo departed the *Pillager* with Wanlo and Wolfdog in the rowboat, she left behind a lot of fine fellows looking over their shoulders.

The ride to Hastur was a brief one. The slaver had found an old blanket and thrown it over her. It smelled rank but afforded some warmth. She'd asked to have her wrists freed but if he heard her he didn't respond.

"Listen," he said, rolling his neck. "Fadumo Aneleh, is it? I know ye understand my words."

She nodded.

"My name is Anse Gargery and I'm yer master now. Best to get that straight right from the start."

Bound as she was, she pinched herself and sucked her lips to avoid laughing at this. Luckily, he was no longer looking at her.

"When it comes to conjuring, Dagon help me, I'm just another crawler. I don't know the why of it and I don't *want* to know the why of it, but I've been led to believe ye can deliver on certain dark matters. Dealing with the dead and so on."

Rigid-featured and stoop-shouldered, Anse was easy to understand. Ruthless and greedy, aye, even evil. Not one to carelessly cross. But thoughtful in his own way. A schemer. He asked her bold as day, without mincing words, if she could really do as he requested. He seemed relieved and somewhat surprised to hear her acquiesce so readily.

The rest of the trip they were silent as Anse let this realization of her powers sink in.

By now, she was familiar with the household's tiresome routines, the principal players, the hierarchy of authority, the layout of the home. She could, of course, strike down her captors, one by one, but then she would face the same quandary as the mage in her dream. *Where would I go from here?* Better to appear to cooperate. After tonight, she could begin setting her own course.

The servants were frightened of her, as they should be, which afforded her a wide berth and a measure of privacy. The one called Bartine emptied her chamber pot and brought her meals, laying out the dishes carefully on the dresser top just inside the door. Sometimes Bartine's eyes sought out the fadumo's but not usually. Usually, Bartine was gone almost at once. The other one, Olalla, when she wasn't attending the boy or his demented, invalid mother, kept herself occupied as much as possible beyond the fadumo's study and reach. Both slaves carried a burden of sadness, but Olalla especially so.

The slaver Anse Gargery doubtless took liberties with the two, which was his right. She had expected him to call on her, as well, but he did not. Instead, he brought her the things she needed and left her to her preparations. Amongst the items procured was the heart of a cat, which she boiled and nailed to a rafter over her door to protect her from evil influences.

The other slaver, Cletus Gargery, she dismissed as Anse's toad, but he was a formidable presence. Part of a rare breed of Ligeian giants.

Ligeians believed that the world before this one was populated with the First People, who had been plentiful and had ruled peacefully. Then the Great Old Ones came from the sky and mated with them. Their offspring became gods, giants or what were now considered regular human beings.

Over time, the First People mixed with the Great Old Ones and the offspring they had with the Great Old Ones until the First People were mated out of existence. Ligeians never quite got along as well after that but they became more creative and better at solving problem. All Ligeians had strains of the First People and the Great Old Ones in their blood.

They believed at one time there were hundreds of gods, but warring amongst them reduced their number to four: the gods of wind, water, fire and earth.

The Old Ones, though, were not mated out of existence but kept a pure bloodline amongst themselves. One day they vanished. Underground, it was believed, into the deepest reaches of caves and long-buried hollows. To rise up again one day and reclaim the world.

She learned all this from Odgar Gargery, one of the ghosts who lived in the main room's floor. The living claimed old Odgar had died of the fever but really his body was destroyed by drink and carnal ravages.

Foolishly, there was no mention in their pantheon of Anarach, the greatest of the gods. But she would remedy that when her time came.

The mother, a mad malingerer, held court in her bed when she wasn't too deep in her nostrums. Her husband seldom visited her.

Then there was Andaman Gargery, the one with the knife. A case all to himself. Solitary, a lurker, handsome but in a haunted and disheveled sort of way. Always on the periphery. A blister poised to pop. She could see something in his eyes that disturbed her; something that turned, something gleaming and watery that guided his thoughts. That seemed to command him. He bore the unmistakable stench of death, thick as gutter mud.

The boy remained the odd one out in this lot. Slight, trim, elegant almost. Little malice in him that she could see, though the sprouting of lust could change that, especially confined as he was in this mausoleum. No teacher, no friends. Must live a rich inner existence. She sensed in him an untapped reserve of strength that was capable of bending the pure energy to its will, given the proper provocation. But, of course, he was clueless of this unused power.

The other occupants of Gargery House were an outlandish gathering of the gone—querulous and raging. Odgar Gargery, Anse's great grandfather, was the calmest but that wasn't saying much. It was Odgar, after all, who launched into the cup smashing spree in the scullery. That had come after the last time she had engaged him. She had not opened herself to any of them since then. Better to leave these dead unpestered for the time being.

So far she had not been collared, which afforded her a curious ambiguity of station.

She climbed out of bed and knelt down in worship. She breathed slowly, eight times in and out. She pictured the circle of light. "*Indrin Anarach, indrin retpus,*" she sang softly. "*Gwael khadath uphursin mewn. Ulthaar trianda hrath. Obassi czatael oia bharzai.*" Eight times she touched her forehead to the floor, circled round to her left, then to her right, threw back her head. A surge of power coursed through her.

She began anew, "*Indrin Anarach, indrin retpus.*" And so on.

In her mind, she plucked at the strands of the gossamer web, saw the red eyes glow, felt the brace before the surge.

Take my hand, dark lord. Tonight we dance and our piper's tune will tremor the land and roil the heavens.

***

Andaman knew it was time to leave. He set the straw doll down amongst his growing hoard of toys and trinkets, said a brief prayer to Osric, blew out the lights except for a single candle and left his room at Nilus Margrave's Inn. On the stairway he passed an islander with deep clefts at the chin and nose and a wine-colored mark on one cheek. The stranger stonily took his measure. Down the steps, through the dining room and the entry, to the street and the embrace of the night below.

Hastur was snowy and slick and all but vacant, though a few souls braved its nighttime tangle of shadowy lanes. The wind had died down but the air was still sharp as an icy blade. For the most part, the gamblers, drinkers and lechers would already be in their haunts, commencing to feed their weaknesses. He expected the back alleys and some of the side streets to give up an occasional derelict or possibly even a brigand, but nothing he couldn't handle. A dollop of snow fell on him from a rooftop.

Ruffling out of the gloom came a pair of watchmen in their ribbons, briefly affording him their pointed attention.

He followed the east wall to Maule Square, looking up whimsically at a familiar house. Around the corner, a stab of moonlight caught a half dozen black rats scaling up the side of a building. He passed a street whore with hieroglyphs on the soles of her sandals that read in the dim snow: "Follow me." Passing the iron gate of Spaulding Stables, he circled round back and ventured downward into the Horrocks district. Mount Dnarden and its grim monolith leered at him. He may be visiting there yet tonight, depending on the outcome of this other errand. From somewhere out of sight, a dog barked at him.

For an instant, light and commotion spilled into the night in front of him. A drunk stumbled from an inn, supported by his slave. The drunk had rotten teeth and wiry hair and put him in mind of an oyster seller he'd once gutted in Wharf Town. The drunk cringed at the unexpected sight of Andaman. Andaman walked on.

Dagon Fane lay just north of Mount Dnarden in a cluster of buildings surrounded by a low, snow-covered wall of sandstone blocks stenciled with seaweed and threadlike confervoid patterns. The compound buildings were enormous: thickset minarets, colonnades, inscribed obelisks and, in the center of it all, a mammoth, greenish black temple, its steps etched to resemble overflowing water dripping and running in rivulets. A great marble figure of Dagon, risen from her depths, her face a vengeful scowl, tentacles writhing, lunged from a mosaic walkway of ominous sea creatures to welcome her worshippers.

Various windows were lit and Andaman sensed activity within. He had never been inside Dagon Fane and hoped tonight would not change that. He had never understood the allure the sea goddess held for so many but he understood the fear generated by the compound's assurance she walked in their midst.

He took up a position embedded in the shadows of a cramped side street across from the front of the fane. Leaning into a corner, he passed the time tossing the dirk lightly from hand to hand. Long minutes elapsed. An acolyte ferried a brass bowl filled with steaming liquid from the temple to one of the minarets. Sometime later, a patron, accompanied by a figure in a pinguid, green robe and a mitered hat, trod to the compound's entrance and out into the street. They whispered together sullenly. When they parted, the mitered official offered some ritual valediction before ascending back inside.

The secret to waiting was to have no expectations. Whatever the outcome. Andaman was no philosopher but he'd learned this long ago. He had his own mind to keep himself occupied. He had his light show and his projections and delicious memories of carnage past.

All told, something like an hour went by. The wind began to pick up again and a light snow resumed. The compound went still in the dark, and Andaman worried he would have to knock at the fane's door and make an inquiry, when from down the street came a figure with a chin beard and a lion's mantel. The general had traded his uniform for a simple tunic. He walked through the compound's entrance, past the statue of the enraged sea goddess, up the temple steps to the door and opened it.

***

The handing over of the conjure woman had been unsettling from the start. The Council of Elders at Presage Cay in their somber vestments had been at the waterline to greet the two pirates, if the word "greet" could be used in that sense. The gathering was more in keeping with a forced ceremonial courtesy or perhaps a memorial for someone distasteful.

"Salutations, yer worships," Wolfdog had said, hoping this was the correct form of address.

Drogo splashed out of the landing craft. "Wanlo sent us," he said, "for the prisoner."

Wolfdog interpreted Drogo's words for the assemblage, then stepped out, as well, and the two pirates tugged their boat ashore.

Presage Cay was a small sandy low-elevation island located on the surface of a coral reef. The shore was lined with well-made thatched huts and docks. Several fishing boats bobbed and swayed in the overcast afternoon sun, as flesh-footed storm gulls circled overhead. Coarse vegetation, mostly spear-frond trees and spiny branching shrubs, packed the central island, along with sedimentary rock formations. Villagers clustered warily outside their huts, all eyes on the strangers.

One of the elders, hoary and age-spotted, approached with a feathered fetish of some kind in one hand. He had an islander's light ochre coloring and the clefts at the chin and nose. The elders were all thin, but this one was especially so, bony and overlong as though held together by wires. "I am Mage Medji Zant wa Zant," the fossil said. "The prisoner is my daughter."

Wolfdog interpreted, then exchanged glances with Drogo.

"Families," Wolfdog said lightly, as if selling a daughter to pirates were an everyday occurrence.

"She has become a danger to us and must go. It saddens me greatly—and her mother. But it cannot be helped. I hope you know what you are taking on."

Wolfdog smiled, one hand nonchalantly on the curved handle of his sword. "That's between ye and Wanlo. All I know is a prisoner needs transporting. Drogo here's got yer money."

Wolfdog gestured to Drogo, who winked at the elders. "Drogo Scuttin, at yer service," the Pym said, scratching his flattened nose. He held up the coin purse in one hand. "It's all here."

They waited on the shore whilst a pair of brawny half-naked islanders dragged out an unconscious woman with a sack over her head. Reedy cords bound her wrists and ankles. When they approached the water, the two pirates helped them load her into the rear of the craft. Drogo handed over his purse to Mage Medji, who didn't even count the coins.

A third islander, with lusterless eyes and a fearsome spider tattooed on his bare chest, brought her things: a droopy jute sack and a box of some sort. He tossed the sack into the boat but carefully laid the box, as if something living resided within.

The elders' ancient eyes hung on the pirates for a long time.

"Well," Wolfdog said in the stony silence, "been a pleasure. Best of luck." Glancing at the boats rocking in the water, he added, "Good fishing."

When they pushed off and made their way out into the open sea, Wolfdog looked back. The elders were being joined at the waterline by the villagers, a vast collection of ochre-skinned humanity gathering like wordless sentries to watch the pirates leave. The sight made Wolfdog's stomach crawl.

From that point, everything began to unravel.

First was Wanlo's slow descent into the quagmire of malady. Whatever had taken hold of him, before it was done, had all but sucked the flesh from his bones. Day by day, it crippled him a little more. Soon he was half days at the mast, and half days on his back. A woeful sight indeed, the bringer of bloody death reduced to a dazed stupor.

And that wasn't even the worst of it.

Wolfdog had heard the hollow laugh, had seen Red Judoc's tumble, had heard the spectral taunt, "Watch yer step, sealegs." The pirates had all flash-frozen in dread at the sound of that voice. They had all known Piran. They knew how he had been treated. His vengeful specter had now apparently risen, and a lot of fine fellows were sorrowfully regretting their cruel behavior toward the cabin boy. Luckily, Wolfdog was not a member of *that* club.

Red had barely been laid to sea when the naysayers began questioning if what they'd witnessed was not merely a drunken pirate blundering to his death. If what they thought they heard was not the sea winds playing tricks on the ears. Their explanations seemed almost plausible in the light of day.

Then there was Drogo, a favorite of the pirate brothers, cheery and reliable when danger got close up. A flagrant tale spinner but good company. Wolfdog had been below deck when the yelling had started. Flying up the steps to where the crew congregated at the bow, Wolfdog looked over just in time to see the Pym gasp a final breath and disappear in a bloody churn. A more helpless feeling would be difficult to imagine.

Perhaps Drogo had gotten too close to the edge and been jostled overboard. It had happened before to other crewmembers. But, coming as this did, so near on the heels of Red's demise, the timing seemed curiously coincidental and there are, after all, no coincidences at sea.

Then there was the fate of poor Obie Morag, a fierce fighter and fair carpenter but loose lipped to a fault. It was he who had given up Piran's hiding place to Red that murderous night, though it was unclear how widely known this was. A half-step to the right and old Obie might have landed smack dab on Wolfdog. As it was, the sudden violence of the fall from the mast came like a comet crashing out of nowhere. Combined with the image of Obie's head and neck collapsing into his spine in a splatter of blood and grisly bits, the event had shocked the living breath from Wolfdog. And from the other pirates, as well.

That's when Wolfdog had first heard whispers of mutiny.

Luckily Hastur approached on the horizon and, with it, the prospect of ridding themselves of the conjure woman. Perhaps that would be the end of it and the *Pillager* crew could split its bounty and head up the coast to Blackwood or Ulalame for some well-earned debauchery.

They set anchor that moonlit night on the outer rim of Dagon Bay and lowered their landing vessel into the water. Wobbly Wanlo and the bound conjure woman joined the craft. Wolfdog was about to follow them when yet another maddening cry went up. The fine fellows, who had all been on deck for the launch, hurried below to see the cause of the howling. What they saw knocked them numb.

Rance Philo, the ship's surgeon, lay in a lake of his own blood, watching terrorstruck as his left hand sought to hold off his right hand, which clutched a razor that was slashing at his face and neck and chest, slicing and chopping with wild abandon.

A collective gasp went up.

"Help!" he cried, twisting from the blade. "It's not me! It's not me!"

But his pleas for assistance had no takers as his pirate brothers stood dumbfounded on the steps and around the lower deck entrance.

Slicing off the thumb, then three fingers from his struggling left hand, the appendage was rendered useless. Now unabated, he hacked away, his prone form flinching spasmodically as each thrust of the treacherous razor threw off his blood in gushes.

Somehow Wolfdog found the strength to walk away. Whilst the rest of the crew was swallowed by the spectacle of horror, Wolfdog grabbed a rope and rappelled down the side of the ship into the waiting rowboat.

As they shoved off, the air still rang with the wincing gasps of awestruck pirates and then another sound: the echo of ghostly laughter.

As they made their way ashore, Wolfdog told the others about the surgeon's death, leaving out some of the gruesome details. Wanlo went ashen. The conjure woman's heavy-lidded eyes sparkled. After that they rowed in silence, amassing their thoughts.

The exchange with the slaver was made: the woman for a bulging sack of coins. As the ox-drawn wagon headed up Old Coast Road, Wanlo turned to his shipmate and said, "What say ye, Wolfdoggie? Have we the sand to return to that ship with this money and sell those hardcases on the notion of journeying on? Maybe a quick guzzle at a harbor tavern first?"

Wolfdog shrugged.

Wanlo the Freebooter turned his gaze to the sea. Slumped and sickly, the pirate was a mere vestige of his former self. "Some days," he said, "it scarcely pays to get out of bed."

Wolfdog's eyes went leaden.

There was a time, not long ago, when Wolfdog would have followed Wanlo into the direst of straits. They could have waded into a black storm together, chewed up its lightning and spit it back into the sky. That's when fate had been their ally and they had been invincible. That was not now.

Plain as day, there was no going back to the *Pillager*.

Wolfdog quietly drew the sword and closed on an old friend.

***

When the general passed through the threshold of the great temple, all lingering visions cleared. All voices quieted. The weight that had been with him all day was with him no longer and an exquisite calm took him. It had always been this way for him at the fane. He paused to wrap himself in the feeling, now glad, after all, that he had come.

At the shrine just inside the door, he lit a candle from another. From mounds of fish scales and bone-colored seashells, stone figures stared up blankly at him, their shadows flickering. He laid down his offering of coins.

The dead were gone. They could not judge him. But a reasoning beyond logic suggested otherwise, a reasoning born in the hollow of this fane, where seaweed draped the walls and sacrificial blood dripped from the altars. A reasoning proselytized by pale-eyed men with curled lips in oily robes and mitered hats shaped like severed fish heads.

The general walked softly through the vestibule. In the presence of his mystic deity, he felt part of a community, of a greater cause. The Esoteric Order of Dagon. Yet, he itched with the suspicion that in life's greater scheme all of this quite possibly amounted to nothing at all.

He stepped through a gateway flanked by two huge sculptures: gilled sirens, finned, web fingered and frog eyed, their long tresses floating as if underwater, their faces corpselike. In the ceremonial chamber beyond, thick garlands of seaweed hung on damp, greenish-black walls that were carved in a grim salmagundi of fearsome aquatic images. Torches in iron stanchions cast wavering light and shadows deep into the chamber. Rows of onyx benches, unoccupied at this time of night, faced seven colossal statues rising up to support the soot-stained ceiling. The Seven Oblations. Oddly angled and obliquely edged, the granite statues were vaguely human, vaguely piscine, cloven into neat sections on ribbed colonnades, their wounds red jewels, their mouths and eyes glaring metal.

Past these figures, three altars topped with blue-veined Ligeian marble, arranged in a slight semicircle, hunkered imperiously in a grotto guarded over by a spectacular wall painting of the goddess Dagon, in all her seductive and maleficent splendor. This was how the general pictured her when he prayed: slipping up from her murky depths, ringed fingers sinuous, hair lustrous, tentacles menacing, amphibious eyes casting their spell.

Somewhere water dripped.

"General?"

A stunted woman, remotely gnomelike, had joined him from a back passage. Though the size of a young child, she was middle-aged or older, and wore the scaled-down vestments of an acolyte, spayed and circumcised for her faith.

"I need to see the oracle," he said. "It's important."

"Aye. She's expecting ye," she said and left to fetch her.

A moment later, a high priest in a mitered hat and a green robe that gleamed with fish oil stepped from the back shadows, carrying a jeweled censer. The general recognized him. His name was Cosmas and he was the priest who had led the mourners to Mount Dnarden the day of Lucrezia's funeral. In the harsh torchlight, Cosmas took on a sinister quality that formed in the deep creases that lined his square face and the luminous whites of his blanched eyes. Prepared for ceremony, he wore rouge and dusty blue lip coloring. Around his neck he wore amulets and talismans charmed with specific powers. He chanted, "Queen of the trident, queen of the sea. We, yer loathsome, we, yer vile call to ye. Goddess of dark water, hear us and grace us with yer terrible presence." Smoke rose in puffs from the censer.

Next came the servitors. They were iron-masked and naked to the waist, including the women, and wore skirts around their loins. There were six altogether. Four were carrying eel-shaped scepters over their heads. One carried a flat, covered tray and one held a thin black vase with a tear-shaped stopper. They made a curious humming noise in their throats that rolled like a low rumble of thunder. The nightmare imagery of their masks was all twisted, with misplaced features—ridged and cavernous—and jagged-toothed sneers. They fanned out to either side of the central altar and brought their scepters to the floor.

Out stepped the oracle.

He looked upon the legendary Saga Eldritch, seer of Dagon Fane, with the trepidation that had always gripped him in her presence: the fear any mortal being would feel before the manifestation of the soul in bodily form of the great deity Dagon, goddess of the ocean's depths.

A tall woman, thin and hawk-faced, with a shiny bald head and elongated hands and feet, she was barely recognizable as Ligeian. She wore a yellow-gray, fish-leather frock, high necked and bell sleeved. Her expressionless eyes, seldom blinking, were of the oddest color: a reddish dark green. They seemed to look through him. They seemed to look through everyone and everything.

She walked with her arms in front of her bent at the elbows to keep her long fingernails from scraping the ground. They cascaded in sequences of gray arches that swayed with each step. The weight of the nails curled her fingertips.

She took her place at the central altar. The high priest joined her at one side with the censer, shaking out wafts of smoke. The servitors with the tray and the vase met her at the other. On the altar top, one laid down the smoking censer, one laid down the tray, one laid down the vase. The servitors ceased their humming. The cloth covering on the tray roused.

Cosmas regarded the general bleakly through the smoke. "Ye have a question for the oracle?" The voice boomed in the spacious chamber.

The general cleared his throat, keenly aware of being an audience of one. "If I make a promise to the dead, then change my mind, must I be held to my word?"

Cosmas' faded eyes narrowed. "What kind of promise?"

"A promise I made to my wife before she died. I promised to endorse her cousin in the upcoming archon race. But now I feel I should support another. A better choice for Hastur."

Cosmas nodded. "So, ye want to know whether yer wife will view this change of heart as a betrayal?"

"Aye!" The word leapt from his mouth. "That's it, exactly. Will she be disappointed in me if I do this?"

Cosmas lifted his chin and turned toward the oracle. He leaned into her and whispered. She remained impassive. If she understood him, she gave no sign. He gestured with a hand and one of the servitors unstoppered the black vase, then held it to Saga Eldritch's nose. She inhaled and a blue vapor rose into her from the vase. She sucked the vapor deep into her lungs repeatedly. When she had enough, she pulled back and the servitor removed the vase, stoppled it and carried it off.

Saga Eldritch took on a glow: ethereal, uncanny. She focused darkly downward on the altar top.

Cosmas gestured to the remaining servitor, who slid the flat tray under the oracle's gaze and lifted the covering. A spiny, needle-jawed sea creature writhed belly up: a scowling, deepwater cousin of the lobster, perhaps, but much larger. Eight-legged, barbeled, pulsing translucent, the creature's exposed underside was ridged and covered in sucker-bearing bristles that crooked and curled in the air. Tubular eyes hovered on threadlike stalks.

Reaching over, Cosmas thrust his hands into the creature, piercing and tearing open the stomach. Digging around inside, he seized up bloody globs of entrails and held them for the oracle to inspect. The creature's stalked eyes stared into the chasm of opened bowels. Mounds of viscera squirmed in the priest's opened hands, as the gelled blood dripped onto the altar.

Saga Eldritch bent low to study to the offal, practically sticking her face in it. She muttered to herself, then gestured with her head for the priest to show her more. He dug in deeper until his hands were overflowing. He rippled his fingers and moved his thumbs around in it. She surveyed it all intently as if looking for something specific.

Her eyebrows raised in startlement.

She turned to Cosmas and began to gibber excitedly at something she had found in the entrails. Then she yielded up an inhuman scream that set the general's teeth on edge. Her wail froze time and left the general paralyzed, his heart beating wildly. Still screaming, she turned from the priest to the general, regarding him with her red-green eyes, looking through him yet *into* him. There was no shrinking from that gaze: malevolent, accusatory. She raised her hands and the long nails clattered. Then her head fell back and rocked from side to side and she muttered as if in her sleep. She emitted a lulling sound that trailed off. Then she cut silent.

The servitors rushed forward to clasp her elbows and torso. They held her upright to prevent her nails from dragging. As her strength returned, they guided her away from the altar, limp and exhausted, into some tenebrous back niche.

Cosmas, his hands still heaped with viscera, watched the oracle and her servitors disappear. He let the two wet mounds plop down onto the open stomach. The stalked eyes had fallen limp.

"Yer answer, I'm afraid, is not what ye hoped for, General." Cosmas rubbed his hands together, then cleaned them as best he could with the cloth from the tray. "There can be no doubt. Lucrezia watches to see what ye'll do." His pallid stare leveled on the general. "Don't disappoint the dead."

The general, still shaken, could only nod.

CHAPTER 5
Sacrificial Blood

Her da was Zed Mallock, the silversmith. He bought roundheads from us. With their little hands, they do well at that kind of work. Hammering with those little hammers and snipping and fanning the forges. Zed and his son, Zath, were talented and industrious smiths, but Zed always seemed strangely unaffected by things. Simpleminded almost. In the end, he wound up living entirely in his own head. Some say he was touched by the holy ones and had the second sight. But what he had was no gift. Nor was it a sudden change in him. Ye could see the vacancy building for years.

Her brother, Zath, fell in with Cletus early on. They went through their budding days of debauchery together. Whoring and drinking till all hours in the sailor stops in Wharf Town and Carmilla. Tearing things up as young men are apt to do. They parted ways after Zath joined the Shrikes. His breast plate and shield now hang on the West Wall not far from Spaulding Stables.

After I turned 17, Da informed me of talks under way to marry me to Zed Mallock's daughter, Grace, a girl I barely knew. I had no feelings about it.

Gracie was 14, skinny, pasty and knock-kneed, with nervous eyes and mousey hair. No one's idea of a beauty but not the ugliest quim in Hastur. My strongest impressions of her at the time were that she would never look directly at me and she always smelled of lilac water and sweat. In quiet moments, ye could hear her breathing. And this was long before she fell so ill.

After we married, she moved into my family's black brick three-story in Maule Square. When Momma died, Gracie took over the house, keeping the molts busy, and she was passable as a weaver and a seamstress. But her heart was never in it. She struggled over small things and became increasingly prone to fainting and illness. I got used to having her around but that's as far as it went. Although we had relations, we've always kept separate rooms.

She surprised me when she became pregnant with our first son, Ring. I didn't expect it to happen so fast and I guess I thought maybe she'd be too frail for motherhood. That she would come up short in that way. Gracie tried to be a good momma to him, at least for the first few months, but it didn't come easy for her and it didn't really stick. She did try, though. Ye could see it meant something to her. If she's ever had a true connection to anyone in this world 'twould be Ring, though maybe that diminished. Because of her ways.

97

For one thing, Gracie has always dreaded the outside world. Taking her anywhere was an embarrassment. She'd say all the wrong things and become so jittery and clumsy that people noticed. Always dropping something.

Early on, she let me know she didn't want to go outside the house anymore, and after he was born, she didn't want the boy outside either. In his case, she somehow got it in her mind that he is deformed. To her dying day, she talked about him as if he were hideous to behold. To me, he doesn't look any different from anyone else, but I had other concerns like growing the family business, and I saw no gain in arguing with her about it. And I thought it better to keep the boy at a distance anyway, my temper being what it sometimes is.

Then, after we lost the second whelp, Darius, her illness just took over. That's when her room became the sickroom. I don't want to talk about Darius. It still pains me to think of it. Maybe someday.

On the rare occasions I needed Ring somewhere, I took him, despite her objections. But those occasions were hardly ever. Funerals mostly. Otherwise, I just let him be home with her. I know that left him unprepared for what I needed him to do later.

But, ye see? Things were what they were. There was no helping it.

At the western edge of Wharf Town, just beyond the Redgauntlet River, there weaved a shabby lane of single-room shacks known as Auseil Thoroughfare, best known for its cramped taverns and a cut-rate whorehouse called the Surly Oyster, last stop for many a fading daughter of joy. Populated chiefly with aging sailors and the widows of aging sailors, the byway connected greater Wharf Town by bridge to Gondemar and its marketplace.

Willa Lumen returned from her long day at the stables to a shack two blocks from the Surly Oyster. Already, at the green age of 13, Willa had become adept at assuring greasy libertines that her virtue was not for sale. She hurried through the ice and snow to get supper on the stove before Da arrived with Artemis and the ferrets, run ragged as they often were by the never-ending quest for vermin.

To her, it was life as usual, as it had been anyway since Momma died.

That night, Da was in rare form.

"So, Artemis and I are headed to the marketplace, going to collect from Cleonice the fishmonger on what she owes us from cleaning out the rodents from her fishhouse last week"—Da leaned forward over the table, his small eyes were twinkling like he couldn't wait to tell her this story—"when this cobbler's wife calls us over, all flustered but trying to be businesslike. Isn't that right, Artemis?"

Artemis, a spotted, apricot-coated terrier with droopy ears, woofed his approval.

"She tells us there are rats in her husband's shop and could we take care of them right away?"

Willa set down her spoon, already swept up by his enthusiasm. The early bubbling of a giggle threatened from deep within her.

"I say, 'Maybe. Depends on how many rats there are. We'll have a look and let ye know.' Now, I'm thinking, this woman is going to tell us where the shop is, and we'll swing over maybe the next day or so, maybe when the snow lets up, but she's going to show us right now. 'This way,' she says. So, we follow her."

Da gnawed at a wedge of dry bread he'd dunked in his soup. Bread crumbs sprinkled his whiskers.

"So, she leads us to Allhollan, to a little shop where her husband and a pair of roundheads are trimming sandals. They're cutting off the edges of the soles where the sandals have been chewed. Her husband, this big ox of a man, glances up at us from his work and kind of grunts a greeting but otherwise says nothing. I get the impression that he's a little embarrassed that a big guy like him can't take care of this rat problem himself."

A grin spread Willa's lips. Her father was not a big man and she could see he had enjoyed the cobbler's embarrassment.

"Anyway, she leads us to this hole chewed in the base of one wall. We can see where they tried to cover it up with a chunk of wood, but ye can't dissuade rats that easily. They just chew through it or around it, whatever ye block their hole with."

He spooned up the thin soup and slurped at it, chewing a bit of carrot in quick, little bites. A dribble of the soup ran down his whiskers.

"I can tell at a glimpse, this is going to be a problem. Sniffing about, Artemis is alerting me to the presence of rodents. I look around the shop, ask if they keep food in there. She says no. The rats just like to chew on the leather. There are droppings everywhere. I listen at the wall and can hear them skirting around a little."

Artemis seemed as interested in the story as Willa, perhaps because Da mentioned him by name.

"As I'm listening, one of the rats, a dark-brown little fellow with a long, scaly tail, darts out of the hole. It's rare for rats to be roused that easily during the day. Of course, Artemis goes after it, but before he can catch it, it rushes across the floor and goes right up the woman's leg."

He shook his head and tittered in that small laugh of his, the spoon filled for another slurp but just hovering over the bowl. Willa's eyes widened and her first wave of hilarity yielded up a chortle. Artemis' head swiveled from Da to Willa and back again.

"She starts screaming, beating at her tunic to try to dislodge the rat. The husband and the two roundheads just stare at her."

A rising maelstrom of glee threatened to overtake Willa. She held it back but not for long.

"The woman is out-of-her-mind panicked, slapping at her lap and kind of dancing around but the rat won't drop."

Solid belly hoots rolled up, as Willa pictured the dance.

"I run over and lift up her tunic because this is no time for modesty. Of course, she has nothing on underneath. The rat has sort of wedged itself up into her nether regions. She's got brown hair, so for a moment, I have trouble telling what's hers and what's the rat's."

Willa crowed, her sides shaking uncontrollably. Artemis gave a little howl of his own.

"Finally, I grab the rat off her and snap its neck. She falls on her bottom and the hem of her tunic comes flying up *over her head.*"

The room went blurry as tears streamed from Willa's eyes.

Da tittered some more, too. "Of course, at the time, I'm busting a gut to hold in the laughter. I've got the husband scrutinizing me, seeing what I'm up to and how I react, and I'm not about to aggravate that situation. So, I carry the rat outside and give the woman a moment to get herself decent again. Then, come back here for the ferrets."

Da always had a story. Not all of them were funny but most were. He made tracking rats sound like more fun than a three-day festival. Momma tired of hearing about his workday but not Willa. She enjoyed listening to him, though it made her job in the stables seem awfully dull by comparison.

"Ratter" is what people called him, though his given name was Bodac. Bodac Lumen. A small man with gray-brown whiskers, a pointed nose and small, keen eyes, he could talk a blue streak or move for hours on end, as his work sometimes required, but he was always fully engaged. Sharp and alert, right up to the end of the day when he just sort of collapsed in a fitful exhaustion. He and Artemis were alike that way.

His da and older brothers cast nets for tasseled blobfish and goldeneye eels in the Sea of Broken Light and sometimes stilt-fished Dagon Bay. Fishing never appealed to Da though and he just drifted from job to job at the shipyard until he took up ratting. That was his true calling, he liked to say. Not that there was much money in it.

When the sickness carried Momma off, Willa feared it might cost Da some ardor for his work but, if anything, he dug into it more deeply and seemed to enjoy it more thoroughly than ever. It's always tricky for children to gauge the relationship of their parents; the strength and closeness of it. Children see what they want to see and what their parents are willing to show. Momma's death left a void but the transition to life without her was smoother than Willa would have imagined.

After supper, Willa washed the dishes in a tub of cold water, singing a Ligeian song about a boy coming home from a trying day at work, forsaking sleep to be with his true love. Da sometimes teased her about her singing, said it reminded him of frogs croaking, but that was just his sense of humor and he encouraged her in other ways. She couldn't tell funny stories like he could, so singing was her contribution to the evening's entertainment.

This song came from Carcosa. Her momma had taught it to her, though where Momma learned it from was anyone's guess, since she had never been outside of Hastur a day of her life. The song reminded them both of her, sweet Jemmy, fading into memory. Sometimes Da and Willa visited Momma's grave at Mount Dnarden, when there was daylight left and they weren't too tired.

"We had a visitor today at the stables," she said. "A war hero."

She shared her news about General Drummer Maule's visit, about the chariot with the broken wheel and the powerful grays. His argument with Sirrah Luster. The general's peculiar behavior—which Da dismissed. "A man like the general lives with ghosts," Da said as he moved over to his chair by the hearth.

She didn't mention Sirrah Anse or his son, Ring, though the boy kept returning to her thoughts. Straight away, she'd noticed him milling at the white foal's gate with his da and the giant. He seemed struck with the beast, like he was disbelieving his own vision, which was how she reacted, too, when she first saw the foal. So white. So pure. No one at the stables had ever before witnessed anything like it.

She'd seen his da knock him to the ground with a vicious blow, watched him stumble to his feet and wipe the blood from his nose. As Paulus, Verger and she led the grays past him, she was careful not to stare but couldn't resist a glance. Though thinner than other boys, he was a healthy Ligeian bronze with piercing gray eyes and sandy hair. At the grooming station, she watched him approach the three of them from a distance. He looked frightened as a trapped rabbit. She wondered what he was afraid of.

When she looked over again, Da was fast asleep in the chair, chasing vermin in his dreams, no doubt. Artemis slept at his feet.

After finishing the dishes, she threw a blanket over Da and blew out the flames on the candle stubs. Grabbing a blanket of her own, she curled up on a quilted pad on the floor in the toasty glow of the hearth. The ferrets made small noises in their cages and Da and Artemis had both begun to snore. The soft, familiar sounds somehow reassured her.

She said a small prayer to Nebo and thought about the boy Ring Gargery until sleep disjointed her thinking and carried her off at last.

***

A reddish moon, convex and swollen, rose from the dark waters at the edge of the world, sending sparkles rippling across the Sea of Broken Light and Dagon Bay in the east and casting a silver glow over snowy Hastur and the sweeping snow-blown Ligeian plains to the north and west. At the crest of Mount Dnarden, which offered a view of this whole panorama, the great scarlet moon lit a clearing near the base of the Beckoning Stone, where Fadumo Aneleh Zant wa Zant and her warders had just emerged from snow-topped woods.

Anse Gargery, head and shoulders bent forward into the snowy wind, led the way, crunching a path across the clearing with his sandaled feet. His lean frame cast oddly angular shadows in the moonlight. He rubbed his long hands together, then held them up to his mouth and huffed warmth into them. He turned to his two followers. "Come along, come along," he chided loudly, his high voice all the raspier in the swirling night air.

The woman came next, carrying a flambeau with a bright, ruffling flame. The torch smelled of burning oil and wax.

As he waited for her, he wedged his hands into his armpits beneath his sheepskin cape.

She wore a hooded, mauve robe flattened by the wind against her generous bosom and apple-shaped body. Despite the weather and the graveyard setting, she appeared serene inside her cowl. Her oval face pleasant and round cheeked and framed in soft strands of dark, frizzy hair. Her eyes were a hypnotic azure in the moonlight and Anse fought to keep from falling under their spell. Bright and steady, they focused directly on him, and he felt himself responding as a man to them.

He forced himself to unmeet her gaze.

Instead, he looked at Cletus, who was bringing up the rear. Under the giant's steerage, the hand cart trundled effortlessly through the snow. It contained mostly the fadumo's things and a few tools that Anse thought might come in handy, all tied down under a flapping canvas tarp. They could have carried these few things but carrying things up the mount wasn't the sole purpose of the cart.

"Where's Andaman?" Anse said to no one in particular. He rolled his neck. "Dagon help him if he's late."

Cletus set the hand cart down in the snow. He spat. "He'll be here. If nothing else, Andaman is reliable."

Anse knew this was true, but he didn't relish waiting for his cousin at night in the snowy graveyard with the wind howling like a great wolf and who knows what afoot. "Let's find the tomb and be done with that much, at least." He rubbed his arms and resumed walking.

Cletus' big sandaled foot slipped on some ice, and the giant crashed to one knee but was up with surprising quickness, pulling the cart behind him.

The way forward was a whirl of falling snow and wind. Though the path was covered, it was outlined clearly by tombs and grave markers that rambled into the distance. To either side, lay similar rows, grayish and ghostlike. The three walked their chosen path like restless spirits.

"Aye, here it is," Anse said at last, stepping up to a tall marker before a burial chamber. He wiped the clinging snow from the marker's front.

The carved surface bore the likeness of a woman on a throne, her long hair swept back to best reveal the smooth countenance of her face. There was a butcherbird perched on one shoulder, a jumbi owl on the other, and all three—the woman, the bird and the owl—looked straight back, past the viewer, as if searching for something in the distance. Engraved above their heads in wedge-shaped Ligeian hieroglyphs hung the name MAULE.

Anse tested the door to the vault. Locked, of course. "Cletus, the pry bar."

From under the tarp, Cletus produced a heavy length of iron, curved at one end. Anse snatched it from him and set to work at the jamb. The door popped with a sigh, breaking the seal on imprisoned air that puffed out dense and moist. The door pushed slowly open on the sunless final resting place of Lucrezia Maule.

"The torch," Anse said, and Fadumo Aneleh handed it over.

The three intruders entered the chamber and it was like passing the threshold into another world.

A hefty dampness draped the air. The mephitic vapor of decay sprang at them. The coffin sat directly ahead, confronting them, fully ornamented with small statues and fetishes, many in silver. These overflowed the lid of the red box, spilling over onto the chamber's floor.

The building itself was composed of bulky granite blocks expertly masoned into neat walls and a floor. Though deep and spacious, it imposed on the interlopers a claustrophobic sensation. The low roof was arched and sculpted in a likeness of the goddess Dagon. She glared down at them.

Anse and Cletus exchanged looks. "Get started, then?" Cletus said.

Anse nodded, trying to look untouched by the surroundings.

The coffin was set off the ground on a low bier. They cleared the coffin surface of burial bric-a-brac, placing the items carefully out of the way. The coffin, formed of red-painted planks of blood-thorn greenwood, was spotted along the bottom edge with the dark brown of decomposition.

Cletus took the pry bar from Anse. Determination lit his face.

Contained as it was in the chamber, the sound of prying wood created a clamor of screeching and squealing. The first slat rose, and Cletus yanked it free. The gap fed light from the torch into the coffin's cavity, revealing a strip of shroud and a desiccated hand. Cletus turned his head away as a cloud of acrid vapor was released. When the worst of the smell passed, he then set to work on the next board. This one came free easier. One by one, the planks were pulled away until the coffin was fully open and the remains of Lucrezia Maule, beloved bride of the famed general, lay exposed to the glare of Anse's torch.

Framed by black, wilted petals barely distinguishable as flowers, the corpse lay sunken and discolored, rigid as the boards that bound her. Her hair and nails appeared unnaturally long from the shrinkage of attached flesh. The positions of her hands and feet, twisted by the stiffening of death, were painful to observe. Her cerements hung loosely over her warped form and settled breasts. But the most terrifying of all was her face. It was fixed in a toothy grimace, the unseeing eyes fallen in, and all but shedding its bones.

Anse and Cletus gaped at the spectacle.

Seemingly unaffected, Fadumo Aneleh went to retrieve her implements from the hand cart, parked in the snow outside the sepulcher's door. Returning with an armful, she sat on the granite floor and began arranging things.

***

General Drummer Maule sat up and swung his bare feet to the cool floor. Wood coals glowed in a pan beside his bed. He warmed his cold toes by them.

Outside, the wind surged and the glass panes of his window rattled passionately, stirring something uneasy within him.

Da and Uncle Lafe were asleep when he had arrived home from the temple, as was Ash, but Huldra came down in her nightclothes and fixed him hot, spiced wine to take the chill off. She'd asked him no questions but wore the same concerned expression he'd seen earlier. He carried the piping cup to his room. Later, when she'd brought the pan of coals, he barely acknowledged her presence.

He had returned from Dagon Fane in a daze, the things he'd witnessed haunting his every step. The high priest's warning still rang in his ears: "Don't disappoint the dead."

He remembered how artfully Lucrezia had ensnared him in the first place.

"Drummer, dear, I have some wonderful news."

It's probably prosaic to observe that her brilliant blue eyes sparkled, but they did.

"As ye know, Aylmer Wilf is retiring from the Conventicle of Archons at the end of his term."

Aye, the general nodded. He was aware, though politics bored him.

"Poor man suffers from the gout and dimming sight. And who knows what else."

"So far, yer news isn't sounding very wonderful."

She laughed. Her laughter had a bell-like quality that never failed to lighten his heart.

"Well, it's not good news for Aylmer but it's good news for Cousin Seth, who is going to run for the open seat."

Seth Spaulding was not the general's favorite in-law. To begin with,

Cousin Seth had never served in the military, which was a strike against his character from the outset. No able-bodied Hasturian who refused to defend the city could be totally trusted. Then there were assorted incidents that cast further doubt on the man: the killing of a slave which was later determined to be an accident, the killing of a whore, of which he was found innocent, the drunken ravaging of a fisher's wife in Wharf Town, which was hushed up by a generous payment from the family funds. And those were just the highlights.

Still, the average Hasturian was largely in the dark about these matters and the Spaulding name carried with it a certain currency. Given the proper campaign, Lucrezia's cousin could win.

But beyond his indiscretions, Cousin Seth bore an air of entitlement that the general found distasteful. The man had a not-so-subtle way of talking down to people.

In the end, the general supposed he would vote for him. He was, after all, family.

"Well, of course, I wish him the best of luck. Has he any idea who's running against him?"

"Not yet," Lucrezia said, "and I was just wondering...."

She wanted more from the general than just his vote. He sensed it.

"I thought that maybe Cousin Seth could get a leg up in the contest if the proper people threw their support behind him. Early on, I mean."

She toyed with the open-hand amulet at her throat.

"The proper people, such as the commander of the Shrike's Fourth Legion," he said.

Her smile was dazzling. "Well, 'twould go a long way to calming concerns about his lack of military experience."

"I'll take it under advisement," the general said, knowing this was one battle he had already lost.

Shortly after, he had reluctantly given his word. Then she fell ill. Then she was gone.

Struggling through the loss of his wife, beset by visions, his doomsmen relying on him as the enemies of Ligeia struck at Scylding Tangle and then Tull Fennel, his closest friend and clearly the superior candidate, announcing for the archon post. It was all too much. Lucrezia, of course, had passed on news of his planned support for Cousin Seth before her death. When he failed to make the announcement, pressure from the Spaulding clan had quickly built.

Now, it appeared, even the gods were lining up against him.

**

In the dream, the ghost horse was huge, larger than any horse Ring had ever seen, with the strength appropriate to so large a beast—so powerful that, at the slightest movement, great muscles furrowed and bulged the creature's white flesh—and a fierceness of nature so compelling and tangible it dared all comers and obstacles. The creature raced in long strides through a waning night over a lake of ice and snow whilst Ring bounced on the horse's bare back, his fingers clutching the white mane for dear life. All around, cold howled and rushed at them, and loose snow swirled like smoke beneath the crashing hooves.

As the shore approached, the sky blushed with first light. They pounded aground, leaped a ridge and roared into the mouth of a deep and rocky valley. He felt the horse's footing slip and give, but the steed charged on. It was all he could do to lock his legs to the creature's heaving sides to keep from pitching or falling.

They skidded to the bottom, and then lurched off in a shot across the valley floor. Here the snow formed an icy crust that crunched beneath them in violent chugging sounds until the valley walls opened to the farthest reaches of sight, and the frozen ground rose to the surface. In the thin light of dawn, the way ahead lay desolate, fractured into angled shards and veiled in whirling snow, like a pathway to the Netherworld or a place where wooly animals came to die. The demon steed tore into it at a screaming pace and Ring gritted his teeth as he leaned into the bite of the wind and accepted the thousand torments the vast passage visited upon him.

Soon, he could not feel his feet. He could not feel his face. His hands became throbbing, club-like things he could barely move. His thighs and bottom chafed. The small of his back clenched. Cramps knifed at his legs and sides. He fought to keep his balance, his seating and his clarity of mind as the behemoth horse charged on, gouging through the barren landscape.

Then at last the creature, sweating and frothing, jerked to a halt, reared, and cried skyward in a savage neigh. The way ahead vanished into nothingness. Foreboding seized him as he realized they had arrived at the end of the world.

He looked behind and saw still figures watching him, hundreds of them, their clothing tousled and their features blurred by the whipping snow. Some he recognized: Da, M, Uncle Cletus, Paulus and Willa from the stables, Digna Greavor, associates of Da who sometimes came to the house, Killman the spy, Luster Spaulding, Cousin Andaman, a neighbor woman long dead now who had always feuded with M, the naked prophet from Aungier Street ... and, surprisingly, General Drummer Maule, whose bright green eyes glared at him with enough venom to burn through the churning mist.

Numb and exhausted, he turned back to face oblivion. Thunder rolled in, carrying with it a great cloud of snow and ice that filled his view, looming for an instant before raining down in an avalanche that whited everything out. He hugged his horse's neck as the weight of the deluge crushed down.

***

Fadumo Aneleh set aside the spirit box with the spider clasp. She picked up a loosely bound bundle instead, untrussed it and spread the contents on the floor of Lucrezia Maule's tomb.

Anse and Cletus turned from Lucrezia's corpse and stared at the fadumo. Anse was still clutching the torch. Cletus still gripped the pry bar.

The fadumo's hands were large, mannish things, decorated on the backside with raised scars that seemed to undulate in the torchlight. On the middle finger of her left hand she now wore a ring fashioned from ebony coral collected at Presage Cay. This, too, resembled a spider. With that hand, she reached out and picked up a wedge of chalk from the items before her. Moving on her knees and using her right hand for balance, she drew a circle just large enough to encompass her and, soft and low, she began to sing, "*Indrin Anarach, indrin retpus.*"

Having completed her circle, she set down the chalk and picked up two handfuls of blue-green prickly-edged leaves with which she outlined the outer margin of the circle. The leaves rocked from the swirl of outside air but stayed in place. "*Jandra m're corpo incubo magicis.*" The pure energy began to flow.

Next came the vial. Her mother, the Grand Fadumo Olisha, had presented her with it on the occasion of her first menses. The roughly-shaped vial was made of crude glass formed by lightning-blasted sand. Still chanting, she poured a thick, carmine liquid she had spent the better part of a week preparing. She had sent Anse and Bartine out in search of ingredients from herb sellers, beggar priests, perfumers and butchers. She had carefully ground the ingredients with a pestle and mixed them with her own blood. The formula was amongst those she had learned from long-dead spirits in the charnel caves. The liquid smelled sharply of cloves and copper, a fragrance that mixed with the waxy smell of the torch and the stench of the dead that dominated the chamber. As it was poured from the vial, the liquid disappeared at once into the bricks and mortar, leaving only a thin, purplish glaze. "*Indrin Anarach, indrin retpus,*" she sang softly over the stain. "*Andakode masmerdo sutyara.*" *Dark lord, the tongue of your servant cries out to you.*

An emerald flame sprang to life and spread in a wave across the glazed surface of the bricks. Cletus dropped the pry bar to the ground with a booming crash. The emerald fire, confined by the edges of the glaze left by the poured liquid, seemed to rise from some source beneath the tomb. The fire neither smoked nor emitted heat; neither did it tremble before the wind let in by the sepulcher's partly opened door. Nor did it cast shadows.

The green flame danced in the fadumo's eyes as she turned to Anse. Palms up, she held out her hands in a wordless command.

Just then, there was a commotion outside. Andaman shouldered his way into the chamber, holding to his chest a tiny clump wrapped in dingy linen that he quickly handed over to Anse who then set it into the fadumo's uplifted palms.

She placed the linen clump on the floor, between her and the fire, and reached for the spirit box.

"*Indrin Anarach, indrin retpus.*" The ancient words were resonant in the tomb. *Hear me, bornless one, boundless and silent.*

"*Punra triada alhuren.*" *Ascend from your dark abode to this place of the gone.*

She placed the box beside the linen wad.

A sinister presence entered the tomb, its thrumming not quite audible. The fadumo sang: "*Punro yakh mudaren obles.*"

The lid of the spirit box popped opened on its own. The contents stirred, eager to be released: the warding stone, traces of blood still on it; a human finger wearing an immense ring; a fragment of skull, not quite human, old as time itself; bark from the hollow tree at the opening of the charnel caves; a pouch containing the dried and powdered lungs and livers of three Morellan hopfrogs; an amulet formed from the gilded shell of a giant hermaphrodite snail; a specially cast handbell etched with obscenely dancing skeletons; and a jade knife with a curved and canted blade.

From the box, she took the warding stone with both hands and laid it carefully before her.

She lifted the amulet and placed its braided, red cord around her neck. The gold shell hung heavily between her breasts.

"*Upro gewogen Anarach. Sor cordyas.*"

She pinched powder from the pouch and sprinkled it on the linen clump that Andaman had brought to the tomb. The fabric shifted slightly from side to side in the flickering torchlight.

"*Upro gewogen panis mortuum.*"

She took up the handbell and shook it violently and repeatedly, its peals jolting the air.

"*Panis mortuum. Lunjara t'ro mel pcuvus.*"

The emerald fire rose in a sheet of roaring flame. Anse and Cletus recoiled from it whilst Andaman froze wide eyed.

The fadumo clutched at the bell in a stranglehold, shaking it as if it were a living thing.

"*Indrin panis andicode, indrin mortuum retpus.*"

Setting down the handbell, she spread open the linen wrap and revealed a roundhead infant, newly born, short legs kicking at the air as if fighting back the cold, tiny fists clenched and trembling in the light of the emerald fire. The infant's eyes were closed, which was just as well.

"*Indrin Anarach, retpus hrobosa.*"

She cradled the jade knife loosely in her fingers; kissed its haft, kissed its blade. Then she drew it up over her head with both hands and shrieked, "*Indrin panis Anarach, indrin mortuum retpus.*" Startled, the roundhead baby wailed at the sound of her voice. But not for long.

The curved blade became a flash of green as it sliced downward through the infant's breastbone and into the tiny heart.

The fadumo shivered all over and the azure of her eyes rolled up under her lids. Her mouth went long as if drawn open by the weight of her chin. The pure energy jerked at her spine as, again and again, she brought down the blade, heedless of the blood splashing up at her.

Outside, thunder cracked sharp and loud.

Inside the air roiled, throbbing in her ears.

She rose to her feet, still gripped the knife. Blood dripped from her hands and the front of her tunic was spattered. A wave of delirium rocked her. She opened her eyes; saw the carnage at her feet. Spinning round, she caught a glimpse through the partly open door of Mount Dnarden bathed in a blinding flash of light. She reeled toward the coffin. The head of Lucrezia Maule's corpse begin to loll amid the wilted petals.

Cletus, Anse and Andaman, stood pale and horrorstruck, unable to even breathe. The fadumo, trembling, dropped the knife.

Lucrezia opened her sightless, shriveled eyes. Opened her teeth, which had begun to rot in her mouth. Drew cold air into her moldy lungs and let it pass back out in a fetid swell. Something of the fullness of life returned to her shrunken form, though the flesh remained discolored and barely clung to her skull. She struggled to move.

"Help her to the cart," Fadumo Aneleh ordered, and the men rushed forward to obey.

The tower of flames receded into the granite brick floor. Some remnant of it flickered and hissed momentarily on the surface.

The fadumo flew from the tomb, out into the snowy graveyard. Unfazed by the biting cold, she soaked up the full wonder of what she had accomplished. Aye, Lucrezia Maule had been evicted from the slumber of death, but that wasn't the half of what the fadumo had wrought. All around her, hundreds of corpse-lights glowed and hovered over the burial places of Mount Dnarden, setting free the spirits if not the bodies of countless dead.

And the same was true of the dead across all of Hastur: those robbed of life shined and rose from their hidden places.

The dogs of Hastur went wild, baying and howling their warnings in the night.

Cletus and Andaman worked Lucrezia Maule's tired corpse into the handcart. They covered her up and, still shaken, began to trundle her downhill. Fadumo Aneleh and Anse, who now stood outside the tomb, watched them disappear into the swirl.

Then the fadumo whirled. By the moonlight, she could see the blood returning to Anse's face. The trembling that had wracked her thick frame had transformed into something surging and powerful that animated her with boundless energy. She broke into a circling dance, pumping her meaty legs with blurring speed and shaking her manlike fists at Mount Dnarden and its fabled Beckoning Stone. She threw back her shoulders, lifted her great breasts and the amulet that hung between them, tossed her head back and laughed into the night sky.

When she had spent the joy of her triumph this way, she turned to Anse, her breathing loud and deep. Her azure eyes widened, then narrowed, like those of a predator spotting its prey. She rushed at him and it was his turn to tremble.

She threw all her weight into him, driving him to the snowy ground. Carnal desire came unleashed. They rutted savagely amongst the dead.

CHAPTER 6
The Two of Him

Ye could see it wasn't headed for a good place. Darius had that glint in his eye and Old Dolge at the ready. Momma was out, looking after a sick friend, and ye could tell he felt this to be some kind of personal injustice. When these black moods took hold of him, ye just kept from his path and prayed to Dagon for the best.

Cletus was about seven. Old enough to know better. But he was oblivious to it, lost in his own world, as young boys can sometimes be. I don't remember what he was playing at, but he was running about, laughing. I could see Darius fixing on him in that grim way of his. I wanted to shake Cletus. Quiet him down until the blackness passed. But it was already too late. This time, it wasn't going to pass.

Darius leapt to his feet, knuckles white on that wretched staff, raising it up over his head and taking a step toward Cletus.

Somehow I broke free from the powerlessness that gripped me. My hands flew out as I rushed him, my mouth forming the single word, "Nooooooooooooooo."

Old Dolge lashed out, a solid crack to the temple that stunned me from my feet. The next blow caught my shoulder, then my chest, then my neck, another to the head, and that's when I lost track. They just rained down on me, one after another, my young body shifting under the violence of Old Dolge and Darius' black temper. I remember begging. I remember screaming. I remember swimming off into a pit of darkness from which I hoped to never return.

And, for some days, it was unclear if I ever would.

Like in fever dreams, I recall fighting off Momma, the wet cloths she held to my forehead, the cups to my lips, the strokes designed to soothe me. Plunging back into the darkness where my bones weren't shattered and my skin wasn't broken and all my senses weren't jangles of agony. Emerging again to the wakefulness of a blurred and wavy world awash in pain, to a beggar priest applying a poultice to my legs, to Momma spooning broth into me.

Gradually, alertness returned. After more than a month, I sat up in bed, sore and stiff, fearful of sudden movements and noises, overly sensitive to light. In the coming weeks, I rose to my feet, walked around, reacclimated myself to life amongst the living. My focus returned. I became less fearful. The pain was largely diminished, but the beating had left me with a stoop.

It also left me to live out my life with the knowledge that my own father had nearly beaten me to death.

112

Mouthless messengers, their voices like softly pouring sand, whispered to him as, once again, Ring slipped off. In the dream, he became two boys, back to back, fused at the shoulders, walking through a grove of spider oak trees at night with a full moon overhead and, all around, a pearly haze. The two of him moved in concert, one stepping forward and one stepping backward, perfectly synchronized. Each of him viewed the passage through the nighttime grove from the appropriate perspective—one advancing, one withdrawing—and he experienced these two perspectives simultaneously. This way of seeing felt familiar and completely natural.

A faint breeze stirred, and the branches of the approaching and receding spider oaks filtered by haze glistened and flickered in the moonlight.

As the two of him walked, they spoke to one another or, rather, spoke together over one another and there was no distinguishing where any thought began or ended nor who originated or completed it. The two of him spoke calmly, saying as much with silence as with words. They spoke about experiences they had shared in the languid oscillations that predated memory—that cherished time after their rise from nothingness but before their entry into the sensory world.

Theirs was a closeness that transcended all physicality.

The two of him passed into a clearing, silvery and weedy, now lit by the full moon bright as day yet still encompassed by the haze which glowed with eerie purpose. Both of his hearts went heavy. Ahead, two paths cut through the weeds. Behind, the view turned tattered and fell away in shreds. An unwelcome lightheadedness came over him.

In time, every possession of the heart is lost, one way or another, he told himself, as a great emptiness seized him.

The two paths crossed and recrossed in the moonlit clearing, both paths leading to the same place. Having revealed itself, the clearing chose to dissolve. He watched it fade to black and wondered whether he was now about to reenter the nothingness from which the two of him had first arrived. He knew eventually his circle would close, as it did for everyone. Why not now?

He listened vainly for Osric's hooves.

113

Just then he became aware of a pressure on one of his chests that made it difficult to breathe. He felt half of himself peel away and drift off into nothingness as he emerged from his dreamscape. He tried to move but couldn't budge. His arms were pinned back at the shoulders and wrists by powerful legs. He writhed and lurched against whatever was holding him. Panic set in and he redoubled his efforts. All to no effect.

Ring's eyes opened on a vision of sheer horror.

When he had first found the courage to ask him about it, Tutor Will Boyle had responded by affixing the vision with a name.

"Shiny Man?" the teacher had said, a puzzled look clouding the onyx eyes. "Comes to ye in the night?" The eyes lit with realization."Oh, ye must mean Gloamer Brom. Is he all stretched out? Long and spiky?"

Ring had looked up from his lesson. "Aye."

"Ah. The Gloamer." Tutor Will paused to collect his thoughts. "Poor boy. Well, I can tell ye what I know of him. First off, yer not the only one he visits. I had an uncle cursed with visits from Gloamer Brom. He used to tell me of it when the adults weren't about. Said he did all he could to keep the Gloamer out of his bedroom, even boarded up the window, but when the Gloamer wants in, he used to say, there is no keeping him out. Of course, Uncle Ubald was known to sip a bit freely from the fruit of the vine. But I always had the impression it was the Gloamer drove him to drink, not the other way around."

"Did he know why it came?" Ring asked.

Tutor Will cocked his head to one side. "Uncle Ubald said that when he was a child he witnessed the execution of a highwayman named Filan Gowdie, as brutal-hearted a brigand as ever roamed the countryside. Filan and his crew had set upon a family coming to Hastur from White Worm. Set upon them with swords and axes, all for a few paltry paldins. One of his victims, though badly butchered, managed to survive. A girl. One day she spotted Filan at the marketplace in Gondemar. Buying figs. She told her story to a pair of watchmen and they hauled him off. The trial was over almost as soon as it began, and everyone came to the execution. It was the talk of the town."

Ring became lost in the story.

"At the execution, a curious thing happened. They put the rope around the villain's neck and dropped the floor beneath him. He started kicking and twisting, as the executed sometimes do but, in his case, he just kept it up. Uncle Ubald said Filan Gowdie was jerking and twisting and kicking defiantly, all red faced, the veins popping from his temples and neck, until it seemed like he would never die. The crowd was quite shaken by this vision of a killer who, through raw will and evil determination, seemed to be successfully rebelling against the very laws of life that govern us all. How long did this go on? For hours. Aye, hours. Uncle Ubald said it was nearly dark and most of the crowd, weary of waiting, had gone off to their homes when Filan Gowdie at last succumbed to the call of the Netherworld. But, before he did, he twisted one last time on the rope and his eyes came to rest on Uncle Ubald. The wicked glare in those eyes burned into my uncle's young heart with a malice that shook him at his roots. That day, when he witnessed the light at last fade from Filan Gowdie, it marked the first night Gloamer Brom came to call on Uncle Ubald."

The memory flared in Ring's mind as he looked up in terror.

Here-I-come, here-I-come, here-I-come.

Only this time he hadn't heard the footfalls approach, hadn't felt their familiar pounding echo in his chest, hadn't had the warning of the blue light crossing the room, hadn't perceived the blinding flash. This time Gloamer Brom was simply upon him, sitting on his chest and pinning him down in the night sanctity of his bedroom, a figure of dazzling light making that sizzling hiss, three times Ring's size and half as wide, with blue fireballs for eyes and long clawlike fingers that curled menacingly toward the boy's face. Powerful beyond all reason. Riding Ring.

The ghastly eyes, the only features in the shimmering visage, seemed to be deciding what to do with him next.

Meanwhile, behind the Gloamer, at least a dozen other figures were loose in Ring's room, swooping from one side to the other in great arcs. Willowy, rag like figures, flying about recklessly, their laughter a cacophony of cackles that should have roused the whole household but beyond Ring's bedroom door Gargery House remained undisturbed.

Gloamer Brom jabbed at Ring's chest with a cold, stiff finger, slapped him, played with his hair, tugged his ears, and slapped him again. The icy fingers found his throat and choked him in an iron grip until his face went hot and his lungs burned and blots churned in his vision. The Gloamer leaned into him and Ring, barely conscious, could now see a ripple in the creature's shimmering countenance, a ripple that parted, at first reluctantly, as if it entailed breaking a gelatinous bond of some sort that clung to the parting's edges before snapping away. The Gloamer's head popped open and revealed three huge rows of glistening teeth. Ring felt his heart stop.

The next thing he knew, he was floating.

All background sounds dropped away. In their place, there arose a noise like a soft roar combined with a faint, high-pitched whistling. A vibration rolled through him: a tingling swell that swept from head to toe, slowly, repeatedly.

A light-blue circle of light encompassed him. The circle moved in synch with the oscillating vibration within him, throwing off wave upon wave of blue light.

He reached up and touched the ceiling.

With a flex of his fingers, he pushed off from the ceiling and spun around until he faced downward. As he turned, he became aware of a cord attached to his back. The cord, a bundle of fibrous tendons, pink shot through with pulsing blue veins, wound to figures on the bed below. There was Gloamer Brom, ablaze with radiating light, kneeling on the chest of a prone form, choking gleefully and chomping his horrendous teeth, foaming at the mouth like some rabid dog. The figure beneath the Gloamer, the figure to which the tendoned cord ran was, of course, himself. Ring looked down on himself and saw he was wide-eyed and dripping sweat.

At this moment, he was glad to not be down there.

Raggedy silhouettes streamed through the room. Some sort of hags, perhaps, coughed up from the darkest reaches of the Netherworld. Like night birds, their blurred forms cast a flutter of shadows that swirled in the Gloamer's light.

He became aware of some new disturbance across the room. Outside his window, a brilliant incandescence lit the tiny pane. He tried making his way toward it, to see what caused it, but he was unsure how to move about in his current state of being.

Then he awoke to the familiar warmth and contours of his bed. Cold sweat covered him. His shoulder ached from where Da's thumb had gouged it in the stables. His feet and legs were cold, having kicked off the blankets in the night.

When he sat up to look for them, he was bewildered to find a figure standing at the foot of his bed.

At first, he thought it was Gloamer Brom, returned to torment him. But the form was of average dimensions and unlit. Then he thought this might be part of his dream. But the realization quickly dawned he was no longer dreaming, that the form before him was real and watching him. One of the figure's hands grasped the footboard. He listened to it breathe.

Gloom made a silhouette of the figure, but a ray of moonlight from the far window limned part of it in silver and he could see from the wisp of outline and from the figure's basic shape and bearing it was not Da or M—certainly not hulking Uncle Cletus—nor did he recognize it with certainty as anyone else he knew. However, as his sight adjusted, he could see it was a boy or a young man in a heavy robe, and now it did remind him of someone, but he couldn't think who.

What reason would anyone have for lurking in his bedroom in the black of night?

It must be a thief. Or worse. But the figure did not react in any discernible way. Instead, it waited, as if to allow the boy time to recognize it.

As he studied the silvery edge of the form near its hip, a new perception jolted him. He recognized the cut and the crimson thread at the seam of the robe. It was one of his own, a flax-colored winter robe Bartine had bought from the market at the start of the season. The intruder was wearing his clothing!

He tried to remember if he had left his jade knife on the bedstand. Dull-edged and rounded, it was only a ceremonial instrument, but it might serve as a weapon.

The intruder leaned closer and, in the shift, a reflection of stray light cast a muted glow on the eyes, revealing them as intent and sorrowful. The sight startled him. The eyes were trying to express something as their gaze pressed upon him.

Maybe he should shout for help and hope to bring some rescuer crashing in?

Instead, he looked into the mournful eyes and asked, in a voice as level as he could muster, "Who are ye and what do ye want?"

The figure stepped back from the bed and positioned itself at an angle where the window's light fully found the face.

Sitting bolt upright, he gasped, appalled at what the moonlight revealed. This intruder lurking in his bedroom in his clothing was the one person he would never have suspected. Pale and ethereal in the fragment of moonlight, wearing a countenance both dismal and commanding was he, himself, Ring Gargery.

Terror roared through his veins.

"H-h-how?" he managed.

But the form gave no reply. Instead, it began to flicker like an object viewed through turning spokes. It swelled and contracted rapidly, going from larger to smaller to larger to smaller with no perceptible transitional phase. Ring stared awestruck in disbelief.

He watched himself reenter the gloom, cross to the doorway and depart.

Hurriedly, he fetched the blankets from the floor and pulled them up over his chest. Gaping at the fisted clutch of his hands on the covers, he listened for footsteps beyond the wall but heard none.

For long hours, he kept a terrified vigil, his eyes darting at shadows until, at last, the kiss of morning arrived and he heard the servants stirring in their room down the hall.

***

Hers was a place of emptiness. A place of dense stillness, buried in the blackened bowels of a thick-walled citadel, hewn in low channels with stunted pillars and the likenesses of fish-faced ghouls swimming in vitreous quartz all around her. A sacred place, to be sure, but a lonely one. Seldom visited, even by her diminutive acolyte, who aided her with dressing, eating and toilette. She needed this place, far from the turbulent voices of the world above. But the endless loneliness had long ago eaten away whatever trace of humanity she had once possessed. The loneliness and the vapor.

She slept sitting up to keep from damaging her long nails. She generally slept through the night this way, as comfortable as she could be in the oversized chair with the padded back and the padded seat and the smooth-worn arms of blood-thorn greenwood. But tonight slumber evaded her, even though physically she was done in.

The reading for the general—her third that day—had sapped what little strength she had remaining. Three times she had sunk into the oblivion, in search of answers. Three times she had huffed the vapor. The cumulative effect on her psyche was numbing. After, the servitors had had to help her all the way back to her chamber.

Sleep should have come at once, a welcome respite. But worry at what she had seen this evening had kept at her, tormenting her from the edges of perception.

A single torch lit the sitting room. Its familiar waxy sputtering sought to comfort her in her restlessness. Once she had awakened in the night and the torch had gone out, leaving her alone in the vast dark until morning. Totally helpless.

Directly across from her, a statue of her deity looked back at her. The sculptor had captured the goddess roiling sensuously, eyes gleaming with passion, one hand outstretched in invitation. Even the tilt of her tentacles promised pleasure.

But tonight Saga Eldritch, oracle of Dagon Fane, was oblivious to the goddess' solicitation, to the fizzle of the torch, to the comfort of sleep. When she recalled what she had seen at the general's reading, she trembled anew. Some crisis loomed that threatened to shred the veil between the two worlds she lived in. Some crisis that threatened this night.

This second sight had been a blessing and curse from the day she was born.

Her people were cunning folk from Carcosa who fled to Hastur at odds with the law. Her da was caught up in some misdeed involving black hens and fortune-telling gone awry and the family had slipped off in a caravan, headed for a fresh start. She was little more than an infant then but already having extended visions. Maybe two years old. She had an older sister but she was left behind with cousins, never to be seen again.

On the trip, Da had sold a tonic to a die-engraver troubled with a nasty cough. The tonic killed both the cough and the die-maker. For his part in it, Da was left to dangle by his neck from a spider oak tree, just outside of Smee. Momma had hastened the end by tugging at his legs. Luckily Momma and she were spared any further wrath and allowed to make their way on to Hastur, though with their prospects now dramatically dimmer.

Hastur was not a welcoming place to outsiders seeking to resettle. They stayed at a broken-down inn in Auseil Thoroughfare. Momma sold charms and curses, told fortunes and sometimes worked at a brothel called the Surly Oyster. There she met a bachelor miller named Flem Wilf and learned he lived in a two-story house on Aungier Street. On the night of the next full moon, she went naked to the bedroom where he slept and, whispering an incantation, cut off a lock of his hair. This she wore from that day on as a ring on her finger. The miller? He fell hopelessly in love with her and they soon married.

For some time, things were uneventful.

Then one day, when the oracle was five, Momma fell ill and began vomiting blood. Before she could cure herself, she passed on to the next world. She was interred in a simple tomb at Mount Dnarden, a luxury for which the miller went to a money lender. But the ring of hair was still on her finger and the miller's love for her lived on. All day at the mill, he pined for her. When he wasn't working, he was at her tomb pouring out his heart to her withering corpse. The love felt for his departed did not, unfortunately, extend to her child, who was all but abandoned in the house on Aungier Street.

One day the oracle was found delirious inside the gate of Dagon Fane. Hungry children were not altogether rare in Hastur, but this hungry child was speaking to the statue of the goddess. Asking questions and responding. And seeing—aye, seeing—into the dark and murky lair at the weedy bottom of the sea. Into the surreal face of the goddess herself.

An older man with faded brown eyes watched the child. He wore a mitered hat and oily robe. Andro was his name. After studying her for some time, he took her by the hand and brought her inside. He fed her some dry bread, which she devoured heartily, and asked her what she and the goddess had talked about. That was 30 years ago. Since then, Andro had passed to the next world. The oracle never again left the compound.

The vapor's intoxicating fumes came from a liquid that oozed up from a chasm deep beneath the fane. So powerful was the vapor's effect that the first time the oracle breathed it she hallucinated for weeks. The servitors who ladled the liquid into the black vase wore thickly wrapped linen over their faces to filter out the fumes. For added measure, they held their breaths.

Over time, the oracle had learned to master the vapor, to make it serve her as a gateway to her other way of seeing. True, the fumes had cost her her hair. And they often left her unable to speak intelligibly, especially when what she saw excited her. But Cosmas had learned to understand her jabber and translate for her. Sometimes, though, she suspected him of altering her messages, whether by accident or design.

Sitting in the still, torchlit chamber with the sense of dread heavily upon her, the oracle could only hope Cosmas had given the correct information to the general. That, rather than worry about what the dead think of him, the general must act immediately to end the plans of those around him who threaten to shatter the barrier between this world and the next.

Otherwise, Dagon help us all.

***

Beneath snowy Mount Dnarden, a blanket of soil shifts loosely as the shepherd god stirs from his deep slumber. Yawning, he wipes away a thousand years of eye crust. Aboveground, something has appeared in the dark. Something that crawled from a primeval forest. Or a mossy swamp. Or perhaps a torrid veldt. Judging by the deafening baying of the city's hounds, something profoundly sinister.

He listens to the faint sounds of the creeping predator. A foreign god? He stretches and sighs. Was it worth being drawn away from his golden, lotus-garden dreams for this? Was it even worth a brief wakeful interval? He blinks into the darkness.

Up to now, they had somehow survived without him.

Forgotten scenes come flooding back. Civilization amok: living trees cut down and burned until the sky turned black, waterways fouled with all manner of filth, beautiful creatures tormented and slain to extinction—that is, when they weren't too busy slaying brothers and sisters. Land divided with artificial borders, wealth hoarded whilst little ones starve, consciences soothed with weekly tributes. Where once had lived endless possibility, now resided meanness and sorrow.

He had never expected things to go so terribly wrong.

He tips toward sleep, tips toward wakefulness.

A pleasant rush of warmth washes over his skin, down his belly to his loins. He pictures her as he had left her: his bearded goddess, in that moment, possessor of a greater wisdom, breathless, sweat glistening on her naked pinkness, offering up to him her countless breasts. She had wrestled and writhed with him on luminous clouds through a thousand years of dreaming. Leaving this world without her had been his one regret.

He dozes.

He reawakens.

Up above, the mount lights bright as daylight. Hundreds of souls who slept deeper than he awaken from their repose in a shimmering mass. Their glowing essence rises from their tombs and graves like smoke roiling from a furnace. They look down on the darkened city.

Some with yearning. Some with spite.

The shepherd god rolls over and returns to his interrupted dreams.

***

In the dim glow of early morning, Olalla, in sheer rose-colored linen, stepped barefoot in through the threshold to where Ring's mysterious double had departed in the night. She carried a tray with a water basin and a sponge. Over a shoulder and across one breast rested a towel of loomed cotton. She looked pretty, as always, her chalky, silver-white features smoothly contoured in pink, as was the skin on her wrists and hands and, he imagined, the throat beneath her collar. Her hair was a lacework of tight braids.

Diligent and dependable, she had been with the family for four years. He worried Da would replace her soon. Da sometimes changed out the servants without warning.

"Morning, Master Ring," she said, sweeping aside some of his things on the bedstand to clear room for the tray. He had looked there for the jade knife after the intruder had gone, but it wasn't there. He must have left it somewhere. Maybe his double had taken it, along with the robe?

"Morning, Olalla," he replied. Shaken as he was, her presence helped calm him, introducing as it did a welcome dose of normalcy.

Setting down the tray, she carried out his slops and when she returned his chamber pot was clean and dry. In it was his jade knife.

"Yer lucky that didn't get tossed with the rest," Olalla said.

Once again, he was lost for words.

She picked up the sponge and squeezed it in the basin water, wrung it and then brought it, dripping slightly, to where he sat. Whilst she was out, he had stripped off his clothes and waited docilely in preparation for this daily routine.

Olalla lifted his chin. She wiped his face with the sponge, paying extra duty to his forehead and the sides of his nose. The cool freshness seeped into his pores. She patted his face with the towel.

She sensed his agitation.

"Nightmares again?"

He shrugged.

Easing his face first one way then the other, she worked the sponge over the swirls of his ears, into the burrows and behind into the creases where the ears met his skull. Then she patted his ears dry.

"Bartine is making groats for breakfast."

Again she wet and wrung the sponge, this time taking it to his hair firmly but gently, using her free hand to move the hair around so she could get to the skin beneath.

She cleaned his chest and stomach, his hands and arms, and under his arms, pausing several times to wet and squeeze the sponge. When she bent him forward and cleaned his back, her breast touched his cheek.

"Yer back is bruised. Near the shoulder."

Instinctively, he rolled it.

She returned the sponge to the basin and moved the tray to the floor.

She squeezed the sponge in the water, took one of his feet by the ankle and, crouching down a bit, lifted the sole close to her face. She began with her knuckles in the sponge, scrubbing his calloused heel, then she poked a stiff finger into the sponge and gently traced the underside of his toes. Holding the sponge loosely, she swathed the tenderness of his arch before finally drying it all with the towel. She raised the other sole and repeated the procedure. When she finished drying it, he stood.

She began working the sponge between his toes. She did the tops of the feet and his ankles, his calves, his knees, behind his knees, his inner and outer thighs, and then, his pubis and groin.

Several times, he felt her breath on his skin.

When she washed to where his legs joined, his flesh pointed back at her.

She lifted him slowly with her smooth fingers. When she took hold, she pretended this was still a routine act of hygiene until he moved in her grip. She looked up at him. Her neck twitched, and for a brief moment, she was lost in thought. It pained him to reduce her this way, but today he needed her.

All expression left her face, and she looked straight ahead through him and introduced the friction.

When it was over, she wiped him, dabbed at a spot on her robe, then wiped the floor.

The tension had left him.

She turned him gently to finish in the back. Then she brought him a fresh robe and he was amazed to see it was the same one his double had worn last night.

Had it just been a dream, after all?

"I'll call ye when breakfast is ready," she said, scooped up the tray of bathing items and slipped out the door.

The thin light of early morning entered the small window at the far side of his room, casting an eerie glow. He left the room and climbed the steps to the third-floor landing where he looked out on his city, trying to shake off the night's events.

Hastur was slowly coming alive in muted gray sunlight. The sky was thick with clouds and dark to the horizon. A faint drizzle had developed from the sea and was eating away at the snow.

Below, a stocky shepherdess in a clumsily-sewn, brown tunic escorted a dozen sheep into Maule Square. She paused to study the general's statue, and her sheep paused too. Holding a hand to her forehead, she looked at the sky, concerned.

Cleonice the fishmonger, her hair oddly disheveled, hurried across the square in the direction of Gondemar, where the marketplace had already opened without her. She appeared confused.

Breaking away from a trio of boys carrying the fighting sticks that were popular then was a wide-stepping, black-haired boy with a clubbed foot who also carried a stick.

As if it were the most natural thing in the world to do, Paulus Spaulding confidently stepped to the front door of Gargery House and loudly knocked.

"In the depths of every heart, there is a tomb and a dungeon, though the lights, the music, and revelry above may cause us to forget their existence, and the buried ones, or prisoners whom they hide. But sometimes, and oftenest at midnight, those dark receptacles are flung wide open."
—Nathaniel Hawthorne, "The Haunted Mind"

PART THREE: CITY OF THE DEAD

JOE PAWLOWSKI

CHAPTER 7

An Eddy in the Fabric of Space

I was against it. From the start. Naming a new-sprung life after that villain. I didn't do it with the first one and I thought it ended there. But, of course, it didn't. Dagon help me. A curse I laid on that little whelp. But they wore me down. Gracie and Cletus and Andaman. And the old devil himself, though he never actually said as much. I could read it in his glance. Give a dog his bone, they said and, in the end, I agreed. I gave in and named the boy after him.

Like the past was over and done with. Like all was forgiven.

But I could never forgive that crawler for what he did to me and Cletus and her.

He killed her. Not all at once, but in bits. There's no misbelieving it. Killed her as much with fear and indifference as with that staff of his. In the end, cowering in the shadow of Darius and Old Dolge, half crippled, her fingers twisted, her voice whispered and hands shaking, her step a limping shuffle, the light in her eyes pinched out like a candle's flame— that was all of her that remained when Osric came to call.

Even in death, anxiety marked her features. Aye, she had escaped the villain but not before he had emptied her.

When we put her in that box, she felt so weightless. Half expected her to crumble to dust. He was there—him and that vile stick of his—lording over the proceedings, mourning patch on his arm. Like he was deserving of anyone's pity. Poor Darius, deprived of the companion who served him so loyally. Who he abused so remorselessly.

He even had that old scowl face from Dagon Fane lead her to the tomb, though she was more drawn to Hastur, the shepherd god. Didn't matter, though, what she would have wanted. He had ruined her life. Might as well ruin her death, as well.

"Someone to see ye, Master Ring."

He turned from the window.

Olalla stood on the stairs, the stain of their intimacy still faintly visible in the way she looked at him. He wanted to thank her in some way but realized that what she had given him was not a gift, and it was best not to mention it, as doing so would only make things more awkward.

"Says he's Paulus Spaulding, from the stables."

"I'll be right down," he said with all the kindness he could muster. He watched her walk away.

He was, of course, curious why Paulus was calling for him. No one ever called for him. He doubted it was with news he would relish.

He was about to head down when a noise on the stairs stopped him. By then, Olalla had made her way to the entry, so it wasn't her. The noise was a creak given up by the heavy shifting of weight on the ancient steps. But there was no one there. He listened intently. He distinctly heard the sound of a foot come down, and the stairs groaned again. It was the sound of a bare foot slapping wood. He listened intently. It happened again: the same shifting weight, the same slap of skin. It continued, down to the second-floor landing, step by step. Then the sound paused before slowly vanishing down the hallway.

A remnant of last night?

Cautiously, he made his way down, with a nervous glance at the shadowy second floor. No one there. He remembered the stir of motion and the fluttering thing in the stables and wondered if those occurrences weren't somehow connected to this.

But something about the sound of the step was so familiar.

"Gargery," Paulus said in greeting, gesturing with his fighting stick. "Don't tell me yer just waking. The working day is half over." He grinned widely.

"Morning, Paulus."

"Must be a challenge, dealing with all yer leisure time." Paulus' brown eyes were either mirthful or mischievous, Ring couldn't decide which.

Olalla, fighting off a smile, turned and headed toward the main room.

"What brings ye to Gargery House, Paulus?"

"What brings me? Why, ye do, of course."

"Me?"

"Is that groats I smell, coming from the kitchen?"

"I was about to eat breakfast."

"Don't mind if I do join ye. I'm feeling a bit peckish this morning."

Paulus swung his clubbed foot toward the main room and walked in.

Ring, unsure what to do or say, simply followed.

"Peckish" wasn't how Ring would describe Paulus' appetite that morning. More along the lines of "ravenous." Paulus wolfed down a second helping of Bartine's groats before Ring had finished a first.

"Ye still haven't told me what brings ye here," Ring said.

"Yer very businesslike, aren't ye, Gargery?"

"I like to know what's up."

They sat at the main room's table in the center of the conch-patterned carpet. Paulus' fighting stick leaned against the back of an empty chair. The usual morning activity went on about them. Olalla brought groats to the boys and to M, who was curious and somewhat alarmed about the visitor in her home. Bartine took bowls upstairs to Da and Fadumo Aneleh and then set about her cleaning chores.

"What's up, my friend, is yer relocation."

Ring felt his appetite leave him. "My what?"

"Relocation. It means to change one's residence."

Ring grappled with the meaning of Paulus' words.

"To move, Gargery. To move."

"I know what relocation means. I just don't understand how it applies to me."

Paulus viewed him in amazement. "Don't tell me yer clueless on the subject."

Ring just blinked.

Paulus licked his spoon and set it in the bowl. "Well, not informing ye seems a glaring oversight." He folded his hands and looked at Ring thoughtfully. "Ye're being relocated to Spaulding Stables. To quarters on site. Very comfortable quarters, I assure ye."

"For what purpose?"

"To work, of course. In the stables. Yer our new stable boy."

Ring felt sick.

"In exchange for housing the white foal, yer to work at the stables. It's all been arranged by our fathers." When Ring didn't reply, Paulus added, "I didn't expect to be the one to break this news to ye."

"How long?"

"How long do ye work at the stables?"

"Aye."

"That's a subject on which we apparently share ignorance. I was just sent to fetch ye. That's all I know."

Ring pushed away from the table. He crossed the room and climbed the steps slowly. He thought for a moment he would leave his body again, so disoriented was he. *Relocate? Him?*

At the third floor, he cautiously approached Da's bedroom. He tried to remember the last time he had knocked at this door. He wasn't sure he ever had. He balled a fist and rapped his knuckles on the old wood.

"Dagon help me," the high, coarse voice hollered. "What now?"

"It's me, Da. Ring."

"What has possessed ye to knock at my door, young villain?"

"Paulus is here. From the stables."

"And how does that concern me?"

"He says I'm to accompany him. To the stables."

"And?"

Ring bit his lip. "And ... is it true?"

"Are ye suggesting that Luster Spaulding's son is a liar?"

"Not a liar. Maybe ... misinformed."

The door flew open. Da, in his loose, fringed sleep gown glared at him. Behind Da, on the bed, Fadumo Aneleh combed her hair with a tortoise-shell brush. Her legs were crossed and her robe revealed a meaty calf.

"Paulus Spaulding is not misinformed. Listen to him. He is yer boss now."

"But...."

"Go! Go! Off with ye. Before I box yer ears and drag ye down to the stables myself!"

And with that, Da slammed the door so hard, the resulting boom echoed throughout the house.

***

Andaman gulped air as if coming up from being too long under water.

Some ruckus down the corridor had woken him, mercifully.

Thump, thump, thump. "What's going on? Open up in there." Niles Margrave's voice.

For a moment, his room appeared entirely alien to him. He sat up and looked around, confused. Why was he so wet? Perhaps he *had* been underwater. He held out his arms and shook them. Sweat flew. His face and hair were slick. His bedclothes clung to his body. Even his bedding was

130

damp.

When he climbed out of bed, his heels nearly slipped from beneath him.

He remembered dreaming of the whirligig. Its colors sparkled and flashed at him in a small room with no doors or windows. A room only he knew how to enter. The colors, some not even recognizable as colors, spun in fragments and bars that bumped and washed into one another, spilling outward, sliding across his eyes and skin; colorful textures and shapes sucking in through his pores and pupils.

Then, amidst the light show, the song began. A young voice sang about the king of suns who made everyone laugh. About summertime and golden dreams and wanting to get back home. It floated to him, as if across a snowy clearing, filling his hollow heart with ... frost-blackened witchweed. Aye, witchweed. He'd taken his medicine, but not like a man. Like the creeping coward he knew himself to be. The witchweed lurched in his chest. It choked up into his throat. He tried to cough it out, but it wouldn't come. The dirk was in his hand, slicing upward. The charmers wilted, one by one. The goat herder's corpse danced in his arms.

The king of suns, drenched in blood, laughed madly as he lashed out with his barbed whip. Lightning tore across the summer sky.

In the darkened alley, in the darkened bedroom, in the darkened tomb, in the darkness that unifies all terror and dread, accusing eyes popped open, even as the life in them began to fade. Or the faded life began anew. This was the only way back home. Beneath him, the tiny forms writhed. He jabbed and ripped, bathed in their sticky warmth.

His body shuddered with all the sobbing.

First his mother, then his father, then his brothers. Empty-eyed, they stared at him. Somehow, this time, their smell wasn't so bad. The space folded in around him, hugging him until his bones cracked. The sound dropped away, and the silence became total and everlasting.

This time, Cletus wouldn't find him.

The house of the dead had claimed him, at last, as one of its own.

He shivered at the memory of the dream.

He dressed hurriedly. He wanted out of the wet clothes, out of the awful room.

From down the hall: "Open up, I say. Don't make me break in the door."

Sandals affixed, tunic in place, he ran a hand through his still-moist hair and was about to step out sharply when he noticed the straw doll, sitting up, facing his way. He was sure he had left it lying flat with the other toys. He didn't even know the doll could be sat up.

***

Artemis poked a wet nose at Willa Lumen's cheek. Da's hand was on her shoulder, gently shaking her. "Up and at 'em. Don't want to keep the boss man waiting."

Willa could tell immediately that something was wrong with Da.

She rose from her quilted pad near the fire, which was all but out, and folded her blanket. It was not as cold as yesterday.

She put out some warm milk for the ferrets. Then she set out a chipped flask of olive oil and the last of the dry bread. They poured oil on the bread and ate their breakfast. Da was subdued. There was no doubting it.

He chewed thoughtfully. "Does something seem off to ye?" he said at last. "Like the day is upended somehow?"

"Upended?"

He chewed some more, talking through it. "Maybe I'm not making sense, but I feel a sort of crawling in the air. Ye know? All about. Like someone's walking on my grave."

Willa was unsure what he meant but detected no oddity in the atmosphere.

"Well, I think it stormed last night," she offered. "Maybe that's what yer feeling? Some trace the storm left behind."

Da poured oil on a second piece of bread. Crumbs were already collecting in his whiskers. "That must be it," he said, but with no conviction.

He eyed the ceiling, where a drop of water was forming. He stared at it, as if in disbelief. "What does that look like to ye?" he asked. He pointed to the drop.

"Looks like a leak," she said, finding a wood bucket to set under it. "Must have soaked through the roof. Must be drizzling."

"That looks like rainwater to ye?"

"Aye. What does it look like to ye?"

Da shook his head, as if clearing it. "Nothing. Looks like water is all." But when the drop fell into the bucket, Da turned a shade paler.

After breakfast, Da and Artemis took their morning walk as she washed for work. A spit bath Da called it. Sometimes they would spring for a soak in the public bathhouse but mostly it was spit baths for her. Every three or four days, she washed her hair, usually at night, to keep it from getting too greasy. This was common practice in the poorer quarters of Hastur.

When Da and Artemis returned from their walk, Willa said her goodbyes and headed off to the stables. The image of Da staring at the ceiling was still fixed in her mind.

It was an overcast day with on and off again drizzling. To avoid getting too wet, she walked close to the buildings, well, closer than normal being as Auseil Thoroughfare was already a fairly tight passage. The drizzle was eating at the snow and, combined with warmer conditions, had turned the streets all slushy. The sky of oppressive clouds offered little hope for relief.

The pedestrians this morning seemed noticeably distracted. As they walked along, some swiped at the air as if bothered by blister flies, though none seemed to be about. Others looked suddenly to their backs or to their sides, as if expecting to be surprised by someone. Many just looked sorrowfully skyward.

She cut through the market in Gondemar, crossing over the cracked mosaic of Nebo and Hastur as young lovers. Merchants were slow to open this morning and many stalls remained shuttered. A thickset shepherdess in a crude tunic was dickering with a wool merchant, her sheep baaing in the light rain. Cleonice the fishmonger was laying out tasseled blobfish and some viper-shark flanks, lost in her own thoughts. Normally Willa would wish Cleonice a good morning but today she left the fishmonger to her ruminations. A lute player tuned his instrument, though the resulting clang sounded no different to Willa after than before. When a heavy-browed halfwit with an overbite approached her selling apples from a barrel, on a whim she bought one, though she felt guilty afterward for spending the money.

She passed a shrine to Osric. A half dozen believers were gathered around it, praying to the god of fire and death. Praying for deliverance from whatever demons haunted their lives. Praying for safe passage on their eventual journey through the Netherworld. Odd to see so many gathered there at once.

But Willa was again thinking about Ring Gargery, about whether she would see him today or anytime soon. Why she had taken such a shine to him, she was unsure. Perhaps it was the cautious way he carried himself. Perhaps it was his trim looks and piercing gray eyes. Or maybe it was the touch of melancholy in his spirit that was the lure. In her mind, he could see past her crooked nose into her heart. She imagined his arms embracing her. She imagined soothing away his fears.

Then as she entered Maule Square, it became unnecessary to imagine him at all because there he was, him and Paulus Spaulding, stepping from the threshold of a black-bricked three-story house. She felt her heart ball up in her chest as she advanced toward them.

***

Wolfdog was awakened by a cold stir of air. It was more than a winter draft. It was as if something had moved nearby.

To all appearances, the small room lit through the window by an overcast morning, lay empty. But the pirate felt a presence of some kind. Those who live dangerous lives learn to trust their instincts. Sitting up, Wolfdog snatched a dagger from the bedside table.

Once, on the northern coast of Ulalame, where inlets and streams abound, Wanlo the Freebooter had directed a nighttime raid on an outpost of miners who panned for gold on the Black Rat River. The pirates, about 40 in number, had waded ashore downstream from the settlement and proceeded with stealth through thick woods to a clearing of darkened huts. Assuming the miners asleep, the pirates crept into the huts with swords drawn and minds alight with the promise of golden spoils.

Wolfdog had partnered with Drogo Scuttin and a thick-lipped fellow with a crooked ear named Jubel Kite, part Morellan, part Ligeian. They entered a large hut and were deep in the shadows when they came upon an empty bed. Wolfdog felt a presence tingling behind in the dark. The pirate whirled and ducked just as a blade whizzed by. Jubel screamed as the point of the blade found him. A glimmer of moonlight revealed blood shooting from Jubel's gashed neck, as he collapsed into the gloom. Drogo immediately sliced out with his sword and somehow, gauging perhaps from some glint or motion, struck the shadow-obscured ambusher a deathblow. It all happened too fast for the senses to register it in real time. Instinct saved Wolfdog's life, steered Drogo's aim. That night, poor Jubel just didn't have it.

Again, the morning stirred coldly, and Wolfdog's keen eyes searched out the source. Across the small room, near the window, something moved: an eddy in the fabric of space. *Some trick of the light?* No, it was the very air itself visibly bending. First it bent into a wrinkle, then into a wave. The wave rolled, crooking and warping perception in its wake. It rolled outward in all dimensions, forming an outline that gradually took the shape of a man.

Too frightened to move, the pirate stared helpless.

Whilst never completely shedding its transparency, the image gathered fullness, substance, texture. As it grew clearer, Wolfdog made out a small, lean man with a long mustache. The figure's thumbs began tapping the tips of its fingers and to Wolfdog's horror, one dead eye peered back.

Wanlo?

The bringer of bloody death himself, Wanlo the Freebooter, shorn naked of his fanciful clothes, and having cast off his ailing carcass, replete with renewed vigor. There was no doubting it.

The freebooter took a grim step forward.

"What's the matter, Wolfdoggie? Ye look like ye've seen a ghost."

Chills savaged Wolfdog's spine and cold beads of sweat popped and ran in rivulets. The dagger tumbled to the floor with a clatter.

134

"Looks like ye dropped something," the ghost said, growing in clarity and malice, as it took another step forward. "Ye wouldn't mean me any harm, now would ye, old friend?"

Wolfdog flung the blanket from the bed and scooted to the floor, away from the apparition, not taking eyes off it. "Stop, Wanlo. Stop! Listen to reason."

The specter of Wanlo approached the bed that now stood between them. It leaned over and picked up the dagger. "Last time I saw ye, ye were doing yer reasoning with a blade across my throat."

Wolfdog held up hands in a reassuring gesture. "Think about it, Wanlo. Ye were sick. Deadly sick. It was an act of mercy."

The dagger looked surreal floating in the ghostly hand. "Mercy, was it? Well-compensated for yer mercy, weren't ye? With the money for the conjure woman, I mean? Somewhat disproportionately compensated compared to yer shipmates, wouldn't ye say?"

Wolfdog backed to the door. "The crew had turned against ye, Wanlo. What with Red all broken up, then Drogo eaten alive, then Obie crushed like a melon. And Rance was the worst of the lot. Butchered to pieces like chum. A true horror to behold."

"I've talked my way out of tighter scrapes."

"Ye didn't see the look in the crew's eyes."

"An opportunity denied me, I guess."

In a flash, the specter was across the room, blade held high. Wolfdog tried to open the door but it was too late. The ghost swept in, hatred stamped in its airy features. Hatred so bitter it boiled over—soul-blackening hatred radiating like a nimbus from the baleful figure. The heat of the hatred was so great it scorched Wolfdog's face and hair and bedclothes as the struggle turned to control of the dagger.

They smashed into the door. They twisted. thrashed, lunged. Wolfdog held firm to the ghostly wrist of the hand clutching the dagger whilst the phantom's free hand tore at Wolfdog's face and chest, ripping through flesh and cloth. They crashed to the floor, Wolfdog squirming on the bottom, face bloody, bedclothes shredded, the blade edging ever downward. Feeling the inevitability of the downward progress of the treacherous blade, Wolfdog pushed and coiled to one side. The knife struck down and across one forearm, the flesh parting in a gaping wound, but the dagger drove into the wood of the floor. As the ghost labored to free it, Wolfdog curled from beneath the spectral attacker and crab-crawled backwards in a trail of blood.

Someone pounded on the door. Niles Margrave. "What's going on? Open up in there."

Perhaps it was the interruption. Perhaps the ghost had merely exhausted its energy. Perhaps it was what the apparition witnessed as it

135

turned to its prostrate victim. Looking at Wolfdog curiously, as if suddenly seeing its former shipmate for the first time, the specter lost tangibility and vanished into nothingness.

Wolfdog would always believe that, in that moment, the ghost had been stunned back through the doors of death by a discovery it made whilst viewing its longtime comrade all but bare-chested in shredded bedclothes.

The ghost of Wanlo had seen, plain as day, that Wolfdog was a woman.

***

Fadumo Aneleh Zant wa Zant stretched and yawned, the pure energy rising with her to greet the new day. Anse lay beside her, relegated to the sliver of bed she had not claimed for herself. The old slaver snored smugly, his petty dreams of power lapping at him from the far reaches of sleep.

In the dreams, she saw, he was no longer crooked and scheming but upright and magnanimous; hordes of fawning Hasturians stopped him on the street to compliment him and to seek his opinions on matters of local governance. He made profound pronouncements, paring every problem to its crux. He told clever jokes with double meanings. He was quite full of himself, as she wanted him to be. He would never see the end coming until her trap had already sprung.

The night had been glorious, thanks to the aid of her spider god Anarach. Together, they had breathed life into a shriveled corpse and raised the spirits of the dead. She felt the presence of these ghosts all around, wending themselves through the lives of those they had left behind, for good and for ill. Mostly, she suspected, for ill.

Awakened by his own snoring, Anse peered at her with one cold, gray eye. "We did it, then?" he said, groggily. "It wasn't just a dream?"

She wasn't sure what "we" had done but she allowed him the illusion of involvement. "We did it. Lucrezia Maule lives again." She smiled. Men are always fools for smiles.

"Hah!" he said, bounding to his feet. "Let's see what the general has to say about things now."

Bartine brought breakfast, careful to avoid eye contact with the fadumo.

Beyond the bedroom door, a naked footfall slapped on wood. Bartine and Anse did not appear to hear it, distracted as people often are by their own discursive thoughts.

***

136

"Outside?" M said. "I see. Ye're leaving me."

She was angry. With him, with Da. He was sure she'd heard the yelling, the door slam. Her lips turned inward and tightened. She looked at him accusingly. "Is this arrangement ... permanent?" She retained the pucker, even as she talked.

"I'm not sure," he said. He tried to be calm for her but it was an effort. "I'm hoping not."

"I see. Well, this is very troubling to me, boy." She turned her head away from him.

He wanted to add that it was troubling to him, as well. In fact, it was worse than troubling. It was terrifying. But he didn't want to sound as if he were going against Da. Not in front of her. Better to put on a brave front, even if it took every measure of his resilience.

"Paulus Spaulding is here to escort me to the stables."

She turned back to him, gently weeping.

"I have to leave, M. But I'll be back soon. I promise."

She nodded. "Don't let them make fun of ye, boy. Don't let them tease ye. Fight, if ye must. For yer honor. For the Gargery name." Her eyes were red now, and they looked very old. "Ye can't help the way ye are, but ye can hold yer head high."

"I will, M." He kissed her lightly on her damp forehead.

He left her room, feeling, with every step, as if he were dissolving.

Paulus had declined a third bowl of groats but eyed the uneaten portion in Ring's bowl.

"What do I bring?" Ring asked.

"Why, just yer own fine self, of course. Someone will bring yer things later. Are ye going to finish those groats?"

When they stepped out into the diffused light of the winter morning, Paulus, fighting stick in hand, turned to him and said, "Come on, Gargery. We have a stop to make along the way."

Ring had retrieved the jade knife, which he carried in his coin purse, and the adder stone, which he now worked his thumb against frantically. He brought these and the clothes on his back. He wondered who would bring his other things. He wondered if he would even be allowed back to Gargery House to visit as he had promised M.

Almost at once, they were joined in Maule Square by Willa Lumen in her dull tunic and scruffy sandals. Upon seeing him, her oval face shined like a copper paldin. The three of them walked abreast as Paulus said, "So tell me. What do ye think of the stables, Gargery?"

Ring felt as if his insides were being tugged at by a riptide. The last thing he wanted to do was make conversation. He shrugged. "I like the horses."

"Of course ye do. Everyone likes the horses. But the stables, what do ye think of the stables?"

He thought for a moment. "They seem ... busy," he said.

Paulus laughed. Willa had to grin, so infectious was Paulus' laugh.

"Ye carry things close to the chest, don't ye, Gargery?"

Ring was unsure what Paulus meant by that but took no offense. Instead, against his best efforts, he allowed himself the faintest touch of a smile before succumbing again to his malaise.

It was a dreary morning. The on-again, off-again drizzle was on again. It slowly weighed down his cloak, soaking through the robe to his skin. It collected in pools on the slushy surface of the snow, which soaked his sandaled toes in cold and splashed up at his legs. It dripped from his hair. The citizenry for the most part reflected the dreariness, gray clouds in their eyes.

A gap-toothed palmist wrapped in a threadbare blanket offered to read their fortunes but Paulus begged off, good-naturedly, leaving the fortune-teller with a pleasant "good day." A man with a bandaged hand crossed the street by hopping from foot to foot, all the while looking nervously about. He stubbed a toe on a heaved pavement stone and would have tripped if Paulus hadn't caught him. The character studied the trio of stable hands curiously for a moment, and then skipped off into the crowd. The rank smell of rotten fruit suddenly wafted up at them from some dubious side street and Paulus comically pinched his nose and walked in that exaggerated, high-stepping way of his.

But the stable boy's good cheer was not widely shared.

A sightless indigent with swollen lips felt his way along the West Wall, clattering amongst the armor in determined search of a specific shield. "Where are ye, Cyril Carver? Ye can't hide from me."

A giant funeral clown with widely spaced teeth hovered over the masses as he dragged his way toward the trio, his disposition no match for the garish merriment painted on his face. He kept looking around, as if he suspected everyone. Of what, Ring had no clue.

There was a woman who kept tugging at her garments as if someone were toying with them; a stern-faced Pym slave with anxious eyes, nearly white-faced with fright; a drunken stumbler with shocking saffron hair swinging fists, blotchy and gnarled, at some invisible foe.

They passed the cracked shrine to Nebo, which teemed with worshippers.

"People seem to be feeling especially devout today," Willa observed.

In front of the leaning, rust-stained building adjacent to the shrine, the man with no arms and one leg was being prodded by a boy with a fighting stick. The boy was laughing as he poked at the helpless beggar's chin and nose. "Knock out his teeth," a second boy goaded. "Piss on him."

The boys found these suggestions uproarious.

Sizing things up, Paulus hurried to the beggar's aid. "Now, boys," Paulus said, "fun is fun, but this here is none other than the war hero Hedwig Geb, who sacrificed himself nobly at the Battle of Hex River, fighting off Usher invaders. Ye owe yer very liberty to this man, isn't that right, Sirrah Hedwig? Ye could be speaking Usher right now, bowing to their heathen gods and whatnot, if it wasn't for men like him." Paulus laid down his fighting stick and helped Sirrah Hedwig to sit up. The tormenters stepped back.

Sirrah Hedwig looked confused.

"We were only playing with him, Paulus," one of the boys said. The bottom lid of one eye twitched. "Didn't know he was a war hero and all."

"Of course, not. How could ye know?" Paulus righted Sirrah Hedwig's alms bowl and, fishing into a coin purse, pulled out a shiny silver paldin, which he placed in the empty bowl. "For yer trouble, Sirrah Hedwig," he said, smiling down at the beggar. The old soldier's mind was elsewhere, as he stared at some fixed point beyond them. His mouth formed the word, "Petrus?"

"Now, boys," Paulus said, "I would consider it a personal favor to me and my family if ye could keep an eye on our war hero here and maybe intercede on his behalf, should ruffians affront him."

The boys blinked at one another. "We could do that."

Paulus fished out another silver paldin and handed it over to one of them.

"Ye have my everlasting gratitude," Paulus said. He picked up his fighting stick and rejoined his workmates.

Ring was unsure what to make of this display. The concept of stepping in at possible peril to assist a fellow Hasturian, who wasn't related and didn't even realize what was going on seemed downright outlandish. A beggar, no less. And paying out silver paldins on the beggar's behalf. He couldn't have been more stunned if Paulus had turned himself inside out. Ring looked to Willa for her reaction but she wasn't even watching Paulus. She was looking at the apple she carried, as if attempting to judge its weight.

They walked on in silence for a time.

Then, Ring said, "Why did ye help that old beggar, Paulus? What's he to ye?"

"Well, Gargery," Paulus said, taking on a scholarly tone, "he's nothing to me, as far as that goes. Except he could be me. Or he could be ye. If our lives had turned out differently. Ye see?"

Ring really didn't.

"If ye were that old beggar, a war hero and all, being terrorized because of yer lack of limbs, wouldn't ye favor someone coming to yer rescue?"

Ring had to admit he would.

As he thought about that, they came to a throng of boys in an alley. The boys had cleaned away a section of slush near a wall and were tossing copper paldins to it. A light-skinned Ligeian boy with broader-than-normal thumbs tossed his coin just a smidge from the wall, closer by far than the others. He laughed heartily at his good fortune, baring a dead front tooth.

Paulus returned to his purse and plucked out a half dozen copper paldins. "Try yer luck, Gargery?" he asked, offering a coin.

Ring declined, but Paulus handed him the fighting stick and lined up with the others for a turn to throw.

"Do ye want this apple?" Willa said.

Ring looked at her, looked at the apple. "No, thank ye. I had groats."

She smiled and nodded.

He sensed it was his turn to say something.

Forgetting himself, he reached out and touched her broken nose.

"How did this happen?" he asked.

She didn't flinch, didn't make a move to brush away his hand, but watched his face closely. "I forget about it sometimes."

"Tell me about it."

Her eyes were truly beautiful. "Does it repulse ye?"

Withdrawing his hand, he considered the question.

"It interests me," he said, weighing his words carefully. "Did someone do this to ye?"

"Aye. But it was years ago. I was eight or nine. I was staying over at a cousin's house when an uncle of mine...." The sentence trailed off. "He had been drinking. It doesn't matter. There are hateful people in this world. People who hurt little children for selfish reasons."

"Yer father's brother?"

"Aye. Uncle Silas. Da was furious. I'd never seen him that angry before. It doesn't matter though because Osric soon came for Uncle Silas."

"How did that happen?"

She sighed and looked down. "They're not sure. After he hurt me, he just vanished. His body was discovered later in an abandoned building in Carmilla. He'd been dead for weeks." She paused. "There wasn't much left of him. The rats had been at him pretty good."

"The rats?"

She didn't answer.

Paulus returned whistling. Of his six throws, he'd won two, which put him up a dozen copper paldins. He jingled them in his hand a while before adding them to his purse.

Passing Spaulding Stables, Ring looked over at the side street where he'd seen the barefoot little girl yesterday. She wasn't out this morning but the wharf rats were, down the way, chewing on something. He thought about Uncle Silas.

As they swung down to the Horrocks district, they were passed by a swarm of Hasturians: water bearers, watchmen, a diminutive acolyte from Dagon Fane, one of the harlequins he had seen yesterday, immaculate patricians, laborers, sailors, ragged trolls, humanity in all its forms, for the most part clammed up and dour. On a street corner a reed piper was attempting to lighten the mood but was repeatedly jostled by unseen hands, disrupting his melody with shrill dissonance. The drizzle had stopped but the snow was still eroding, running downhill in a dismal soup.

"What's the errand, Paulus?" Ring asked at last.

"The general's chariot is fixed and prepared for battle. The mighty Fourth is ready to ride again. We're letting him know."

"We're going to General Maule's house?"

"'Twould seem to be the simplest way to let him know, don't ye agree?"

But as the trio arrived in the general's neighborhood, they found their way blocked by a massive crowd gathered in the street outside his door.

CHAPTER 8
The Luminous Choir

I never took to eating animal flesh. A lot of other crawlers do it. At the festivals and so on. They fill their cheeks with animal muscles and guts. Gristle. Who knows what all? Like it's some kind of treat. Fat dripping down their faces, picking bits of skin from their teeth. Blood on their plates. Gnaw it right from the bones, if given the chance. Da, Cletus, Andaman, they all do it, Dagon help me. But I don't. I stand firm on that.

I know, big-hearted for a villainous old slaver. But some things are just barbaric and eating dead animals is one of them. Says me.

It was toward the end of summer and we were coming back from delivering a wagonload of Skalks to the Cannera Iron Mine, north of Melmoth. It's a cold-blooded business, supplying the mines. They go through man-footed beasts like wood through a mill. Work them to death, then dump them in nearby pits. I've seen the pits, seen the gone ones stacked like kindling. Worked till there was nothing left of them. Then covered over when the smell gets too bad. And the slaves themselves dig a new pit. We only sell Skalks to the mines. Skalks ye can't give away anywhere else. Besides, the mines' coin is always good.

It had been an awful summer. Momma went a few months earlier, then the little whelp. Seemed like death was our constant keeper. Andaman had a run to Morella, so I joined Cletus with the Skalks. Why Darius came along is anyone's guess but I knew right off it was a mistake. Because of his size, Cletus rode in the back, even after we dropped off the Skalks at Cannera.

We were halfway back to White Worm when we made camp. It was getting dark and we were tired. Darius had been going on about adjusting to life without Momma, trying to wring sympathy out of us but I wasn't buying it. Cletus was nodding but of course he wasn't buying it either. We unhitched the oxen and were starting a little need-fire when a stirring rose from the low weeds and this wild boar comes lunging out. We all of us jumped at that.

This pig was huge. I'll wager he weighed as much as two men, though he was lean by boar standards. He had long, thin legs and was dusky matted, his high back ridged. The pig's snout looked almost like a rat's except it had a phenomenal set of tusks wrapped around it, shaped for business and sharp as blades. He was watching us with those beady pig eyes, deciding whether to charge or walk away.

"Good fortune to us," Darius said, and he edged on the beast with Old Dolge held high.

Me and Cletus just looked at each other. We weren't sure what Darius was planning to do with that stick of his but we sure hoped it wasn't whack that monster boar on the snout. Yet, that is exactly what he had in mind.

The pig grunted a warning, the hairs on his back bristling.

Darius took another step, holding Old Dolge with both hands. Moving slowly, creeping up on the beast, talking to him. "Hey, ye little rooter, yer just in time. Just in time for dinner."

We had a bow and some arrows in the wagon but that did us no good at the moment. Cletus held a knife, but I was empty-handed. Not that a knife would do much good against a charging wild pig.

The boar sprang at Darius, his hooves thundering, his head low, the tusks widening.

They say with a charging boar ye can skewer him with a pike and he'll still come at ye, moving down the shaft, mindless of the pain. Old Dolge came down with a loud crack, but the boar didn't even blink. Somehow, Darius managed to twist out of his path, Old Dolge flying one way and Darius the other. The boar, a living embodiment of terror and hatred, rampaged around our campsite, with me and Cletus fleeing for our lives.

I bolted up a spider oak and clung to a branch as the boar rammed the tree's trunk not once but twice, trying to shake me loose. But I wasn't going anywhere.

The pig reared toward Cletus. The giant leapt into the wagon. I shouted to Cletus to find the bow and arrows. He grabbed hold of them and was trying to notch an arrow when the boar crashed into one of the wagon wheels, cracking it lengthwise, and almost spilling Cletus to the ground. As the boar readied for another strike, Cletus' arrow found the string and with a twang it surged into the thick hide of the creature's back. This just seemed to anger the boar further, bringing out the sheer wildness in him.

Spinning, the pig charged again, this time toward one of our oxen. A vision of savagery, jowls frothing, the arrow jutting from his back, he slammed into the side of the ox, leveling him with an ear-splitting din, the ox wailing. Tusks flashed as they scissored into the ox's underside, breaking open the skin in clean lines, pouring out the blood and the filmy innards as a second arrow struck the boar's back.

Infuriated, the boar reeled and raced around the campsite once more, then charged off into the undergrowth.

When I dropped to the ground, I was shaking. I had never seen Cletus so pale. Darius rose to his feet and brushed dirt from his lap.

Moving toward him, not saying a word, I picked up Old Dolge. As my hands formed around the gnarled wood, anger generated by 30 years of tyranny came to my forefront. Darius could gauge by my approach that his time had come. He didn't even raise a hand to fight.

How long I continued to swing that wicked staff, I couldn't say. I guess, until all the strength was gone from my arms.

As he made his way through the marketplace, Andaman couldn't shake the notion that things were going on all about him. Things beyond the ordinary that had appeared out of nowhere, hidden from the light of day. Noises, shifts in the air, hints of motion behind him or way off to this side or that. His eyes never quite catching them, his ears, straining, unsure what they heard, his skin tingling as if traced by feathers. Illusive things, but nonetheless real, snacking on his nerves.

Every few steps in the cold and slushy muck, he looked around. He noticed others were doing the same. Some did more than just look.

Down an alley, someone battered at a door, screaming, "Let me in. Hurry. Let me in." At a sundial, a grimy figure draped in rags gave up a soul-wrenching howl, as if lamenting the very passage of time itself. To the left, a potter hurtled one of his wares to the snowy bricks. To the right, a painter excitedly swatted stretched canvas at thin air.

Crossing deeper into Gondemar, Andaman approached the Gargery slave pens. Enoch Glister was due this morning with a load of shouldna-beens from Usher. Shouldna-beens were what slavers called infants abandoned to die of exposure by their parents, a practice sadly common, especially in the poorer regions. Usher brokers rescued and nursed these little ones to adolescence, then sold them to traveling slavers. Andaman hoped to throw off some of the morning's madness with the routine work of preparing these children for auction. Scrubbing the dirt from them and replacing their tattered rags with simple robes. When it came to the collaring, they would wait for Cousin Anse.

But, as his hand neared the door, it flew open on its own. He jumped back.

Enoch Glister, eyes bulging, mouth agape, came bolting from the shadows. Red-faced, he held his neck crunched down, as if fighting the grip of some invisible strangler at his back. Darting past Andaman into the street, splayed fingers clawing the air, he let loose a gurgling cry and rumbled off into the crowd.

"Enoch!" Andaman shouted, but Enoch was already gone.

For an instant, Andaman froze with uncertainty. In the darkness inside the doorway, a chaos of commotion was under way: blurred movements, gasps, a thud, a scream, a pounding that shook the walls. Someone called his name.

He spun, sought a break in the crowd and ran off as fast as his legs would carry him. Down a winding side street, crashing to the pavements,

144

skinning his palms, scrambling to his feet again, nearly falling a second time. Shoving pedestrians out of his way, he scurried into an alley, crossed a yard, clambered over a fence. He wasn't even running toward anywhere, just away, away, away from it all.

The whirligig coughed to life, but this time it was strangely subdued in the distant background. In the foreground, in what was supposedly the real world, appearances were losing their luster. Color drained, surfaces went flat, and every line wavered. All sound mashed together in a way that robbed it of meaning. It swelled and diminished like the breathing of some malevolent beast. Whiffs of reeking dross heaved out at him, leaving him choking back dry retches. He ran on, oblivious to time and space.

How long he ran was anyone's guess.

Reality smeared past him. He broke through wood. The whirligig angled and sputtered, tossing off random shards of light. His lungs were catching fire. A sandal flipped off, but he ran on, barely aware of the snow and wetness and the stones and refuse vexing his naked sole. He bounced off a wall, cracking his head. Blood dripped into one eye to mix with the sweat that streamed down his face. He crashed into something else, his hands tearing away at it as he wedged through an opening. Fabric ripped. He tumbled and scrambled and crawled until his knees were bloody and his shoulders screamed and his fingernails were ravaged to the quick. Until the last burst of energy shuddered from his frame and he didn't even have the strength to close his gaping mouth. Until the whirligig ceased to spin and darkness crashed upon him.

He awoke indoors.

He had been bleeding on the carpet and had probably ruined it, which was a shame given its impressive weave. Lifting his head, drool trailing from his lip, he listened intently. The only noises he heard were the crackle of a fire and his own breathing which had resumed a normal tempo. Satisfied he was alone in the house, he sat up and squinted down, not sure how he had made such a mess of himself.

His robe was soiled, bloody and torn. His knees and palms and elbows were shredded. The cut on his head still trickled. The sweat on his body had gone cold. He glanced down at his unsandaled foot and shook his head at the swollen and bruised sight of it.

He peered up at the fireplace, burning brightly under its bunting. He knew this place. He recognized the bunting of the Fourth Legion, the dented Arnheimian helmet, the feathered spear, the coin, the obsidian dagger. He knew the shield and pennant on the far wall and military-style dinner table. To his right was the stairway with its carved griffin forging and fern-colored runner.

It pulled at him. It made him rise to his tortured feet and walk toward it. It made him—*made* him—lift his damaged foot to the first step, one hand on the griffin's nubbed horns for balance. Shakily, he lifted the sandaled foot from the floor and climbed to the second step. This more than satisfied the urge to revisit the scene of his crime. This was the crime itself demanding he come. This was his being owned by it.

He was halfway up the stairs when he became aware of a sudden glow behind him.

Pausing, he twisted his neck toward it.

The room had filled with brilliant light. In the light moved figures he labored to see. Turning full around, he sat on the steps and, shading his face with one hand, squinted into the glare. There was Digna Greavor, holding her dolly and looking up at him. There was Tilda Tambernich, his very first charmer. There were other sweet nothings he had put the dirk to, coming in and out of focus in the bright white light. And the oyster seller and others. He adjusted to the glow and his hand fell from his brow. He was not so much afraid of these apparitions as wearied by them. They stirred like some luminous choir gathered for his benefit but no song came to their lips. He deserved to walk amongst them, he saw that now. But he hadn't the heart to do it, even though the dirk had now magically appeared in his grip. He thumbed the ribbed handle, thoughtfully.

Then, stepping to the forefront of the glare came a figure he only dimly remembered. A woman, naked as were all the spirits, her great breasts pendulous, her arms outstretched toward him. Her eyes, which he had last seen staring blankly, now warm and moist, and looking at him with the total love that could only be offered by ... a mother. Andaman gasped. It was Momma. Behind her he could see Da and his brothers. They were smiling at him, their heads tilted to one side, their arms outstretched in welcoming gestures. Tears came to him as he rose. Aye, they had left him alone amidst a punishing world but now they had returned for him.

"Momma," he cried, putting the dirk to his own throat.

The last sound he heard was the benevolent approach of hooves.

***

Fingers of sunlight, groping deep, stir murk from the bottom of Dagon Bay. Bloated discs cut through a stew of algae and seaweed: a school of blood-colored moonfish. As they swim, they shudder en masse, as if connected somehow. A goldeneye eel, ray-finned and spiny, circles a community of crabs whilst ghoulish bottom-feeders send up clouds of fish debris. Vegetation erupts everywhere in shocks and plumes.

Time has not been kind to the kingdom's structures. It has nibbled away at them and encrusted them in coral and sediment. The massive bricks that form them—irregular and roughly fitted together—ooze dank water freely. The towers, turrets and ramparts now acclivitous and caved, harbor the eroded bones of a lost civilization, the city's roofless haunts now largely claimed by eyeless predators.

The palace lies at the black heart of the kingdom: once an imposing monument to domineering rule, now a ruin, drenched in shadows. It may be unfair to suggest that all that keeps it from crumbling are delusional followers and profiteering priests. There are those who draw true authority from this place. But their numbers ever diminish.

In the throne room the blue-veined marble floor, covered in silt, crawls with centipede-like creatures, horned crustaceans and barnacles. Ageless jellyfish pulse ghostlike amid rafters festooned with streamers of kelp. Though rusted, the throne remains the focus of the dreary chamber. And the goddess of the sea holds court with her advising familiars.

Dagon's sleek, scaled body shifts forward, the ringed fingers of one hand snaked around the scepter that bears her mystic sigil. Her tentacles drift languidly in the deepwater tide. Her eyes rivet on the imp called Aldinach, a hairy little demon known to whip up earthquakes and tempests: Aldinach the destroyer, always eager to deliver vengeance in the service of his queen.

"If we don't step on this spider quickly," Aldinach says, "it will ensnare all of Hastur in its web."

Dagon's eyes flicker. Translucent lids slide open and closed. "And how would ye have me attack this spider god?"

"A great tide could sweep up at it from the sea. Or a terrific temblor, rending the ground, could swallow it whole. Or...."

"Ye would have me destroy the city to save it from this islander god?"

Aldinach looks suddenly sheepish. "Not the *whole* city."

Dagon sighs.

She turns toward Bar-Lgura, a stumpy, winged grotesque known for her avarice and lust. Keeper of a legendary horde of gold, Bar-Lgura haunts the mines in search of dying men with whom to perform cruel sex acts.

"We could creep up on him whilst he sleeps," Bar-Lgura offers. "Then we could stuff his spider eyes with pepper, hack off his legs, and send him floating back to his island where he belongs."

"And ye would do this?"

Bar-Lgura freezes. "Well...."

"I see. Unless yer prey is helpless as a tasseled blobfish, ye lack vigor for the hunt."

Bar-Lgura looks away.

Dagon turns to her third familiar, a tall woman in white with no skin and eyes like a cat's. This is Gresil, only 500 years old, still a demon of the second order. Gresil is said to exist on the roasted bones of dead men and the breath of babies.

"Even if we slay the spider," Gresil says, "assuming we can, the city is still overrun with ghosts. The question is why? What is the conjure woman up to? Until we know the answer, we act at our own peril."

"Wait? Is that what yer suggesting?" Anger blooms on the sea queen's face. She slams her scepter on the ground, sending an infant octopus off in a puff of ink.

Aldinach grimaces. Bar-Lgura flinches. Only Gresil remains unmoved.

"It would be the prudent approach," Gresil says.

"Very well," Dagon replies. "We'll wait, but not for long." Her serpentine eyes hold nothing but fury. "We'll see what this fadumo is up to. Then we strike, and when we do, teeth will gnash and blood will flow and horror will find our foes, no matter where they hide. And they will learn the painful lesson of what happens to those who entice the wrath of Dagon."

An impressive display for an audience of three, but the words ring hollow. Gresil could see how it was. She could see the old ways crumbling like the walls of this sunken palace.

***

Cletus Gargery was one of the first to awaken from the tangle of bodies. The floor, black marble set in gold relief, was sticky with spilled wine, olive oil and other fluids. In order to extricate himself, he carefully moved a woman's thigh from his stomach and a man's hairy armpit from his throat.

He had only slept for a few hours, so he was still slightly drunk. He sat up a bit too quickly and suffered a chill swirl of nausea. Spaulding Inn's great orgy hall wobbled and, at his foundation, so did he. Murals of copulating merrymakers quivered on the stanchion-lit walls.

There were maybe two hundred naked people spread out all around him on couches and on the floor, including two other giants: one a brick manufacturer named Elam Larch who snored on his stomach as a Hastur maid with hair like curling flames rested fitfully on his buttock cheeks, and the other was a honey seller from Carcosa, a woman whose name escaped him. She lay on her back, hugging to her bosom the long, pimpled face of Cleve Wilf—the architect. Some of the sleeping revelers wore garlands of ivy to ward off drunkenness.

From somewhere, bowels rumbled, threatening flatulence.

A coppersmith named Ormas Illing slept with a terra-cotta cup poised on his hairy chest. The cups, featuring scenes of brutish satyrs buggering nymphs in a vineyard, were part of the general litter which also included wild thyme and roses, masks, castoff clothing, oyster shells and, in one corner, the remnants of a sacrificed goat. A sacred prostitute struggled to extricate herself from beneath a corpulent bald man who failed to awaken despite her virulent prodding.

Spaulding Inn hosted its orgies more or less monthly to correlate with various religious observances. Each event was rigorously planned and governed over by a designated official of the appropriate fane. Attendance was by invitation only and many in the city lamented being snubbed. He looked upon these gatherings as his times for forgetting. Cletus Gargery had much to forget.

Last night had been dedicated to the Holy Ascension of Light and Darkness held by the Loyal and Benevolent Order of Nebo the Merciful. It recognized the Old Ones' separation of day from night, symbolic of dividing good and evil, a distinction that had been unclear amongst the First People and, if truth be told, was still somewhat hazy to the average Hasturian. Some suggested that the observance symbolized the divide between life and death but Cletus was put off by that kind of talk.

The orgy, if the past was any guide, was marked by a procession of acolytes bearing lanterns that cast off the likenesses of hundreds of stars. The high priestess of the temple, wearing the Silver Mask of Wisdom, had led the opening recitation of ritualized monologues, spoken as though from the mouth of Nebo. Her speech had no doubt taken on a soaring eroticism that held the audience spellbound and climaxed in the sacrifice of the goat.

Flute girls on their slender reeds had treated the attendees to stirring renditions of songs from one of the popular plays. Perhaps "Jocasta on the Hill" or "Jocasta in Black." They had invited the faithful to sing and dance along to their tunes. Rose petals had filled the air. Wine had flowed. Cups had clinked. Tunics had slipped from bronze shoulders. Playfulness and laughter had become the rule of the evening, with the priestess herself joining in once passions fully ignited.

This was the point when Cletus had arrived. He was late, which was frowned upon but tolerated in his case, as he was a longtime celebrant, a resident of the inn and a crowd favorite. He had been to many Ascension of Light and Darkness orgies and knew when to appear without causing too much of a disruption. He had quickly lost himself in wantonness, eager for release from the terrors he had witnessed that night on Mount Dnarden.

Rising now to his feet, he padded off in search of his tunic and sandals, stepping carefully over prone and witless slumberers. The tunic, pried gingerly from beneath the soft curves of an archon's concubine, had been badly stained with pomegranate juice and still smelled slightly of Lucrezia Maule and her tomb. Distasteful as it was, he slipped it on and poked around until he discovered first one sandal then, on the opposite side of the room, the other.

As some of the revelers began to yawn and stretch, he left their presence, climbed a stairway and entered his room at the end of a long corridor.

The room was large but plainly furnished. Everild, who shared his bed, was out at the marketplace rounding up breakfast. When she returned, it was with bread and a sizable quantity of figs, sufficient to conquer even his deep hunger. A lank Morellan with a small chin, broad forehead and quick, large-pupiled amber eyes, Everild was his closest companion and he held her in high regard.

She sliced the bread into thick wedges, and let him eat, knowing how ravenous he was after orgy nights. When he finished with the bread, she wrestled off his stained tunic and sponged him clean. She rubbed his skin with olive oil and a spikenard ointment and then she dressed him.

The washing had opened his pores to the cool morning air and he felt fresh.

She put the figs on a plate, reserved a few for herself, and brought the plate to him.

She watched him eat, positioning her neck very straight to avoid the collar rubbing.

"I should be home for supper," he said when he'd cleaned the plate.

As he descended the stairs, he became aware of a ruckus in the orgy hall. Last minute grab-ass, he thought as he left the building.

Enoch Glister was due this morning with a shipment of shouldna-beens from Usher, but Cletus would trust them to Andaman's care. Instead, he decided to head over to Gargery House. He and Anse could walk over to the pens later for the collar fixings. He wanted to gauge his brother's take on the night's events.

Overall, it was a grim day. Not as cold as yesterday but overcast and drizzly. The sort of day to stay indoors and get lost in thought. But his thoughts this morning were all about the dead: the smell that soured the back of his throat, the yielding and clammy touch he could still feel, the shriveled eyes that stared at him, the labored rasps of obscene breathing.

A stringy oaf with an overgrown jaw and some kind of eye spasm knocked into him. "Watch it," Cletus warned. But the warning fell on deaf ears as the character acted like he had been set upon by some invisible provoker. The offender plowed into a grandfatherly type, jostling the old fellow to the ground. "Hey, no need for that," Cletus said. But the character, beset again by his unseen tormentor, just leapt off into another pedestrian. Unsure what to make of this exhibition, Cletus spat and shook his head.

A clatter came from on top of a tall neighboring house. There was an old woman on the roof but how she had gotten there, he had no clue. Clumsy and unsure of her footing, she motioned frantically with her hands. "I'm sorry, Elmo," she said to no one he could see. "Please forgive me." Tears streamed her wrinkled face and her body wracked with sobs. Then

150

her feet flew out from under her and she tumbled. "Elmoooooooooo," she called on her way down. She hit the cobblestone street with an emphatic *thwhack*.

Cletus turned away, wishing he could unsee what he had just witnessed.

As he crossed through winding, tapered lanes, he was elbowed, poked, jolted and nudged. Given his giant frame, he was unaccustomed to being treated so roughly. But he sensed he wasn't deliberately being bothered. In fact, his assailants were all but oblivious to him, so consumed were they with delusions.

He wondered whether some plague of madness had descended on the city. However, when he opened the door at Gargery House, an abrupt understanding seized him—he comprehended immediately the nature of the panic that gripped Hastur. There, standing in the shadows, he was confronted by the presence of several relatives ... all of whom, had been dead for years.

***

It had been a restless night for the general. He was dozing when his room had suddenly filled with light. The source of the light was the room's rear window. Rising to the cold floor, he cautiously approached the glare and squinted into it.

Outside, it was brighter than day. Great shafts of light cut through the swirling snow in a blinding display. Mount Dnarden had come alive with a glow that sliced the night wide open. *But what does it mean?* His mind raced with possibilities. Was it the return of the Old Ones from their profound depths? Or had the shepherd god finally risen as foretold? If so, would all the other sleepers awaken, as well?

Lucrezia.

Then, just as sudden, the great light dispersed and the city recloaked in darkness.

The general, still staring out the window, curled his cold toes.

"Da!" he called, bolting from his room. "Uncle Lafe! Ash! Huldra!"

"What is it, dear fellow?" Ash called, hurrying down the stairs. "Are ye injured? Is it a burglar?" Following behind Ash came Huldra, straightening her nightshirt.

Uncle Lafe came racing down the hall. "Ye aren't dreaming, General," he said. "I saw it, too. Great flash of light, coming from Mount Dnarden." He hurried down the steps. The front door opened and they heard him run out into the street. The howling wind blew the door shut.

"What is all this?" Da asked groggily. "Are ye alright, Drummer?"

"Da, something happened at Mount Dnarden. There was a light...."

Running back into his room, he found a pair of sandals, slipped them on and rushed down the stairs. He opened the door and flew outside.

A dozen people in sleep garments were gathered in the blowing cold. "Did ye see the light? What was it?" someone asked. "I've never seen anything like it," another chimed in. "It was like Nebo herself opened the heavens." "It was the Old Ones come back, I tell ye." "It was Hastur risen from the mound. We're saved! We're saved!" So they speculated, one over another, on the source of the light and what it meant.

The general scurried around to the back of the house, following in fresh footprints. Standing in the snowy gust, his outline sharp, his concentration fixed on the distance, was Uncle Lafe.

"What do ye think it was?"

"Something foul," his uncle replied. "I feel it in my bones."

They peered into the hazy swirl until it became apparent that whatever the light had been, it was gone. They went back inside and closed the door.

"No more to see, for now," Uncle Lafe said. "Best to return to our beds."

"But what was it?" Ash asked, his thick gray brows pushing up his crinkly forehead.

"We'll know more tomorrow," Uncle Lafe said. Then he and the general herded the others up the stairs.

For the longest time, the general sat on his bed, trembling hands in his lap.

The light appeared again, filling the room with its blinding intensity. His breath instantly fogged. Small snow creatures, horned and rat-faced, frolicked and rolled across the floor, which had become a sheet of solid ice. The walls contracted in the cold. From the ceiling, limned by the great brightness flooding the room, now hung gigantic, frosty icicles that thrust out menacing at him. A huge, leathery snow bat came flapping down, alighting on his shoulder. He looked over its twinkling pink eyes.

When the room at last went dark again, he lay down in bed and attempted to sleep.

He thought about what the high priest had said to him at Dagon Fane that night. *"Don't disappoint the dead."* Was that what this was all about? Was he to blame for all this?

His thoughts lost all meaning as they threaded the fringes of sleep. At last, exhaustion overtook him, yanking him into oblivion. But it seemed that he was no sooner gone than a hand shook him to back to consciousness. "Wake up, General. A miracle has taken place."

Uncle Lafe peered down at him, his bronze face drawn in amazement. Behind his uncle stood Ash and Huldra, clutching one another, and his da, looking older than he ever had seen him before, almost corpselike.

"What is it?"

Instead of answering, Uncle Lafe said, "Come. See for yerself."

They cleared a path to the bedroom door. Alarmed, he got to his feet and walked through the door. He descended the steps.

"Outside," Uncle Lafe said.

The general looked back and saw his family gathered on the landing, looking down at him.

He opened the door.

Assembled outside were hundreds of people, staring at him. When he stepped out, they went silent. He was about to ask them why they chose his door to gape at when he glanced down at his front step and the answer became apparent.

A rotting cadaver, appareled for the tomb, looked up at him. Had he the sense of smell, he might have been overwhelmed, but instead he knelt before the figure on the step and saw that it breathed, saw that awareness gleamed in its withered eyes, saw one hand rise weakly toward him. Around the corpse's neck hung an amulet shaped like an open hand. He looked at the hem of its shroud. It was missing a square of fabric.

Recognition hit him like a bolt of lightning.

Drummer Maule looked down into the sunken eyes and blistered face of his Lucrezia. "My darling, my darling, ye have returned to me." His voice broke with sobs and his heart filled with boundless love. He cupped her face in his hands.

CHAPTER 9
Returning the Favor

Me and Cletus never spoke of it. We fixed up the wagon well enough to get it back to Hastur, minus a gutted ox, which we left for whatever beasts cared to claim him. Cletus rode in the back, as always, as did Darius ... what was left of him. Every now and then, I'd glance back at the villain—all wrapped in a bloody tarp with Old Dolge at his side. I'd always thought doing him in would relieve me of some great burden but on that long, quiet ride to Hastur, I saw the truth of it. I'd never be free of that heartless old crawler.

That would ultimately prove to be the case in more ways than one.

After the funeral, which was a bit sparse on attendance, Cletus left Gargery House and took up quarters at Spaulding Inn. He brought Everild along, so I needed to find a new nursemaid for the boy and Gracie. After these adjustments, things settled back into their rut. The wheels of commerce rolled on.

When Gracie gave birth to the second whelp, I thought, this is it. This is my moment. Fortune was just another man-footed beast I'd collared. My business thrived. My standard lifted. My family bloomed. But the coming weeks brought black clouds of doubt.

Dagon help me if I didn't begin to see in little Darius signs of his villainous namesake.

On first glance, when I looked him over in his tiny cradle, wrapped in his blanket, fresh from the womb, I felt amazement in the presence of this new life. And pride. Pride that this was my progeny. A new Gargery to further seed the line of succession. I pictured this new branch blossoming into a thousand more.

But in passing days, I began to notice things. Disturbing things. For instance, I took notice that little Darius' hands seemed oddly gnarled, with knuckles ungainly for an infant. Perhaps, I thought, I was imagining this. But looking away and shaking my head and reexamining the tiny hands only reaffirmed my original observation.

Then there was the whelp's arms. Ye'd expect a baby's arms to be all plump and flabby but his arms were thick with muscle and nearly as big as his thighs. His shoulders looked carved from granite. I swear he had almost no neck at all. It gave him the appearance, overall, of not a baby but a little man. Aye, crawlers often refer to a baby as a "little man," but not in the sense of half-expecting him to sit up and talk to ye. When I say Darius looked like a little man, I mean he looked in every way like a little man.

It got so I couldn't stand the sight of him. When they brought him out, I would leave the room. I hoped he would eventually outgrow his ghastly appearance, but until he did I wanted nothing to do with him. I left him to Olalla and Gracie and hoped for the best.

One night, I half-convinced myself I was being daft. That the whole business was in my head. After all, this was my son and I owed it to him to at least put in an appearance now and then. So, I went to him at night in his room as the rest of the household slept. I went to him and what I saw chilled me to the marrow.

It was like he was waiting for me. Waiting in his little crib, hands balled in gnarled fists, smiling his evil, toothless grin. As I appeared in the dark, he looked up at me and his eyes twinkled merrily. I saw, to my horror, that they were the eyes of the old fiend Darius himself, gleaming at me from within the little whelp. I gasped.

So, ye see? There really was no helping it.

I closed his mouth. I pinched his nose. And I waited for the wicked gleam to fade from his eyes.

Her father was a fisher renowned for his angling prowess. He cast his nets off Blancmange Cove on the southern tip of the Amethyst Archipelago. Her mother, whom she never knew, had simply gone missing shortly after her birth. Taken by pirates, it was assumed, to be sold as a slave somewhere on the mainland. Some said it was a curse, brought upon the mother's head for delivering a baby with a disfiguring wine-colored mark on one cheek. But the truth was they all lived in fear of pirates and any one of them could have been taken.

As far back as she could recall, the boat was her playground. Here she was Wolfdog the cutthroat pirate, sailing in search of adventure. The rigging and the rudder and the sea taught her all she needed to know from life. The sparkling water provided.

She grew to be a great sailor and angler, hauling in with her father fish one day and squid the next and occasionally octopuses and, mingled in, crustaceans of all orders. She learned to gauge water depths. She learned to read the weather. She learned to always be aware of her position in the sea. When her father became too ill to fish, she set out alone and brought back nearly the same hauls as always. And when he died, she took over the boat.

But she became restless.

One day, whilst casting for tasseled blobfish, she spotted a distant pirate ship, lying in wait in a cove along the coastline of a neighboring island. As a big trade ship lumbered by, the pirates in their sleeker, faster vessel closed in and, amidst a volley of arrows, quickly boarded and commandeered the larger, clumsier craft. It was a thing of beauty, a spectacle of precision and agility. If it had been a performance of acrobats, it couldn't have been more impressive. After cleaning out the stores of cargo and whatever else took their fancy, the brigands swooped back to their ship and cut a path too close to shore for the big boat to follow. They disappeared into the hidden waters of an inlet.

That was when she began plotting her escape from Blancmange Cove.

She emptied her hut, bit by bit, of what she would need, and packed the items into the hull of her fishing boat. Amongst these was a wonderful curved sword bequeathed to her father by a great uncle. This sword had always fascinated her, and her father would sometimes let her hold it and turn it in her hand. It was sharp and heavy, and light glinted from it polished surface. In its reflection, she saw a pathway to power, a seriousness of purpose, a symbolic egalitarianism. Armed with such a weapon, she could live as she chose. Wolfdog could be made flesh.

Leaving behind most of her things, she set off one morning before the sun rose, her bosom bound, and her hair cut short. She didn't even say goodbye to anyone. Her plan was simple: search out a pirate ship, follow it to shore and join the crew.

During this time on the sea, sailing farther from her village with each passing day, she collected some of the happiest memories of her life. Divorced of obligation, living on the catch of the day, the winds of freedom soothed her brow as they filled her sail and the dancing waves beckoned her toward a horizon that shined with promise and adventure.

These were the thoughts that consumed her as she nursed her wounded arm and assorted bruises over a pot of wine in the tavern at Niles Margrave's Inn. She had, of course, hidden her sex before opening the door of her room to Margrave's hammering. She explained that some brigand had attacked her in her sleep. She pointed to her wounded arm. She pointed to the knife pegged to the floor. Though, plain as day, no attacker was to be found in her room, on a morning largely proving in want of explanations, her experience soon blended into the general sense of mystery that descended on Hastur.

Nearly all the tavern's patrons had their own tales to tell. There was the stuffy-nosed dowager who awoke in the early morning to the familiar snoring of her long-dead husband. The needlewoman with the lesions on her face who was joined in her morning walk by a friend who, as a child, had been taken by the fever. A perfumer, oddly devoid of eyebrows and eyelashes, was nonetheless convincing in his discourse on being serenaded by his gone mother. Indeed, experiences with ghosts were so widespread as to leave the unaffected feeling somewhat overlooked.

Wolfdog was having none of it. Even though the ghost of Wanlo the Freebooter had departed, he could reappear anytime. And how was it that she'd fled one spirit—that of the murderous cabin boy Piran—only to be surrounded by countless more? The general creepiness of the coastal town had become intolerable, and she made up her mind right then to leave this cursed place once and for all.

She finished her wine, collected her few possessions, settled her bill with Niles Margrave, and then headed off to Wharf Town to buy herself a boat.

***

They gathered in the entryway to peer at him. Dozens of milky masks swimming in the dark, their attached naked torsos more suggested than actualized. He recognized a few, at least dimly. Others he did not but he saw in their features hints of Darius and Anse and himself. Some wore

157

joyless grins. Some gaped, as if horrified by *his* visage. Some tightened their eyes in a menacing manner. Under their gaze, Cletus felt himself melting.

"Anse!" he said, finding his voice.

Inside, he heard movement on the stairs. Collecting his courage, he ducked into the doorway, but left the door open behind him, letting in the cool outside air.

Anse, in a daze, made his way down the steps, still in his fringed sleep gown, almost as pale as one of these spirits. "I see ye've met the family," he said. His voice sounded as if it came from the next room. "Grand Da Odgar, Uncle Ansgar, Auntie Dula, Momma, of course. And Darius is around here somewhere. Quite a houseful. We've all been reacquainting ourselves."

Reaching the floor, Anse sat down heavily on the stairs.

Momma? Cletus inspected the floating heads until he spotted her in the back, fearful and broken even in death. She wavered in and out of focus.

"Where's the conjure quim?" Cletus demanded.

"Upstairs, talking to one of them. Auntie Photina, I think. I'm still learning some of their names."

"Why is this happening, Anse?"

"We unleashed it, I'm afraid. Dagon help me. When we resurrected Lucrezia Maule, we apparently resurrected these spirits, as well."

"The whole city is gone mad." He frowned. "Unintended consequences, then?"

Anse laughed weakly. "Unintended on my part."

Cletus looked up the stairs to the first landing. The fadumo stood there, spectral companions at either side. "Morning, Cletus," she said. "Invigorating morning, wouldn't you agree?"

"Send them back!"

Fadumo Aneleh was the picture of serenity. "That wouldn't be very friendly, now would it? After all, these are our guests."

"We didn't ask for this."

"And I didn't ask to be taken by force from Presage Cay."

"People are leaping from buildings! The streets are awash with panic."

"People will adjust," the fadumo said calmly. "Or not."

"Get rid of them!"

"No."

He was astounded to hear her deny his command. "What?"

"No. I will not get rid of them. Not until it's time. Not until I'm ready." She smiled. "Some of them I may always keep around. For company."

"Anse!"

Anse Gargery, the hunched and chisel-featured slaver whom he had never seen back down from a fight, looked positively sheepish. He shrugged.

"Run along, Cletus," Fadumo Aneleh said. "Don't you have a shipment of little children to check on? Go feel powerful again."

He took an angry step toward her and the specters swirled at him, forcing him to duck back out the door into the street. As he stood looking dumbfounded, the door slammed in his face and he heard the lock turn.

***

Ring was tired, but he couldn't sleep. The day had been long and full of upsets and unfamiliarity. He squirmed in the strange bed, his nerves humming ceaselessly under his skin.

If he were home right now, he'd be ... probably fearing another visit from Gloamer Brom, if truth be told. That was how most of his nights began. Here, he wasn't sure what to fear. Would the Gloamer find him in these stable boy quarters? Somehow he doubted it, though now he wished he'd put the question to Tutor Will: *Will the Gloamer follow me always, wherever I go?*

Instead, when he'd met last with Tutor Will about a year ago, when the teacher had given him the adder stone, Ring had felt the burning need to ask him something wholly different. Something that had bothered him since he first spotted Digna Greavor across the square. He'd meant to ask this question many times in the past but had always failed to screw up the necessary courage. But, with this wise man about to fade from his life for good, Ring mustered the resolve.

"Tutor Will," he said, "how will I know when I've fallen in love?"

The raven eyes gleamed.

"Some say," the tutor began, "that it's better never to know. That the open hand of love can turn to a fist and strike us in our very hearts. They say love is an emotion that blinds us from our purpose and robs us of our dignity. It interferes with having our mates chosen for us by any reasonable criteria. It's frivolous and holds us back. That's probably the general view, or so people would have us believe." He let the words sink in, then he leaned toward Ring and continued in a conspiratorial manner. "Don't misunderstand what I'm about to tell ye. Love is a leap that seldom works out for the best. But in the leaping lies its value."

Ring hung on every word.

"When ye're in love, yer heart opens as wide as the sky. Waves of euphoria ride yer breath. Elation roars in yer veins. Ye yearn with all yer being for her smell, her taste, her touch. The world becomes a perfect place."

The teacher had raised one black eyebrow and nodded

thoughtfully.

He wondered where Tutor Will had gone in exile. Was he wandering the Valdemar Desert as a mendicant, exchanging bits of wisdom for bits of bread? Or had he settled in Carcosa or White Worm to teach his heresy there? Ring hoped he was somewhere safe.

Ring also hoped that he, himself, was somewhere safe. He suspected he was.

Paulus had been right. The room was comfortable; the blanket a thick, double-layered quilt, the bedding firmly strawed, the frame solid and, supporting his neck, a thin pillow of down that could be folded and fluffed up. He liked the way it felt against his ear. He had slept without a pillow at home, Da being against them on principle. Sharing the room would take some getting used to, though.

He rolled up on an elbow and bit his lip.

Illuminated dimly by the wavering light of a single oil lamp were three more beds, though one remained empty. They were spread out, each boy claiming a corner to himself. The empty bed also had its corner, ready and awaiting the arrival of the next stable boy. In the center of the room was a crude but serviceable table with four chairs arranged crookedly around it. Three of the chairs matched and the fourth one was similar, as if someone deliberately sought out as close a match as possible. The oil lamp rested casually centered on the table.

Paulus had introduced him to his roommates, patting Ring on the back to show the boys he felt a special affection for this stranger, assuring them he had full confidence in their welcoming his friend as an equal, above hazing and other such foolishness.

His roommates' manner indicated that Paulus' confidence in them was well-placed. Of course, they would be friendly toward the new boy. They smiled at Ring and nodded.

They were both Ligeian, about Ring's age, maybe a little older. One was a little taller than the other. They wore plain robes, clean, as were their faces and hair, though the taller one, Zog something-or-other, showed the barest beginnings of a beard. They both wore good-luck charms. The shorter one, Lativius Bendel, wore a bloodhawk feather and an amulet with a shepherd's crook to symbolize the sleeping god, Hastur; Zog wore some kind of bone fragment. They were both dark-haired and of average build, though Lativius was a bit gaunter, with pronounced cheeks and a missing front tooth that sometimes whistled when he talked. Zog's face was fuller and more serious, with watery, lavender eyes.

There was something substantial about these stable people. About Paulus and Willa and Lativius and Zog. Something that fleshed them out more than the sort of people he was used to. Something that seemed to *complete* them.

Satisfied Ring was settled in, Paulus said goodbye, clapping Ring's shoulder, and left for his family supper. Tonight Seth was joining his folks and Addie and himself for the meal and Paulus wanted to be there when his brother arrived.

The stable boys sat around the central table and talked for a while. A Morellan slave girl named Issobel brought them a steaming pot of porridge and bread dipped in olive oil, along with bowls and spoons. There was enough porridge to feed a dozen boys and Lativius and Zog set about the challenge of cleaning the pot. Ring hadn't eaten much that day and he joined in with surprising enthusiasm.

Issobel stayed to visit, taking up the empty chair and cocking back on its rear legs. It seemed presumptuous behavior on the part a slave but neither Lativius nor Zog seemed to mind. Issobel was past middle age and a bit thickset for a Morellan. Her silver-white complexion was reddish at the cheeks and her amber eyes had a merry quality that quickly won Ring over.

When she chatted, she jumped excitedly from topic to topic, from Ring's first day at the stables to his amazing white foal to Sirrah Luster's health (which she feared was getting worse) to mending the collar on young Addie's dress and, finally, to the ghosts that had apparently descended on the city, throwing everyone into a panic.

"There's all kinds of stories making the rounds," Issobel said. "I haven't been out myself, of course, but they're saying that the ghost of Filan Gowdie, the highwayman that was hanged years ago, rode through Auseil Thoroughfare this afternoon on a black horse, dragging some poor woman behind him. Also a ghost, I guess. They say he still had the hangman's noose around his neck." Her amber eyes widened to the whites.

Aye, Tutor Will had told Ring about the grisly hanging of Filan Gowdie.

"And Aylmer Wilf, who stopped by to talk with Sirrah Luster, says he saw a floating head in an abandoned building down the street from him. A horrible sight, the face all dead and evil-looking, the tongue lolling out. And he heard from Cleonice the fishmonger, who he says was trembling like her life had been threatened, that ghosts had been swarming at her all day."

The boys finished eating and Issobel collected the dishes and the remainder of the porridge. She cleaned the breadcrumbs from the table top and wiped away any spillage. Before leaving, she said, "I don't know about ye boys but I'm sleeping with the light on tonight. Don't want any ghosts sneaking up on me."

After she left, Ring said, "There's something going on in the city. Not sure that it's ghosts, but it's something." He told them what he had witnessed this morning on his journey to the stables. When he described

161

the scene at General Maule's house, their jaws dropped.

That night, they agreed to sleep with the oil lamp lit.

All this talk of ghosts had not helped his nerves. He thought about the oddities he had witnessed this morning; thought about Lucrezia Maule, who had seemingly crawled home from the tomb; thought about leaving M and Gargery House; about what Paulus had said about the old soldier with the missing limbs; about Digna Greavor and Willa Lumen and the nature of love; about his roommates Zog and Lativius. And about tomorrow and what new rounds of aberrations the day might bring.

His mind was a hive of thoughts, buzzing around in his head until sometime late in the night when the buzzing finally tapered off and sleep firmly seized hold of him.

***

Artemis was on edge, stopping every few dozen steps to sniff the air and look around. In the deepening dusk, the terrier's ears rose slightly and a barely audible, squeaking sound issued from his throat. He looked at Ratter Lumen as if questioning whether to proceed.

"Come along, ye silly mutt." But the words rang oddly flat, without the usual levity in them.

Most of the snow had been eaten away to slivers of crust by the rain, but a damp chill remained that had chased most of the Hasturians indoors early to perch near their fires. But it wasn't just the chill that sent them huddling with their loved ones. There was a strangeness all around that had ridden the breeze since morning. A fear-swelling, soul-tiring strangeness that threatened from every passage.

Ratter chose to ignore it. Or, rather, he chose it over what awaited him in his own dwelling.

Drip. Drip. Drip.

Willa said it was just drops of rain leaking through the old roof. Maybe that was all she saw because that was all she was meant to see. But him, maybe he was meant to see something more.

Silas always was a bastard even in childhood, though for a child, actions are smaller as are their consequences. However, what's naughty in a child can be, in an adult, evil. Ratter had watched his brother evolve, had watched the sickness in him grow and harden. Had seen where the child taking glee in tiny acts of spite—like putting his grubby hands in other people's food—had degraded into a sadistic man who took full-throated joy in visiting malice on the unsuspecting.

Once, shortly before Ratter had given up on fishing as a livelihood, he and Silas had gone out alone on the boat when Da was down with a cold. Silas had caught a razor-billed gull by the wing and delighted in throttling the poor creature until it was little more than a shattered mass of blood and feathers. Beyond the horror of the pummeling was his brother's total absorption in it, as if he were feeding on it somehow. As if the gull's cries and spasms of pain brought him some measure of peace.

Artemis began to move again, tentatively. Overhead, Ratter heard a gravelly scamper on a rooftop. He and Artemis looked up in time to see several black rats spring from one roof to the next. Artemis growled at them but walked on.

Though he hadn't set out deliberately for any specific destination, he now knew where he was headed. Where he had always been headed: toward a certain abandoned building in Carmilla he had not visited for more than four years.

Silas, of course, had been Da's favorite. He was tinkering with Da's fishing gear, almost as far back as Ratter could recall. When Silas was little more than a toddler, playing with the nets, spears and harpoons, or trying to walk around on the stilts they used for bay fishing, they were forever pulling hooks out of his tiny fingers. He would cry and throw fits whenever Da took off in the boat without him. Part of that was a genuine interest in angling but a larger part, Ratter always felt, was just to get in good with Da. Though Ratter resented it a little, he knew he could never be close to Da in that way, so he accepted it. But Silas used this advantage to wedge his way into Da's thinking and his influence wasn't always in Da's best interest.

There were loans, for instance, never paid back and forgotten over time. There was the ownership of the fishing boat, which Da signed over to Silas for "simplicity's sake." There were the heirlooms and family memorabilia that Silas managed to wheedle from the old man's paws, only to turn around and sell them off. It hit Ratter hard one day in the marketplace when he saw Savina Gargery wearing a gold-rimmed brooch that had belonged to his grand momma. He almost accosted her over it but the poor woman already looked so sullen, so shaky, he didn't have the heart to do it. Besides, it wasn't her fault.

As Ratter and Artemis crossed the Redgauntlet River from Gondemar into Wharf Town, a pair of Pym watchmen hurried by, going in the same direction. Their ribbons flapped in what to Ratter's ears always sounded like the clucking of disapproval. But their disfavor was not directed at him. The watchmen all knew Ratter, knew he was often out at all hours hunting vermin. Some even greeted him. But not today. Today, the watchmen had other, more serious concerns.

At present, they appeared interested in the comings and goings at the Surly Oyster. A woman with her dress torn stood crying outside the building amidst a milling throng. Regarding the source of her tears, Ratter couldn't say, though he suspected it to be, sadly, a concern of this world not the next. Perhaps for the watchmen this represented a welcome respite from a day of pursuing ghosts.

Visitation Day. That's what some people had taken to calling it. Ratter guessed it was a big enough event to require naming. But what if it was really Visitation Week or Month or Year? What if today signaled the start of the Visitation Era, a permanent melding of realities between the Netherworld and the physical world they had come to know? He shuddered.

Fane priests had combed the city streets during daylight hours to perform exorcisms for the well-heeled, who could afford them, but there was no sign of these ministers now. Unaffiliated wonder-workers, though, could sometimes be spotted slipping in or out of doorways with their amulets and strings of boar's teeth at the ready.

It was fully night when Ratter and Artemis left the northern gate at Port Whilom and ventured out to Carmilla. Ratter always had a sense of moving to a wilder space whenever he left the safety of the city walls. He had the same feeling when he went to Horla, far to the south. Though within easy access of the walls and their protection, and perfectly civilized, these two outgrowths of the city had an unmistakable, unfettered quality that Ratter found both liberating and a little unnerving.

Carmilla spread along Hastur's northern coast and up into the hills to the north. Some of the side streets were unpaved but the main ones weren't and generally looked every bit as lively as any in Hastur, sprinkled with taverns and inns and smelling of the breads and cakes baked by the area's renowned bakers. The rest of the citizenry was a mix of millers, fishers, carpenters and masons. There were also several olive-oil wholesalers there and, up in the hills, lived many artists and sculptors, including Varley Antagan, whose remarkable carvings included the tracery and scrollwork on the steps and columns of Hastur Fane.

However, tonight, there was little activity on the streets of Carmilla and signs of the ghostly visitors were everywhere: the oil lamps and candles in the windows to keep out the ghosts, doors hung with sachets of garlic or cloves, food left out for the specters or rats, whoever claimed it first. A beggar priest startled him from an alleyway. For an instant, the priest looked like some ghastly night hag, his tattered cloak resembling thickets of clinging seaweed. "A prayer to keep off the ghosts?" the priest offered, holding out a hand for alms. Ratter hurried past.

The side street was called Rusticula Way, named for a seamstress and wool worker who, according to legend, had been born with two heads. Though one head was largely unresponsive and dangled loosely at her back, the other was talkative and affable and accounted for Rusticula's immense popularity. They say when she died nearly the whole town turned out for her funeral. The street named for her was unpaved and muddy and on an incline. Ratter and Artemis made their way up, taking care with their footing.

The drizzle began anew, pooling and forming rivulets in the mud.

They plodded on for several blocks, when Artemis froze. Ratter's stomach tightened.

Standing before them was the abandoned building where Silas Lumen had met his fate.

Flashes of that night reared up at Ratter. The yelling, the anger, the recriminations. Silas at first denying it, then admitting to having succumbed to his urges but in a moment of weakness, addled by wine and goaded on by the young temptress.

"Just the one time," he pleaded as Ratter hurled at him, clutching his neck. With all his fury, Ratter squeezed. Silas pelted him with his coarse fisher's fists but they were powerless to deter the rat-catcher. Fingers animated with rage not so much choked as crushed the wind from the treacherous brother's throat, as the face went scarlet then purple. The eyes bulged with terror, the mouth became a gagging cavern in which no breath could pass. Then the fists dropped, the knees bent.

"Succumb to this, ye bastard!" Ratter said. When he was certain the life had been slaked from it, he let the limp form collapse to the ground.

He had stood for the longest time, hands still clenched, his fallen brother at his feet. In the building's darkness, vermin scampered.

Ratter broke from his reverie. Looking down through the light rain at his hands, he saw they were clutched, as if possessed of a memory all their own.

Feet still frozen, Artemis looked warily to his rear.

From down an alley came a hollow thumping noise for which Ratter had no association. Peering into the night-cloaked path, he watched a dark, shadowy form take shape in the distance. Wharf rats by the score ran to the sound, drawn to it. The thumping, he realized, was some sort of drum the shadow form was playing, unlike any drum he had ever heard before. It gave off a thudding that was almost more of a feeling than a tone. It swept outward along the ground; it resonated in the solid bricks of buildings; it passed through Ratter as if not intended for his ears.

He was almost upended by a pack of street rats that flocked over his sandaled feet on their way to the shadowy drummer. Artemis bolted, yelping back down Rusticula Way. The terrier stopped at the corner and turned back toward his master, his back bowed, tail tucked, shivering.

"Since when do ye shrink from a few vermin?" But, down the alley, he could tell it was rapidly becoming more than just a few.

They roiled like a river, dancing to the hypnotic rhythm. An ever-growing swarm, called out from all corners, jumping, frisking, romping merrily to the throbbing beat. As the mass grew, it became more excited, prodded on by the sinister form's incessant, nearly sub-audible pounding.

Having gathered in sufficient abundance, the army of rats turned and slowly rallied down the alley toward Ratter.

Every fiber in his being told him to run. Screamed it. Pleaded with him. But his sandals remained fixed in the muck. Though he grabbed handfuls of his whiskers and bared his teeth in horror, he stood helpless in the rain, paralyzed, as the rats moved closer.

"Bodac!" a recognizable voice hailed. "Remember me?"

The patter of the drizzle no longer covered the sound of rat feet scampering across the soggy ground. They squeaked and roared. They bobbed, leapt over one another's backsides, forming a wave of gray and black fur that swelled toward him. Countless eyes shined in the moonlight.

"What's the matter, brother?" the shade drummer asked, marching smartly, "rat got yer tongue?"

It was Silas. And, yet, it wasn't. It had Silas' voice, that much was true. But a flare of lightning briefly lit the form and Ratter plainly saw it was just a dark swirl, more or less human in shape. Perhaps it was some otherworldly representation of his brother. Or of the evil at Silas' core. Whatever it was, it was closing in upon him.

"She was a little girl, Silas. A helpless little girl and ye, a full-grown man with a daughter of yer own. Ye desecrated and disfigured her, and she has to carry that with her for the rest of her life."

But Silas wasn't interested in such appeals.

"Ye know my furry friends, Bodac? They have a bone to pick with ye. Seems ye've been killing off their relatives by the thousands. They'd like to return the favor."

In a surge, the rats broke into a run.

Ratter, regaining his presence of mind, spun toward the abandoned building behind him and pushed open the door. Down Rusticula Way, Artemis still stood, trembling. There was no time to coax him in. "Go!" Ratter yelled at the terrier, and slammed the door shut.

The door had no latch. At one time there had been a handle, but it had broken off. Now all that protected Ratter were boards of wood he held in place with the weight of his body.

Outside, the rats assembled noisily. The smaller ones stuck their heads under the door and Ratter promptly stomped them, crunching their bones beneath his heel. He could hear tearing wood and felt the vibration near his ankles. It wouldn't be long before they broke through.

He peered into the gloom, his back against the quivering door and tried to remember if there was another way to escape. A stripe of moonlight entered with the rain through a gap in the roof but its reach didn't extend far. There, at a distant wall, he thought there was another way out, except he couldn't be sure.

He would just have to hope because once he let go of the door, the rats would come avalanching in. He'd be lucky to get away with his life even with a precise destination. If he had to feel for a doorway in the dark, there would not be enough time.

More heads poked though the widening bottom. He crushed two, but before he could get a third, a sharp pain knifed his right calf. Another ripped the flesh from his left heel. He felt one scurry up his leg as the rats began to swarm in under the door.

He pulled the rat from his thigh, tossed it to the side and darted into the pitch black. A rat leapt onto his back. He batted it away. His feet now hammered the old building's wooden floor. The weight of the rats pushed the door open. More and more rats cascaded, squealing and scrambling over one another to get at him. Piles of rats tumbled in, melding into a knee-high swarm.

Dimly, he thought he a spied an opening to his left. He cut that way and nearly tripped on some debris. Two more rats were on his back, with others underfoot, slashing at his ankles and calves. The room filled with screeching and thudding as rats closed in on him from all sides. He staggered and, his wounded legs slick with blood, began to fail. Daggers of pain jabbed from all angles. Lightheaded, he flailed toward what he thought was the doorway.

Then the floor gave under him.

He plunged and twisted downward into mounds of fur and slicing teeth. The moldering floor had spilled him into a nest of hundreds of rats. From above, they flooded down at him. He screamed and screamed until his screams turned to whimpers.

The last thing he saw was a dark form peering at him through the hole in the floorboards, drumming to its heart's content.

CHAPTER 10
By the River

Little Darius' death was an arrow through Gracie's heart. It wasn't the first baby she's lost. The other was a miscarriage. But this hit her harder. This one, ye see, she'd suckled and held in her arms. He had a name and a face. When I told her he was gone, she cried for days. After that, the light left her eyes.

Now that I think of it, I guess, I'd killed her, too. Some part of her, anyway.

We never spoke of him. None of us. I told Olalla and—I can never remember her name—the maidservant before Bartine that if they ever mentioned him, I'd pack them off to the mines.

Andaman took away the body. I don't know what he did with it and I don't want to know.

People pulled long faces for a time, Cletus, Enoch Glister, some others, but infant deaths were common enough and it was soon forgotten by most.

One thing about it always bothered me, though. I could never be certain, and he never mentioned it, but that night when I done the deed, I looked up into the shadows at Ring's sleeping form and I could almost swear, Dagon help me, that his eyes were open and he was watching me. But darkness can play its tricks, and when I checked again, this time closer, his eyes were definitely shut.

For an instant, I remember hovering over him, considering whether to send little Darius off to the Netherworld with a playmate.

What started as a drizzle on Visitation Day built into a steady downpour that went on and on for weeks. Some said Nebo brought the showers to wash the ghosts from Hastur. But if that was her plan, fortune frowned on it. The ghosts, as it turned out, were in no hurry to leave.

A minor uprising in Smee required the attention of the Fourth Legion, so there was some activity at Spaulding Stables. The uprising was so minor that General Maule did not accompany the Fourth, but left command of the troops to his second, Brigadier Tull Fennel. Nonetheless, the excursion elicited great excitement and enthusiasm amongst the stable hands.

Ring's role lay in helping to get the warhorses groomed and ready for the cavalry, an operation Paulus took charge of handily. He relied on Ring more than he normally would have—with Willa off mourning the death of her father—but Ring learned quickly and proved to be up to the tasks assigned him.

As the cavalry rode off, Ring joined Paulus, Verger, Lativius and the others in cheering the riders and their horses on to victory.

For the first time in his life, Ring felt a part of things, not merely an observer. Others trusted him to do his functions and he trusted them to do theirs. These efforts combined in a unity of purpose that he could now see had real value.

That's not to say the boy was entirely happy. He missed Gargery House and its familiarity: the rooms, the halls, the stairs where he sometimes secretly eavesdropped. He missed his window on the third-floor landing that looked out on busy Maule Square. He missed M and Da and Olalla and Bartine. He even sometimes missed being a world-famous explorer, traversing a mountain ledge on the conch-patterned carpet in the main room.

When Bartine brought his things to him several days later, he pressed her for news of when he could visit.

"Now's not the time for that, Master Ring," she said, her pretty face drawn and haggard. She looked as if she hadn't slept in days. "Things aren't the same there, what with the ghosts and all."

She told him how Fadumo Aneleh had taken over the running of Gargery House. The spirits had moved in permanently and Uncle Cletus was no longer welcome. She spoke of his father's weakness, his mother's growing insanity, Olalla's near breakdown. Of the spirits howling at all hours and constantly breaking things.

She told him of Cousin Andaman's shameful death in Sirrah Alban Greavor's house, which earned his cousin a burial without ceremony outside the city gates at Suicides Crossing.

"Ye don't want to be at Gargery House, Master Ring. Not now."

He found himself feeling sorry for Bartine that she had to return to that madhouse.

It seemed the place Ring missed no longer existed.

When he wasn't busy with his duties, he visited his foal, petting him and giving him extra attention. He decided to call the horse "Phantom," in keeping with his shimmering white color and special lineage. Sometimes Ring would explore the stables, though mischief still lurked in the darker corners, waiting to flutter out at him. When Willa returned he tried to comfort her but he was awkward at it, being still somewhat a novice at certain common interactions. She moved into separate quarters in the stables and they saw quite a bit of each other for a time. Ring became fast friends with Lativius and, to a lesser degree, Zog. Paulus checked on him regularly and Ring felt closest to him.

One day, after Ring had been there a while, Paulus came to him, dripping rain and holding his fighting stick. "Come on, Gargery. Let's get out of here."

They walked through upper Allhollan down Aungier Street. Ring was surprised how quickly he had acclimated to being outside. When he wasn't needed in the stables, his time was his own, and he and Lativius investigated the city. Walking now with Paulus reminded him of his fantasy friendship with Arvin and how they joked with the slave girls and sometimes walked on the beach. Maybe someday he would tell Paulus about all that.

It was wet but the cold had all but departed. Spring was just around the corner. The citizenry of Hastur were back out in force, not about to let a little rain interfere with the daily running of their lives. Nor were they dissuaded by the haunting. Not most of them, anyway. Whether it was a mark of their resilience or subbornness, they adjusted and went about their work and trade.

Most of the pedestrians were wearing hoods or hats of some sort, but others preferred to let the raindrops plop on their bare heads and hang from their noses. Conversations were louder, so as to be heard over the spatter of rain and the sheets of water spilling from the rooftops but, otherwise, the crowded, twisty streets were more or less the same as always, rain and ghosts be damned.

"Where are we going, Paulus?"

"To get ye a proper fighting stick, Gargery. Can't have ye walking around empty handed. What would people think?"

"I'm not sure I want a fighting stick."

"Ye want one. Trust me. Leave it to yer good friend Paulus."

The downpour helped to clear the air of chimney smoke and had the added benefit of giving the unwashed a thorough soaking, but it was irksome and Ring soon found himself weighted down and sopping wet and not at all enjoying it.

With a crash, a second-story window on a ramshackle inn burst outward, spilling shards of thick glass into the street. The sudden noise gave his heart a twist but he quickly recovered. Another display of apparition mischief. People glanced up at the ragged hole left in the broken pane, then walked around the fallen glass; such acts of ghostly destruction had already become commonplace.

He followed along with Paulus who was unaffected by the rain to the point of being oblivious to it. Paulus remarked cheerfully on city sights or chatted up the immense number of passersby he personally knew.

When they came to Hedwig Geb, fixed as usual on the street in front of the abandoned building, Ring's heart sank. The old soldier, slumped to one side, appeared drowned. His hair stuck out spiky in every direction. His skeletal head rested against the broken door, mouth wide open, eyes closed. His tattered robe, heavy with rain, had slid over the stumps of his shoulders, baring his gaunt, bronze chest to the elements, and his one good leg lay naked to the thigh in a pool of rainwater. His alms bowl brimmed with it.

"Sirrah Hedwig, are ye alright?" Paulus shouted over the downpour. The boys rushed over.

Sirrah Hedwig opened one eye. "Morning, Paulus," he said. "Still raining, I see."

Ring and Paulus helped the old soldier sit up. They pulled the robe over his chest and down over his curled leg. Paulus smoothed his hair and Ring emptied the water from his bowl.

"We could help ye into this building if ye like," Paulus offered. "Get ye out of the rain."

"No, I'm fine here," Sirrah Hedwig said. "This is my place. This is where I'm meant to be. The rain will pass. It always does."

The boys looked at each other.

"Besides, I'm waiting for Petrus. Now that he's back, he'll take care of me."

Paulus pressed a silver paldin into the old fellow's hand and they continued on their way.

As they passed into the marketplace at Gondemar, the doors of an adjacent warehouse flew open, knocking a poor flower girl clean off her feet and sending her blooms airborne in a colorful spray. The doors closed just as suddenly with a blaring slam. Before anyone could help her, the girl bounced up and, leaving behind her scattered wares, ran off screaming.

The Redgauntlet River ran from Al Aaraaf in the north along the eastern border of Morella into Ligeia and Hastur where it divided Gondemar and Wharf Town before emptying into Dagon Bay. A stone bridge of generous width, known as Wiley's Bridge, spanned the river. The bridge's arch was sufficient to allow flat boats and other smaller vessels to pass beneath it, given normal conditions, however, the conditions at that time were far removed from normal. The constant rain had risen and widened the Redgauntlet to the point where it not only overflowed its banks but occasionally lapped at the ankles of bridge pedestrians. The incessant downpour had whipped the river into a terrifying force of nature: a roaring, steely surge of foamy whitecaps that knifed past treacherously.

"What are we doing here, Paulus?" Ring asked over the rain.

Pausing at the crest of Wiley's Bridge, Paulus put one hand on Ring's shoulder and pointed upriver with his fighting stick. "Look along the banks, Gargery. There's a bounty of branches thrown up by the river. Make sure ye get a good one. Ye want something long and thick and as straight as possible. Not too thick or ye won't be able to get yer fingers around it. Ye want one that feels comfortable in yer hands. One that feels good to swing."

"Will ye help me find the right one?"

"I can't help ye, Gargery. It's got to feel right to *ye*. Otherwise, it would just be picking out another stick for myself. That would do ye no good. Ye see?"

Ring didn't but knew Paulus couldn't be persuaded to assist, so he set off along the bank, searching for a stick that met Paulus' requirements.

The swollen bank was littered with waterlogged branches of ironwood, spider oak and blood-thorn greenwood, some massive. Walking with his neck bent and frequently wiping water from his eyes, Ring studied the array. Some were long enough but too thin. Some were thick enough but too short. Others were too twisted. He hefted a few, rattling their wet leaves before discarding them.

From nowhere, a dog ran at him, barking. It was the scarred, yellow dog he had seen hanging round the stables. There was no mistaking this walleyed mutt with its missing back leg. It circled him, barking and yapping unremittingly.

"What are ye doing out in the rain?" Ring asked. "Are ye looking for a fighting stick, too?" He laughed, in spite of himself.

The yellow dog seemed to take exception to this, barking now with added enthusiasm.

Ring was about to ignore the dog and return to his stick hunting when he became aware that the cur was backing perilously close to the river's edge.

"Watch out, little fellow," he called. "Watch—"

The dog's single back leg slipped over the edge of the bank.

He dove for the dog's front legs, slamming hard into the mud and sliding. He swiped at the cur but grasped only air as, with a yelp, the dog disappeared into the roaring waves.

All at once, Ring lost control of his momentum and, before he was even aware of what was happening, he, too, plunged into the deadly waters.

***

When Drummer Maule arrived home, the front door was already open; the back door, as well. Rain had entered and slicked the floor, forming puddles. Wet footprints ran the length of the house. Ash and Huldra stood near the table ahead, looking at him wide-eyed and open mouthed, unsure what to say.

In the main room, Da and Uncle Lafe warmed themselves as best they could at the fireplace. Two large panes had been pried from the window in that room to pull yet more cool air into the house.

The general had just returned from doing something he always found distasteful.

"I need to ask ye a favor, my friend," he had said to Tull Fennel over bowls of warm broth at an inn called the Wooden Eye. Inwardly, he cringed. "It's a big one, I'm afraid."

The request came after they had exchanged pleasantries on their families. Tull had heard about Lucrezia's miraculous return and was eager for news on this, which Drummer supplied sparingly. She had come back to him, feeble but alive, the general said simply, and they would remake their life together. Tull appeared surprised to hear him discourse so casually on this but the general only allowed the topic to be breached to a certain point. And, Drummer supposed, given the flurry of supernatural activity in the city, the resurrection of Lucrezia Maule seemed more or less in keeping with the times.

The lanky Tull then reported on the recent uprising, which the Fourth Legion, under his command, had quelled. It was a minor episode between some refugees from Scylding Tangle who resettled just outside Smee and a shady tavern owner named Knucker Pratt who had riled up some of the locals against them. There was some back and forth, some beatings, a hanging, Knucker's tavern was burned to the ground. Then came a night of rioting that left three dead. By the time the Fourth arrived, Knucker was gone, the refugees were all gone and the citizenry of Smee was busily rampaging on wholly unrelated matters.

Smee had a reputation for these kinds of events. The town was chiefly a stopover for travelers who followed Merchant Road from Carcosa to Hastur. Much of its population, at any time, was made up of transients and the remainder was largely rough characters that eked out their livings alternately servicing and thieving from those passing through.

"For the life of me," Tull said, shaking his head of long russet hair, "I'll never comprehend why anyone would choose to live in such a forsaken place as Smee. We stayed for the day to round up the remaining troublemakers, mostly drunks, and to help with the cleanup and to attend to the wounded. The whole thing was just senseless. People turned on each other for no good reason. At least the Fourth didn't have any casualties."

The general nodded and stroked his orange chin beard.

That was when he asked the favor.

"If I were to step down," the general said, "would ye be willing to take command of the Fourth?"

"Step down? I don't understand."

"If I were to retire my commission, would ye consider taking charge?"

Tull eyed the general hard. "Why would ye do that?"

Drummer waved his hand at the air, dismissing the question. "It would require yer full attention, of course. Ye'd have to put off yer political ambitions. At least for the time being."

Tull thoughtfully spooned broth into his mouth. For several moments, he said nothing. The general could see the idea appealed to the young brigadier. He could read, if not the content of Tull's thoughts, at least the working of his mind.

"This is what ye want?" Tull asked.

"Aye."

"Alright, general," he said. "Ye've got a deal."

And, just like that, Drummer Maule had surrendered his calling, his passion, his identity.

Da and Uncle Lafe watched him as he wordlessly crossed to the stairs and climbed out of the cool, damp room. Drummer, of course, had no sense of smell, which was fortunate for him. Perhaps Lucrezia's tomb odors, which so bothered the others, would eventually dissipate. Perhaps not. It made no difference to the general.

Entering his room, he went to the alcove and pulled back the curtains. He stood there for a long time, smiling down into the loving, unblinking gaze of his beloved.

CHAPTER 11
Into a Midnight Black

After the whelp died, I kept watch on Ring. Trying to determine if he'd seen what happened to his brother that night in the dark of his room. But, if he did, he didn't show it. He was sad, as were Olalla and the maidservant. Hard not be sad with Gracie weeping continuously in the background, day after day. I had no indication the boy knew I was to blame, though it was about that time he started having his dreams.

He was always a sullen boy, even when he was a baby. He was four or five when his brother died and he started talking about the Shiny Man. That's what he called it. The Shiny Man coming into his bedroom at night to carry him away. I told him it was just a dream. That there was no Shiny Man. I'm doubtful he believed me but he stopped talking about it and that was good enough for me.

When Ring turned seven, I brought in a tutor. A teacher named Will Boyle. I hoped it would get the boy thinking about something useful for a change. Numbers and history and what have ye. Get him away from that window he stared out of all day or his games in the main room where he walked around and around the carpet, wearing a path in it. Get him talking to someone besides molts and batty old Gracie.

Maybe it would prepare him for something. I don't know, maybe taking over the business one day. It was hard to imagine the boy as a ruthless slaver. Hard to imagine him as a ruthless anything. But one day he would have to do something with his life, so he may as well be educated.

The city fathers drove off the tutor when Ring was eleven. Something about heretical teachings. Didn't see what all the fuss was about, but he was gone in exile and the boy was alone again. I thought about bringing in another. But what's the use? They'd probably just drive that one off, too.

Besides, when I started plotting the Luster problem, it occurred to me the boy could play a role. What if, in the course of things, I could get Luster to agree to take the boy on. In one of his businesses. Get him on the inside, ye see? To where I could maybe maneuver him around a bit. Get the inside information on the Spaulding clan. Maybe even get him over to the boatworks. Dagon help me, but Luster was so taken with Seth's situation that it could work.

I knew the answer to Luster's problem was Drummer Maule. Luster told me Drummer's wife wanted him to support Seth for archon. If Drummer announced for Seth, I had to believe Tull Fennel would bow out. The key was to convince the general that his wife's passing in no way ended his obligation to her family. I had Luster and some of the others start planting seeds of doubt in Drummer's head.

But I knew that wouldn't be enough.

Then Killman told me about the conjure woman. Told me how her people were ready to get rid of her. Said she was raising the dead and killing babies and they wouldn't have it. I thought, here's a wedge that could come in handy. Was it possible she could be the genuine article?

I told Killman to arrange it with Wanlo to bring her to me. I figured even if she couldn't raise the dead, she could be useful. Maybe make it appear that she raised the dead, then drop Lucrezia Maule's bones on Drummer's doorstep. That might be enough to convince him to honor his wife's request.

That and a bribe paid to the priest Cosmas at Dagon Fane to put on a little show at Drummer's expense.

When Queen Samira sent the white foal, well, there ye have it. The final piece. If I moved quickly, I could get Ring inside Spaulding Stables, get Luster to convince Drummer to go to the fane, pay the bribe to Cosmas and see what happened that night on Mount Dnarden. Just like that, it all came together.

And, just like that, it all fell apart.

Ring's body went wet and cold, and his legs flew up from under him. The rushing tide, all bubbles and foam, whizzed past his face. He careened off the rocky bottom of the river, gouging his back. He whirled and buffeted, just another piece of flotsam in the roaring waves.

When he broke the surface, he had a watery view of Paulus, staring at him in disbelief. But not for long. A fresh surge yanked him down and had him flailing. His head knocked a tree branch. He nearly fainted but fought to maintain consciousness. One hand brushed against the dog's coat and he reached out, but the animal spun from his grasp.

He kicked to the surface, opening an eye on the cur before being sucked under again. Projecting himself in a wriggling motion, he stretched out and seized the dog, who became frantic in his grip. He wrapped his arms around him and hugged him to his chest. The dog panicked, clawing and biting his chest and upper arms, in a struggle to get free. Together they bobbed to the surface, gulped air, and went under again. The dog sank his teeth into the flank of Ring's hand but still he held on. Up and down the pair went, tumbling to the surface, dunking again. He banged his knee on something, reviving his flagging senses. Again he kicked to the surface, his knee throbbing. He was bleeding profusely from somewhere—his back or the back of his head or maybe his chest or hand. A great branch swatted the side of his face with a solid *thwack* and the strength drained from him.

He floated beneath the surface, the sun shining dimly orange through his closed lids. He floated for what seemed like forever. He had never felt more relaxed, more at peace. There was nothing left to worry about. No one to please. Just drifting in total tranquility. *If this was what awaited at the end of his time, why had he ever dreaded it?*

He rose toward the veiled sun. The rain drummed on his chin and forehead. Vaguely aware of hands on him, he slipped into an easy sleep.

The sea became a sea of space, vast and void. He felt himself loosening, coming apart. He rolled in scattered bits of himself, images lazily turning over and over, merging and blurring, haloing. He saw now that all limitation was an illusion. An elemental tide of voices heralded him with a dream song from a distance beyond measure. *Set down all sentience*, the singing urged. *Relinquish and relax.*

Phantasms of remembrance formlessly swirled in the starless ebony before vanishing. Leaving him with nothing but emptiness.

He slid out of his sleep for an instant, briefly aware of a burning heat, then down, down, down into a new quiet, beyond voices. Beyond

177

silence and stillness. Into a midnight black with no end and no beginning, where there was nothing left of him but fear and loneliness, hovering at the rim of eternity. He tried to see beyond himself, tried to glimpse the bigger picture. But all he could see was one human being after another: born, living, dying, parading mortality, as if it meant something. As if it had value. And when the parade ends?

Would the universe even exist if there was no one there to witness it?

A tingle cut through him. His heart beat in his ears. The sudden noise startled him.

He felt it before he saw it: a form, taking shape in the void. He prayed it was Osric, hooves pounding dead air, dragging his massive balls through the fabric of time. Giving life some portion of meaning, after all. But he knew it wasn't the king of death who neared; knew from how the form thrummed and crackled in the darkness.

First he saw the front appendages, colossal legs of seven segments covered in urticating hairs that stirred at his presence. The legs slowly crawled toward him, clawed tips moving as if every bend was calculated. Next came the fanged tagma, glistening with rows of prominent eyes, jade-green and unblinking, staring at him. At Gargery House, the spider could have filled his room. It paused, regarding him, flexing its fangs, combing its rear legs, silk beginning to pearl from its claws.

The rear legs began wheeling.

A string of fibrous web hurled out at him. The spider scrambled forward and carefully looped the strands around him, enveloping him, until a thick, sticky shroud covered him. He braced himself for the sting of the fangs, wondering how it would feel to have his insides liquefied by powerful venom and sucked out of him.

Instead, the mammoth spider pivoted and scurried off, dragging him behind like some captive strapped to a kite. On and on, through the dark, soaring through passages he felt certain he wasn't meant to pass back through. Bound tight, surrendered to his fate, buffeted by blasts of night, he drifted off, hoping to be asleep when the creature finally claimed him.

He coughed. His body tightened.

Issobel stood over him, daubing a cold rag at his forehead. She backed away with a start. Her amber eyes studied him. "Ye awake?" she asked.

He coughed again, his throat raw. "Could I have some water?" he asked.

She bolted to her feet. "I'll get some," she said, and ran out of the room, calling for Paulus.

He was in the bed in his corner of the stable hands' room, covered by the double-layered quilt, his head cradled in the thin, down pillow. He tried to sit up, but tried it too fast and made himself dizzy. He fought back the urge to retch. Masses of mossy poultice, held in place with bandages, padded his chest and back under his tunic and the back of his head. The bandages itched. He opened and clenched his bitten hand, then laid back down.

Paulus swung his clubbed foot through the threshold and ambled toward him. "Back to the land of the living, I see. Let me ask ye something, Gargery. Who was it taught ye how to swim?"

No one. No one had taught him how to swim. He had never even been in a river before.

"Did the dog make it, Paulus?"

Paulus nodded. "Aye, Gargery. The dog made it. As we speak, he's, no doubt, off terrorizing the villagers with his yapping and howling."

Issobel hurried past Paulus with a cup of water. Lativius entered and joined the gathering at the bedside. Ring sat up slowly and drank the cup dry. He smiled weakly. "How long was I out?"

"Two days," Lativius said. "How do ye feel?"

"Sore. A little stiff."

Zog and Willa entered next. Relief swept Willa's face. "Thank Nebo," she said.

"Did my father come? Uncle Cletus? Any of my family? To see how I was."

"The conjure woman came," Paulus said. "The one they call Fadumo Aneleh. She came last night. Said some prayers. Burned some herbs. Maybe that's what brought ye back."

Ring thought about the spider that captured him in the void.

"Let's let him get some rest," Paulus said, "so, he can get back on his feet and start doing his share around here again." Paulus smiled one of his contagious smiles. "Good to have ye back, Gargery." He herded off the others. "Come along. Time to get back to work. There's plenty to do, now that the rains have stopped."

Issobel brought Ring some vegetable broth and spoon fed him. When she left, he used the chamber pot and then returned to bed. He fluffed up his pillow and lay back down. Sleep called to him from its distant shore. He dozed, this time dreaming of the three-legged yellow dog, of Paulus and Willa and his stable friends, and of his white foal, whose friendship he was now especially keen to rekindle.

When he awoke, Lativius and Zog were at the table in the center of the stable hand's room, eating barley stew and talking about Tull Fennel taking over the Fourth Legion and Seth Spaulding's unchallenged run for archon.

For the first time ever, Ring felt the caress of fortune. He had come back from the brink to this strange, new life where he was welcome and accepted and part of something. Where his absence had been noted and his return eagerly anticipated. For the first time ever, he knew who he was and who he should be. It had never been like this at Gargery House.

There's plenty to do, he told himself as he drifted back to sleep, now that the rains have stopped.

CHAPTER 12
The Terrors That Haunt

Sometimes Gracie's wailing is almost enough to drown out the startling screeches and inane jabber of our ghostly lodgers. They have the run of the place now. When they aren't shattering my belongings, they're slamming doors or up to some other tricks. They never tire. Least of all my father, Darius, who pads up and down the stairs, calling my name, looking for his wicked stick.

This is what my life has become.

I cannot go outside because they *lurk there. The man-footed beasts who have passed on and hold me to blame for their fates. Is it my fault they were born for the collar? Molts, Skalks, roundheads, Pyms, islanders. The kidnapped, the castoffs. Warriors fresh from defeat. Free-walking foreigners with lives so hopeless they begged me to take them away. The strong and the frail. Beauties and shriveled husks. Little children. They gather outside the iron street door and demand retribution.*

Then there are the others. The ones who come in the night. The hanged First People who wail in the square. Returning to a gallows that no longer stands. Still seeing in Gargery House the shadow of the rope that claimed them.

I haven't seen Cletus for weeks. Corporeal visitors no longer come to me. The conjure woman has even abandoned me, preferring the company of the specters.

Every day, I sit in my room, waiting for Bartine to bring my meals and take out my slops. She'd bathe me if I asked her, but I haven't yet, though my skin crawls with filth and reeks.

Of all the terrors that haunt me, the worst lays down the stairs, down the hallway in Ring's old room. I can hear him down there stirring sometimes. Gooing and gawing. All through the day. It's the first thing I envision every morning, and the last I see every night: my infant son returned, hands balled in gnarled fists, smiling his evil, toothless grin, ever watchful of me from the shadow of his little crib with those gleaming eyes.

Dagon help me. This is the collar that clamps at my *throat.*

She heard the boy was hurt in the flooding and, when the rains stopped the next day, she went to visit him at the stables with the spirit box. It was her first time outside alone in Hastur but Bartine gave her good directions and the fadumo found her way to him with no problem.

When the ritual was over and she had returned to Gargery House, she found herself puzzled by her own behavior. After all, this boy was nothing to her. His own people seemed unaffected by his tragedy. Why had it been so important to her to help him?

Perhaps it was because she felt something of a kinship with the boy. Both of them suffered from parents who had forsaken them. Both had been raised largely in isolation. Or perhaps it had to do with the untapped reserve of strength she sensed in him or the fact that, of all the people she had met in this miserable city, he was the only one with traits worth admiring.

Maybe it was something else. Something beyond all this that she just couldn't put her finger on. Something the boy represented that she did not. Something that kept the scales balanced somehow.

Whatever the reason, it had freed her somehow. Freed her to concentrate without distraction. Freed her to move forward with her own plans.

CHAPTER 13

A Perfect Place

That morning, the stable doors were all flung open and the golden light of spring poured in. Ring stood inside the horse pen, combing the mane of his splendid, white foal. The boy and his horse, framed in wood and stone, formed a picture of quiet composure.

Phantom stood firmly on his forelegs, his head compact and lean, his eyes wide-set and alert. The pink nostrils were hairless and thin, as were his lips. His ears, spaced not too far apart and positioned generally forward, were proportioned exactly to fit his face. His tapered neck, sharply defined, swept elegantly from his ridge of muscular withers and the sloping span of his shoulders. He tipped his muzzle into his feeder and came away with a mouthful of orchard grass, which he chewed contentedly.

In the dazzling sunlight, the colt's white coat beamed.

Without even realizing what he was doing, Ring pursed his lips and blew soft, clean notes into the morning air. It was a catchy tune he had once heard a trio of minstrels play in Maule Square before Da chased them off. It was a song about a man who was nowhere, who had nothing to say and nothing to do. A dreamy sort of song that connected with him as he stared out his third-floor window.

Outside the stall, in a warm corner, the scarred, yellow dog curled on his three legs and fixed Ring in a walleyed gaze. He'd taken to following the boy around at a cautious distance. An odd sort of ragtag companion, not completely trustful of Ring but more trustful of him of anyone else. The cur even followed the boy into his stable hand quarters at night where Ring tossed him scraps of food.

The boy became aware of a stir in the straw dust motes hanging in the brilliant sunlight. Someone had walked in. At first, Ring didn't look up. People came and went from the stables all day long and most of them, if they looked at him at all, looked through him in disinterest.

"Paulus here?" a girl's voice asked.

She stood in the light from a doorway, her skin golden bronze, her features soft-boned and freckled. Judging from her dress, she was not a stable worker.

It occurred to him, quite suddenly, that this must be Paulus' sister, whom he had never met. "Addie?" he asked.

"Aye," she said. Her head cocked to one side. "Have ye seen my brother?"

Her smile was the brightest thing in the room.

Standing there with his curry comb in hand, he opened his mouth to reply when all at once he felt something within him open: his heart. He felt light-headed as euphoria rode his breath. He tried to form words but they were overwhelmed by the elation that coursed in his veins.

In that instant, for Ring Gargery, the world became a perfect place.

Epilogue

He swept her up in his arms and swayed. She was as airy as the lute strains that sang in his head. Loosely cupping the fragile hand, holding her to his breast, her head nestled in the crook of his neck; this was what he had missed most: her touch. He closed his eyes and reeled, soaking her presence in. His feet tapped across the carpeted floor, whilst hers hung suspended. It was a folk dance his mother had taught him as a child: one, two, three, swirl; one, two, three, swirl. He had danced it with her at their wedding. Now his bride and he were dancing through life again, young and laughing, each swirl eliciting a fresh exhilaration. Tilting and listing and banking in a heady swoon whilst the music played.

In his mind, her eyes sparkled again, her teeth glistened. *She has come home to me.* Her frame shuddered against him, her breath on his throat: a voiceless whisper of love. They romped, they capered, they dove through the night into each phrase of the ethereal lute. *She has come home to me and I will hold her to my heart forever.*

List of Characters

Gargerys

Ring Gargery - 12-year-old boy; son of Anse and Grace Gargery, brother to Darius II (deceased)

Anse Gargery - Ring's da, Grace's husband, Cletus' brother, son of Darius and Savina (deceased) Gargery; slave trader

Grace (Mallock) Gargery - Ring's mother (M), Anse's wife, Zed Mallock's daughter, Zath Mallock's sister

Cletus Gargery - Ring's uncle, Anse's brother, son of Darius and Savina Gargery; slave trader, giant

Andaman Gargery - Anse and Cletus' cousin; slave trader, serial killer

Darius Gargery (deceased) - father to Anse and Cletus, grandfather to Ring, husband to Savina (deceased); slave trader, owns walking staff Old Dolge

Darius Gargery II (deceased) - infant son of Anse and Grace Gargery, Ring's brother; named after Grandfather Darius

Bartine - Gargery house slave

Olalla - Gargery slave, nursemaid

Will Boyle - Tutor Will; Ring's teacher

Maules

General Drummer Maule - Commander of the Fourth Legion of the Vermilion Shrikes; husband of Lucrezia Maule (deceased), son of Grady and Undine Maule (deceased), nephew of Lafe Maule

Lucrezia (Spaulding) Maule (deceased) - wife of Drummer, daughter of Garner and Aella Spaulding

Grady Maule **-** Drummer's da, husband of Undine (deceased), brother of Lafe

Lafe Maule - Grady's brother, Drummer's uncle

Ash - long-time Maule slave; common law husband to Huldra

Huldra - Maule house slave; Ash's common-law wife

Spauldings

Luster Spaulding - father of Addie, Paulus and Seth; patron of Spaulding clan

Paulus Spaulding - Luster's son, Addie and Seth's brother; stable boss

Addie Spaulding - Luster's daughter, Paulus and Seth's sister

Seth Spaulding - cousin to Lucrezia (Spaulding) Maule (deceased), Luster's son, Addie and Paulus' brother; running for archon

Islanders

Fadumo Analeh Zant wa Zant - conjure woman from Presage Cay; Tarbula's sister, daughter of Mage Medji and Grand Fadumo Olisha Zant wa Zant

Mage Medji Zant wa Zant - father to Fadumo Aneleh and Tarbula, Grand Fadumo Olisha's husband; presides over Council of Elders

Grand Fadumo Olisha Zant wa Zant - Fadumo Aneleh's mother, Mage Medji's daughter

Tarbula

Pirates

Wanlo the Freebooter- pirate, captain of the Pillager

Piran (deceased) - *Pillager's* cabin boy

Drogo Scuttin - pirate who coaxed cabin boy Piran to the *Pillager* and brought Aneleh from island

Wolfdog - second to Wanlo; islander

Red Judoc - boatswain; threatens Aneleh

Lumens

Bodac "Ratter" Lumen - father of Willa, husband of Jemmy (deceased), brother of Silas; city rat-catcher

Willa Lumen - daughter of "Ratter" and Jemmy (deceased); works in stables

Silas Lumen - Ratter Lumen's brother, has a child, abused Willa at eight or nine - found dead weeks later in Carmilla, eaten by rats

Dagon Fane

Saga Eldritch - Oracle, seer of Dagon Fane

Flem Wilf - married the oracle's mother; under spell, continued to love her after death

Cosmas - high priest of Dagon Fane

Gods, Goddesses, Demons

Dagon - goddess of the sea

Aldinach - one of Dagon's familiars; a hairy little demon known to whip up earthquakes and tempests

Bar-Lgura - one of Dagon's familiars; a stumpy, winged grotesque known for her avarice and lust

Gresil - one of Dagon's familiars; a tall woman in white with no skin and eyes like a cat's

Nebo - goddess of wisdom

Osric - god of fire and death

Hastur - shepherd god; city was named after him
Spaulding Stables

Lativius Bendel - stable hand

Zog - stable hand

Verger - stable slave

Issobel - stable slave

Assorted Hasturians

Alban Greavor - Digna's da; spearman, carpet trader

Digna Greavor - daughter of Alban Greavor; young girl across the Maule Square

Zath Mallock (deceased) - husband to Casilda, father of three, brother of Grace Gargery; spearman and silversmith

Hedwig Geb - father of Petrus; beggar, war hero who lost two arms and one leg in battle

Petrus Geb (deceased) - son of war hero Hedwig Geb; tanner

Cyril Carver (deceased) - father of three; spearman and breadmaker

Killman - spy who sells information to the Gargerys

Aylmer Wilf - retiring archon

Filan Gowdie (deceased) - highwayman; hanged

Miscellaneous

Queen Samira - ruler of Morella; supplier of slaves to Gargerys

Gloamer Brom - Shiny Man; haunter of Ring's nights

Enoch Glister - supplier to Gargery slave business

ABOUT THE AUTHOR

Joe Pawlowski is a retired journalist and author who lives in the Twin Cities with his wife, Debbie, and their rescue dog, Lucy. Besides reading and writing, he enjoys music, movies and socializing with his many friends.

73349723R00118

Made in the
USA
Middletown, DE